"What the...?"

Mary Rose spoke aloud, her tone sounding as puzzled as she felt. It was barely light out, and she was clad in her flannel nightgown, a warm, fuzzy robe and a pair of rubber boots with fluff on the inside of them when she slipped out the cabin door to go to the privy—and found a man!

"Who are you?" she called out.

A cheerful voice spoke from the interior of the privy. "Wait your turn. I would've locked the door, but I didn't think you'd be up this early."

Mary Rose dropped the handle of the door as though it were burning-hot and took a quick three steps backward.

Caleb tried to control his amused laughter. This wasn't the way he would've chosen to meet her. But he should've anticipated that Murphy's Law operated even out here in the backwoods.

Mary Rose pressed her lips together and narrowed her eyes. She was not in the least amused. Without saying a word, she pivoted on her heel and retraced her steps to the cabin.

Caleb watched her stomp off, his gaze speculative. He'd already made a bad impression on her, and if he didn't remedy the situation his plans were going to come to a slamming halt before he could even begin to set them in motion.

ABOUT THE AUTHOR

Jacqueline Ashley is a veteran romance writer who began her career many years ago when the union at her workplace went on strike. To preserve her sanity, Jacqueline started her first book, and by the time she was finished, she was addicted to "creating characters and situations undergoing the very real process of falling in love." Jacqueline has lived in seven different states, including Hawaii, and now makes her home in Oklahoma.

Books by Jacqueline Ashley

HARLEQUIN AMERICAN ROMANCE

HARLEQUIN INTRIGUE

Don't miss any of our special offers. Write to us at the following address for information on our newest releases.

Harlequin Reader Service
901 Fuhrmann Blvd., P.O. Box 1397, Buffalo, NY 14240
Canadian address: P.O. Box 603,
Fort Erie, Ont. L2A 5X3

The Gift
Jacqueline Ashley

Harlequin Books

TORONTO • NEW YORK • LONDON
AMSTERDAM • PARIS • SYDNEY • HAMBURG
STOCKHOLM • ATHENS • TOKYO • MILAN

This book is dedicated to
Charles's and my family and friends—
thank you for the gift
of your love always,
but especially since
December 19, 1986.

Published June 1989

First printing April 1989

ISBN 0-373-16299-5

Prologue

The screen door of Butler's General Store creaked open, and Will Butler stopped whittling for a moment. Turning his grizzled head, he watched as a slender fourteen-year-old girl dressed in a clean but faded blue gingham dress stepped out of the store with a five-pound bag of cornmeal in her arms.

A shiver of uneasiness trailed down Will's shrunken spine as he noted that today the girl's eyes were a clear green. Sometimes they seemed a light brown. But at least her white-blond, hip-length hair was confined in one neat braid down her back this morning, instead of flying all around her body like a shroud.

"Good morning, Grandma Bolling," the girl said, addressing the elderly woman sitting in the rocking chair beside the wooden bench Will occupied.

The girl's voice fell pleasantly enough on a body's ear, sort of low timbered and musical, Will thought, yet he didn't much care for the high-falutin' way she pronounced her words...as if she was puttin' on airs.

Grandma Bolling was no one's grandmother, but had gained the title by dint of age and the respect in which she was held by the general community. In response to the girl's greeting, she peered upward through the magnifying spectacles perched on her nose, nodded her gray head and smiled affectionately.

"Mornin', Mary Rose," she said.

The girl turned her large green eyes on Will. He suppressed the urge to look away.

"Good morning, Mr. Butler," Mary Rose said.

"Mornin', Mary Rose," Will grumped, then stared down at his hands as he rubbed his fingers over the wood he held.

Mary Rose turned her attention back to Grandma Bolling. "How is your arthritis today, Grandma?" she inquired, her young voice taking on a sympathetic tone. "Do you need anymore of Ma's potion yet?"

"No, child." Grandma Bolling shook her head. "I got 'nuff of the last batch your ma made up fer me to do me a spell longer. How is your ma, honey? She over that old winter cold now that the warm's come?"

"Ma's feeling tolerable, Grandma," Mary Rose replied. Then a smile suddenly tilted her pale lips, like a ray of sunshine splitting the clouds. "Shall I bring you a new batch of potion when I come to the store next Saturday?" she asked.

"You do that, child," the old woman said, nodding. "I oughta be needin' it by then."

"Fine. Well, good day, Grandma...Mr. Butler," Mary Rose said, and she descended the stairs of the porch sedately. But once she had stepped onto the road, she broke into a headlong run for home.

"Thar she goes again," Will Butler snorted. "Runnin' like she's got the devil on her heels, 'stead of walkin' like a young lady. That girl is spooky. But I guess it ain't surprisin', seein' her ma's a witch."

"Oh, pshaw, Will," Grandma Bolling replied, peering over the top of her spectacles and searching her knitting bag for the right color skein of wool for the afghan she was making. "She ain't spooky. She's a sweet girl. And her ma ain't no witch. She's a good Christian woman blessed with the gift of healin'."

Having found the skein of wool, Grandma Bolling sat back in the rocking chair, originally placed on the porch of the general store for anyone who might want to sit awhile and pass the time of day after making purchases inside. She appropriated the chair during good weather to satisfy her desire for company, now that she was too crippled up with arthritis to go very far afield from her nearby cottage.

"Humph!" Will scowled and emphatically sliced a long strip of wood from the toy horse he was whittling. "If'n Mary Violet Perkins was such an all-fired powerful healer, how come she ain't healed her own self? She been in that wheelchair 'bout eight years now, ain't she?"

Grandma Bolling shook her head. "Some thangs even them high-powered doctors in Charleston cain't fix, Will, so we cain't expect Mary Violet to be able to fix everthang, neither. But I'll tell you, if'n it warn't for her potions, I'd be in a wheelchair my own self, so I'm jest grateful to have her, and that's all I got to say 'bout that!"

Will knew when he wasn't getting anywhere, so he hushed. But as he stared down the road Mary Rose Perkins had taken, he again felt uneasy. Despite Grandma Bolling's affection for the child, he hoped he didn't never come upon Mary Rose flittin' around the hills in the light of the moon, lookin' like a ghost with her pale skin and white hair flyin', the way Jeb Stouts had that time. Old Jeb had like to had a heart attack, and Will looked forward to a good many more years of settin' and jawin' before he went to meet his Maker.

"I'M HOME, Ma!" Mary Rose called breathlessly as she threw back the screen door to the cabin and quickly crossed the threshold. She was always out of breath these days because whenever she had to be away from her mother, she ran back and forth to where she had to go, terrified that when she returned home, she'd find that her ma had slipped away and gone to Jesus.

Mary Violet, whose once beautiful face was now carved with lines of pain, sat in her wheelchair in front of the back window that gave a view of the beautiful spring-greened hills behind the cabin. As Mary Rose entered, her mother turned her head and smiled.

"You'll never guess what I just saw over on the east ridge, Mary Rose," she said, her voice warm and happy. "A mother doe and her fawn. There are so few of them these days, it was such a treat."

"Really?" Mary Rose dumped the bag of cornmeal on the scarred kitchen table and quickly crossed to her mother to look out.

"They're gone now, honey," Mary Violet said. "But maybe you'll see them while you're out gathering plants this evening."

"I hope so," Mary Rose replied. She turned around, and saw a spasm of pain contort her mother's face before she could hide it. Sobering immediately, Mary Rose said, "You're hurting. Let me get you a dose of—"

"I just took a dose, honey," Mary Violet interrupted. "It'll start to work in a minute. Get the Bible, instead, and read me Corinthians 13. Hearing those beautiful words always makes me feel better."

Trying not to show the fear trembling through her, Mary Rose went to the old walnut table her grandpa had made many years earlier, which stood against one wall in the front room. Picking up the heavy family Bible, she returned to the kitchen and took a chair from the table, moving it close to her mother's wheelchair. Opening the Bible unerringly to 1 Corinthians, Chapter 13, she began to read in her clear, preternaturally mature voice: "Though I speak with the tongues of men and of angels, and have not charity, I am become as sounding brass, or a tinkling cymbal..."

And Mary Violet, a sweet, accepting smile curving her pale lips, closed her pain-filled green eyes and leaned her gray-threaded blond head against the high-topped back of her old-fashioned wooden wheelchair as she listened intently, for what would turn out to be the last time, to the words she had lived by all of the years of her life.

MARY ROSE BURIED HER MOTHER in the family plot on top of a nearby hill, in a grave she dug herself. She was slender, but spading garden plots every spring by herself and lifting her mother in and out of her wheelchair over the years had made her much stronger than she looked.

When the wildflowers she'd dug up and replanted on the grave covered the raw earth, and the wooden cross she'd fashioned from redbud limbs still covered with blossoms was positioned at the head of the mound of dirt, Mary Rose knelt beside the grave.

"Thank you, Ma, for all your love and all your teaching," she said as tears streamed down her cheeks. "Like I promised you, I won't forget anything...not the medicine, the book learning or the way to live among others with love and respect.''

At the last words she raised her face to the blue canopy of sky peeking between the gently swaying tree limbs and peered as though searching for something.

''Jesus, Ma said you had a reason for everything,'' she whispered. ''So I guess You had a reason for taking Ma when it seemed like I needed her more down here. Maybe You took her because she was hurting so badly, and if that's so, I don't blame You, though it hurts so much to have her gone I don't know if I can stand it.''

She paused a moment, closing her eyes and clenching her teeth to keep from sobbing until she was finished with the service. Then she opened her eyes and spoke again.

''Ma also said You answer prayer, so long as a person asks for the right things and answering won't hurt anybody else and won't get in the way of what You have in mind. So I'm asking You to help me keep anybody, especially Aunt Sarah, from knowing Ma's gone until I'm ready to leave here. I know people are kind and would want to help, and Ma's sister is a good woman and will take me in when I'm ready to go. But Ma said since Aunt Sarah moved away to the city, she thinks book learning is all there is that's important, and I don't know if she'll understand why I need to stay here a little while yet . . . until the hurting can be borne.''

Mary Rose closed her eyes again, squeezing tears out below her thick, black-lashed lids.

''Ma always said to thank You for providing before You do, to show faith. So I thank You, Lord . . . and I trust You.''

Her praying done, Mary Rose fell across the wildflower-covered grave and let the sobs come full force.

A long time afterward, when she was drained of tears, she got up and went to the cabin to mix Grandma Bolling's arthritis potion, as she had been doing for the past year. The task kept her trembling hands busy for a while ... but more important, it served as a partial antidote to the lonely agony she felt every time she looked at her mother's empty wheelchair.

The next Saturday Mary Rose made her way to the general store to deliver Grandma Bolling's medicine, also taking around a few other homemade remedies to other folks in the community. And each time someone asked after her mother, she answered that she was doing fine ... better than she ever had before.

It took two months before Mary Rose was able to take her mother's wheelchair apart and burn the wooden portions in the cook stove. The parts that wouldn't burn she buried near the family cemetery. And then she began to heal enough to contemplate her future.

JUST BEFORE the new school term started, Mary Rose watched impassively as an expensive gray foreign car came up the dirt road to the cabin. Her expression didn't change as a stylishly dressed woman in her forties climbed out.

Sarah Zimmerman walked up the wooden steps to the porch, then gazed down into the solemn face of her niece. "When did Mary Violet die?" she asked gently. "You didn't say in your letter."

"In the late spring," Mary Rose answered quietly.

Sarah Zimmerman blinked at her niece, looking bewildered. "But...why didn't someone notify me sooner?" she asked.

"No one knows but me," Mary Rose answered with devastating simplicity.

Sarah took in the implications of that statement, and her straight back sagged a little. "Who buried her then?" she asked.

"Me," Mary Rose replied, and her eyes never wavered from her aunt's.

Sarah didn't look away. "And who said the service?" she asked.

"I did," Mary Rose answered, and there was no apology in her voice.

A hint of sadness joined the bewilderment in Sarah's brown eyes. "You didn't want me there?" she asked in a subdued tone.

"You would have taken me away," Mary Rose explained. "And I wasn't ready to go then."

Sarah continued to stare at her niece for a long moment, then shook her head and sighed. "Are you ready to go now?" she asked. "Is that why you wrote me?"

"Yes, ma'am," Mary Rose said. "I have to go to school."

Sarah considered the statement for a moment, then nodded emphatically. "Yes, you do," she agreed, and some of the sadness departed from her eyes. "You, of all people," she added firmly, "need to be in school."

"Yes." Mary Rose accepted the comment without undue modesty. "I've decided I'm going to be a doctor."

Sarah Zimmerman's eyes lit with the fire of the dedicated scholar. "Of course." She nodded again, smiling slightly. "What else would appeal to you, considering your upbringing so far?" She looked out over the area surrounding the cabin for a long moment, her expression ambiguous, before returning her gaze to her niece. "Let's go to your mother's grave now. I want to say goodbye."

Mary Rose led the way to the family plot, and Sarah walked among the graves of her relatives, finally stopping beside the flower-covered grave of her sister.

"She could have been anything she'd wanted if she hadn't married your father and stayed here," Sarah said to Mary Rose, her tone bitter. "She was smarter than any of us . . . even me."

"She didn't want to be anywhere else," Mary Rose said simply. "If she had, she would have left here after Daddy was killed and she got paralyzed. She loved it here. And so do I."

Sarah got an impatient look on her face and started to say something, then thought better of it. "Well, whatever Mary Violet wanted or didn't want, things are going to be different for you," she said determinedly. "You're going to live up to your potential. I'm going to make sure of that!"

The expression on Mary Rose's face was unrevealing, but her tone was just as firm as Sarah's had been as she answered, "Yes, I intend to do that, but it may come to be that we disagree on what that means."

Sarah immediately frowned. But an instant later a smile replaced the frown, and she gazed at Mary Rose with satisfaction. The child's maturity was gratifying. Apparently, the teaching Mary Violet had given her daughter at home to supplement what she got at school had paid off. Not many fourteen-year-old girls could express themselves so sophisticatedly. Yet while the child might sound mature, Sarah was keenly aware that

Mary Rose was not ready to make decisions for herself. By the time she was, Sarah intended to have Mary Rose indoctrinated in her own thinking to avoid any unpleasant disagreements that might arise concerning her future.

"Let's go home, Mary Rose," she said, and she reached to take her niece's hand in a firm grip.

Mary Rose allowed her aunt to hold her hand as they made their way into the cabin. Inside, Sarah saw that Mary Rose had already done her packing. An old trunk, which Sarah recognized as having been her and Mary Violet's mother's, rested on the floor of the kitchen, its lid thrown back. It contained Mary Rose's scanty possessions and the family Bible.

"I'm glad you're packed . . . I don't want to stay here any longer than I have to," Sarah said, and she barely controlled a shudder of indignation as she looked around at the shabby, but clean cabin she herself had grown up in. After all these years it still didn't have an indoor bathroom. And the old-fashioned hand pump at the sink was apparently still the only source of running water.

Mary Rose frowned thoughtfully over her aunt's words. She fastened the lid of the trunk and looked up with an oddly cautious expression on her face. "Is it true, Aunt Sarah," she asked, "that the cabin and the land around it belong to me now?"

Sarah turned a sharp glance her way. "Yes, it's true," she said, hoping the query didn't mean what she was afraid it did. "Why?"

Mary Rose ignored the question and asked another. "Is it also true that if the taxes aren't paid I'll lose the place?"

Annoyed, Sarah looked away and, without answering immediately, wandered over to the back window. As she gazed out, she thought that at least the view here was beautiful. It had been the only compensation during her growing-up years, when she'd been stuck in this backwater away from all the places she longed to see . . . all the things she yearned to learn.

"Yes, it's true, Mary Rose," she finally answered, and turned to give her niece another sharp look. "Why?"

Mary Rose got to her feet and joined her aunt at the window, thinking hard before she answered. She had a feeling this was one of those times when lying would gain her more than the truth, but lying didn't come easily, so she didn't look directly at Sarah as she replied.

"Some say this land is going to be very valuable one of these days," she said quietly. "So I was wondering if you'd be willing to pay the taxes for me since I can't pay them myself. I may need a . . . a nest egg one day. To set up a practice, for instance."

Sarah was relieved and pleased. She'd been afraid Mary Rose would want to cling to this place the way her mother had. Instead the child was thinking ahead. And the idea made sense. For although Sarah's position as a college professor earned her enough to pay the taxes on this place with no strain, it might very well be a problem to set Mary Rose up in a practice when she graduated from medical school. So this land might one day be the means to give her niece a good start in her career.

"Very well, Mary Rose," she said agreeably. "I'll do that for you."

Mary Rose was careful to keep her heartfelt sigh of relief inaudible. "Thank you, Aunt Sarah," she said softly. "Thank you very much."

And then, as though they were a sign that her long-range plans would one day be fulfilled, she saw the doe and fawn her mother had seen the day she died. They were on the east ridge, outlined sharply against the horizon. The sight brought an inexplicable feeling of peace to Mary Rose's heart.

"Look," she whispered, pointing. "Aren't they lovely?"

Sarah followed the direction of Mary Rose's finger, but by the time she looked, the doe and the fawn had disappeared over the ridge.

"At what?" Sarah asked, frowning. "I don't see anything."

Mary Rose smiled then, and Sarah studied her for a moment, noting that the child was as beautiful as she was intelligent.

Sarah wasn't sure if Mary Rose's beauty would be an advantage or a problem. Mary Violet had been beautiful, as well. And her beauty had attracted Tom Perkins, thereby ruining any chance she ever had of getting out of this backwater. Sarah vowed once again to give her niece the sort of guidance that would keep her from making that kind of mistake.

"Never mind, Aunt Sarah," Mary Rose said, still smiling. And she turned away from the window to go back to the trunk. She started dragging it to the doorway.

"Here, let me help you with that," Sarah said.

After the trunk had been deposited in the car, Sarah straightened and looked at Mary Rose, who was gazing at the cabin, her expression inscrutable. "Have you got everything?" she asked.

Mary Rose nodded. "Let me shut the door and I'll be ready to leave." She started walking back to the cabin.

"Be sure and lock the place up," Sarah advised.

Mary Rose looked at her aunt over her shoulder, her green eyes wide with surprise. "No one around here will steal anything," she said. "And if a stranger comes by, Ma would want them to be able to take shelter here. Anyway, I've already put everything I want to keep in the old wooden box and locked that."

Sarah shrugged. "Well, suit yourself. This old cabin and the things in it aren't worth anything, anyway."

That statement made Mary Rose stare at her aunt in complete astonishment for a moment, but she quickly turned away before Sarah could see the expression. After shutting the door to her home, she returned to the car and climbed into the front seat.

Sarah got behind the wheel and started the engine, but before she pulled away, she glanced at Mary Rose, who was sitting up straight in her seat, her hands folded in her lap. Her eyes were focused straight ahead.

"I know you're sad to leave," Sarah said gently. "But, Mary Rose, I promise you . . . after you've lived with me awhile, there'll be nothing here you'll want to come back to. There's a whole world out there . . . a world full of wonderful things you'll love more than you do this old place."

Mary Rose didn't answer for a moment. She couldn't think of anything in the world she would ever love more than her home. But she knew by now that Sarah didn't want to hear that, so finally she said, "Yes, I'm sad to leave. But it has to be. I understand that."

"Good," Sarah responded with satisfaction, and she put the car in gear and began guiding it carefully over the rutted unpaved road leading to the small town downhill.

As Sarah pulled up minutes later at the general store, Grandma Bolling and Will Butler sat forward, their expressions curious.

"We need to let people know about Mary Violet and that you're coming to live with me," Sarah said. "And I suppose you'll want to say goodbye to your school friends."

All Mary Rose's school friends were at home, and it would take hours to drive around the dirt roads and stop at each place, so she merely answered, "Yes, I want to say goodbye to Grandma Bolling and Mr. Butler and Ina."

"Lord, how long is that old woman going to live?" Sarah said under her breath as she and Mary Rose climbed out of the car. "She must be at least a hundred by now."

As Sarah and Mary Rose approached her, Grandma Bolling spoke up. "Is that you, Sarah Zimmerman?" she demanded, peering shortsightedly over the tops of her glasses.

"Yes, it is, Grandma Bolling," Sarah answered pleasantly.

Grandma Bolling's face crinkled up, and she reached for the handkerchief she kept inside the neck of her faded brown dress. "Then Mary Violet's gone, ain't she?" she said, then buried her face in the handkerchief and began to weep.

Mary Rose quickly knelt beside her and leaned her head against Grandma Bolling's shoulder. She looked solemn, but there were no tears in her green eyes.

Sarah was puzzled. She failed to understand how the old woman had known about Mary Violet's death. But Will Butler informed her.

"Reckon you wouldna showed up back here if it wasn't somethin' like that," he explained, squinting up at Sarah through his thick gray eyebrows. "How long's she been gone? And when's the funeral to be?"

Sarah was annoyed by Will's implied criticism of her, but she refused to show it. She was also irritated by his question, because she hadn't planned to tell anyone how long it had been since Mary Violet had died. There might be legal ramifications for all she knew. But Mary Rose spoke up then and told them everything she'd done.

"But land's sake, child!" Grandma Bolling protested, staring with astonishment at Mary Rose. "You shoulda come and got somebody!"

"If I had, you all wouldn't have let me stay at the cabin by myself," she answered quietly. "And I wasn't ready to leave my home."

"Well, shore we would have brought you down here, but...but..." Grandma Bolling's protest died on the vine as she stared into Mary Rose's calm green gaze. The elderly woman finally shook her head. "Well, if that don't beat all!" was all she could manage after that, but she repeated her verdict several times.

Will Butler merely looked as though he wasn't at all surprised that a fourteen-year-old girl had managed to bury her mother and keep the fact of the passing to herself. Where Mary Rose was concerned, he was prepared to believe anything.

Grandma Bolling turned her attention back to Sarah. "You takin' her with you back up to that there Washington, D.C., where you been livin'?"

"Yes, I'm taking Mary Rose to live with me." Sarah nodded firmly.

Grandma looked at Mary Rose pitifully and sighed. "I don't guess your ma left any more of my arthritis potion already made up, did she, child?"

Mary Rose shook her head. "I'm afraid you'll have to use aspirin from now on," she replied regretfully. "Or the next time you go to the doctor in Charleston, you could ask for something stronger," she suggested. "I've read there are other medications that work better than aspirin."

"Pshaw, child, I ain't got the kind of money them store-bought medicines cost." Grandma Bolling snorted. "Naw, I'll just stick to aspirin. I'm so old I ain't likely to need nothin' much longer, anyways."

"I'm sorry," Mary Rose said. She would have made up more of the potion, but it wouldn't have kept past a certain point, and there would have come a time when Grandma would have run out, anyway.

"Ain't your fault," the old woman reassured her, patting Mary Rose's shoulder affectionately. "I'm real sorry about your ma, honey," she added. "But she was a good Christian woman, so she's up scamperin' through Heaven now on two good legs, 'stead of bein' trapped in that old wheelchair. Ain't no call to feel too sad when you look at it thataways."

"No," Mary Rose agreed, smiling faintly. "Ma's all right now."

Mary Rose's sad tone made Grandma Bolling look sharply at her, then at Sarah. "You take good care of this child, you hear?" she ordered. "She ain't used to your high-toned ways and she ain't used to no city, neither."

"She'll learn," Sarah responded a little stiffly. "And I certainly will take good care of her, Mrs. Bolling. She's my niece, after all."

"Wouldn't nobody a knowed it for quite a spell now," Grandma said tartly.

Sarah ignored the gibe and turned to Mary Rose. "Is there anyone else you want to say goodbye to?"

"No one but Ina," Mary Rose answered, referring to Mr. Butler's daughter, who ran the general store for him now that he was semiretired. "It'll just take a minute, Aunt Sarah," she added, and got to her feet to go say goodbye to the woman who'd sold her the supplies she hadn't been able to grow in the garden or pick wild in the woods.

Of course, Mary Rose had to go through another explanation for Ina, who seemed flabbergasted by what Mary Rose had done.

"Well," Ina finally said lamely, "I reckon your ma will be sorely missed around here. And you, too, a'course. Is Sarah gonna sell your cabin and land?" she added.

Mary Rose shook her head. "Aunt Sarah is going to pay the taxes on the property so I'll have it when I grow up."

"I see," Ina answered with a nod. "Well, good luck, honey."

Mary Rose said goodbye, then returned to the porch, where she kissed Grandma Bolling. After that, she climbed into the car with her aunt, who started the engine and gunned it unnecessarily as she pulled away from the general store.

"I'd forgotten how *backward* those people are," Sarah said with grim distaste as they drove off. "Thank goodness you're getting away from here and will never have to come back. A few new dresses and a haircut and no one will ever connect you with these people again. At least your mother had the good sense to teach you proper speech, so I won't have that to change along with everything else!''

Mary Rose didn't respond. After spending only a short time with her aunt, she already knew how useless it would be to argue with her on certain subjects. But her silence was resolute.

But I will be coming back, Aunt Sarah, she vowed. *When I've got my medical degree, I'll return to my cabin, and no one like Grandma Bolling will ever have to travel as far as they do now to get medical treatment again.*

Mary Rose considered a moment longer, then a faint smile touched her lips as she remembered one more item to add to her list of things she would do when she was grown up.

And if I want to grow my hair to my ankles, she thought as she pulled her long braid over her shoulder and touched the twisted strands protectively, *I will!*

Chapter One

His second drink all but consumed, Caleb Anderson stood on the terrace of his future inlaws' estate in the Virginia countryside, looking out over the acres that could someday be his, and wondered how he'd managed to get himself into such a mess.

Though it was already 6:30, he hadn't even started to get ready for his own engagement party. His tuxedo hung in the vast closet of the suite of rooms allotted him due to his exalted status as the family princess's intended husband, but he stood clad in the dirty, sweaty clothes he'd worn to ride one of the family's Thoroughbred mares all afternoon.

As the hour grew ever later, Caleb still made no move to walk up the sweeping staircase in the front hallway and go into his luxurious bathroom to wash the dirt and sweat from the body Alicia couldn't wait to claim exclusively as her own. Instead he stood silently castigating himself.

You're selling out, he told himself with bleak disgust. *If you go through with this marriage, you can kiss goodbye to your self-respect and the chance to write anything worthwhile ever again. You won't have time to write, what with all the charity balls and the fox hunts to attend. But isn't that what you've been counting on?*

Caleb looked down at the remaining whiskey in his glass, then raised the liquid to his lips and swallowed it, wishing he could get rid of his self-disgust so easily. Then he had a bitter thought. If he was trying to forget the clamorings of his conscience now, what would he be like in another ten years?

For an instant, his fingers tightened on the empty glass and he almost threw it violently against the brick railing of the terrace. But he sighed, shrugged and set the glass down on a nearby patio table. Putting his hands in his pockets, he returned his bleak gaze to the glorious sunset on the western horizon.

What's it to be? he asked himself once and for all. *Are you going to go through with it, or are you going to go stalking, penniless but upright, into what will probably turn out to be poverty-stricken obscurity?*

"Caleb? Darling, what on earth are you doing out here? It's getting late."

Alicia's cultured, normally honey-laden voice was tinged with annoyance. And before he turned to look at her, Caleb had a sudden vision of the future...a future wherein that annoyance grew more and more pronounced. It would be inevitable, considering that the demons that rode him now would ride him harder as the fruitless years of his life rolled by.

Caleb turned. Alicia, a dark-haired, slender vision of beauty in her designer dress, had just reached him, and started to raise her carefully painted lips for a kiss. But when she caught a whiff of his sweat and noticed the dirt on his clothes, she wrinkled her perfect nose, instead, and stepped back.

"Goodness, you're a mess!" she complained. "I'll wait to kiss you until after you've bathed."

And Caleb suddenly knew what his decision would be. He was sorry about it for Alicia's sake. She didn't deserve what he was about to hand her. She loved him...or thought she did. And to his credit, in the heated beginning of their relationship he'd managed to convince himself that he loved her, as well. He knew now that he'd been fooling himself. More likely what he'd loved had been the escape from his own fears Alicia represented. But that was before he'd fully realized that the price of escaping his fear would be his self-respect.

"Honey, you'd better get yourself upstairs," Alicia said coaxingly. "Our guests will be arriving in an hour or so."

Caleb took a deep breath. "Alicia, I have to talk to you," he said, and he could tell by the sudden look of alarm in her normally limpid brown eyes, followed by a flame of fierce negation, that she wasn't going to require much of an explanation.

"Not now," she said flatly, sounding totally unlike herself.

"Yes now," Caleb responded quietly. "Sit down."

"I can't. I'll muss my dress."

Caleb sighed. She wasn't going to make this easy. But, then, why should she? What he was about to do was unforgivable.

"Alicia, I don't want to hurt you, but..."

"Then don't!" Her voice was growing harder. "We'll talk later, Caleb," she added, as though giving an order. "After the party." She turned then, and started to walk back into the house.

He reached out and took her arm to stop her. His hands were dirty, and she looked down with distaste at the one holding her.

"Please, Caleb," she said frostily. "I've already bathed once."

"I'm sorry, Alicia," he said, speaking gently, "but we can't talk later. I'm not going to be at the party."

She stayed perfectly still for a long moment, then raised her eyes to Caleb's, and he almost flinched at the rage he saw there.

"If you do this to me," she said with cold precision, "I will do everything I can to ruin you."

Caleb shrugged and took his hand away from her arm, stuffing it into his pocket. "I'm already ruined, Alicia," he said dryly. "I haven't written anything worth printing in two years, remember?"

Her perfectly curved lips curled in contempt. "I remember," she said coldly. "But I was willing to overlook it because I was sure that once we were married you'd get over your writer's block."

Caleb raised his eyebrows. "How kind of you to 'overlook' it for any reason," he drawled. "But the thing is, Alicia," he added in that same dry tone, "*I* can't overlook it. And if I marry you and bury myself in all this—" he indicated the estate with his hand "—both of us will probably have to keep on overlooking it." He returned his gaze to Alicia and shook his head. "I can't take that risk," he said soberly. "I'm sorrier than I can say, but I can't marry you. If I do, I have the feeling it will be the end of me as a writer, and probably as a man worth respecting."

Alicia's hands were clenched and her patrician face was livid. "Don't be stupid!" she hissed. "What better place to write than here, where you won't have to worry about money and I can protect your privacy."

He shook his head. "However good your intentions," he said gently, "there would always be something you wanted me to escort you to...some attention you wanted to be paid. And it would be too easy for me to escape that way. I may have lost for good whatever it was I had that allowed me to get two books published—I don't know. But if I haven't, living here with you as a kept husband will cinch the matter."

"But what about our love?" Alicia cried. "You said you loved me, Caleb! Was that a lie?"

Caleb hesitated. He wasn't sure whether it had actually been the truth at the time he'd said it. But he knew it wasn't true now. He preferred, however, for the sake of Alicia's pride, not to tell her the truth.

"Alicia, any man would love you," he said quietly. "You're beautiful, intelligent, fun to be with, wonderful in bed..."

She was trembling now, and Caleb felt like a heel for confronting the situation today. Hadn't he known almost from the moment she'd begun to take it for granted they would marry and had started making wedding plans without his ever having proposed that he didn't really want this? Yet he'd gone along, thinking maybe it was for the best. Fear had overridden his common sense...fear of failure.

"Alicia, I'm sorry," he repeated quietly. "I'm so terribly sorry."

"Oh, you'll be sorry, all right," she retorted harshly, her voice shaking with emotion. "I'll make sure of that!" She started to turn in a rush, but checked the movement and stared at him over her shoulder, her brown eyes blazing. "Go on then, Caleb!" she grated. "Go on to hell, for all I care!"

An instant later, she swept away through the glass door, looking magnificently haughty with her shoulders held straight and her head tilted proudly.

Caleb watched her go. And when she disappeared from view, he let out the breath he'd been unconsciously holding. Then, abruptly, he smiled.

He knew he shouldn't feel so good after doing something that appeared despicable on the surface. But for the first time in a long while, he had a deep inner certainty that he had done the *right* thing—for himself and for Alicia.

Half an hour later, as he was speeding down the highway in the red sports car he had bought when he'd been riding high on royalties from his two published books and on his reputation as the new fair-haired author, he was still smiling... and then he laughed out loud.

"Free!" he yelled, and his words were caught by the wind and thrown behind him in the direction of Alicia's family estate.

He was smiling still as he pulled into an automobile dealership the next morning after spending the night in a motel. Sometime later, having sold his car at not too bad a loss, he bought a backpack complete with all the essentials for camping out. He also bought, then donned, a pair of sturdy hiking boots.

As he hitchhiked his way to the Blue Ridge Mountains, where he intended to trudge away the sophisticated cynicism and destructive self-indulgence that had blocked his talent and sapped his energy for far too long, he felt wonderful. When he was sufficiently cleansed by nature to feel whole again, Caleb intended to get an honest job to support himself while working on his writing in his spare time. Then, if it came to be that he truly had lost the muse that had once visited him regularly, at least he would know he'd tried his best. But if he regained the one precious gift he'd ever had, he knew better now than to ever stifle it again by living the fast-paced, hard-drinking playboy's life that had once before robbed him of all that truly mattered.

MARY ROSE WANDERED toward the rose garden in back of her Aunt Sarah's Georgetown home. She supposed it was probably crass to have left the party in her honor to wander out here on her own. But she was so very tired of behaving according to other people's ideas of what constituted proper conduct that she didn't care how crass she appeared.

Besides, she needed some time alone to figure out exactly how she was going to tell Aunt Sarah that instead of accepting one of the numerous offers she'd received to go into partnership with other physicians in the area, she was going back home to Sweet Water to practice medicine alone.

Mary Rose sat down on a small wrought-iron bench under a cherry tree, closed her eyes and let the peace of the garden and the lovely scent of the flowers soothe her soul. She was so tired...so unutterably weary. All the years of unremitting study to get scholarships so she wouldn't feel beholden to Sarah, then going through a residency as an internist, had taken their toll. There had never been enough sleep. But it had all paid off, or at least it soon would. Not the way Sarah hoped...but certainly the way Mary Rose had intended it should.

"Mare?"

A dart of irritation over the way Geoff always short-ened her name joined the resentment Mary Rose felt at being disturbed. But when she opened her eyes, there was no lack of welcome in them. Geoff had done ab-solutely nothing to deserve rudeness from her. He thought himself to be in love with her and she knew gentle handling rather than an abrupt refusal would be better in turning down the proposal she was sure was coming.

"I'm over here," she said quietly. "Under the cherry tree."

Geoff moved his long legs in the right direction, and Mary Rose knew he was smiling, though she couldn't see his face clearly. His good nature was one of the rea-sons she had allowed herself to spend with him what little free time she had. But she wished now her loneli-ness hadn't made her date him. Not when it meant he was going to be hurt.

"What are you doing out here by yourself, Mare?" Geoff asked as he sat down beside her. "Everyone's wondering where you got to."

Mary Rose sighed. "My name is Mary Rose," she said with gentle firmness. "I wish you wouldn't call me 'Mare.'"

"Huh?" He was taken by surprise.

Mary Rose smiled wearily and shook her head. What was the point of making an issue of something so small at this late date? "Never mind, Geoff." She spoke list-lessly, her normal font of energy temporarily drained.

"You're in a funny mood," he commented, and slid his arm around her shoulders to pull her against him.

The position was uncomfortable... and stifling. She suddenly wanted to fling herself away from him. But, mindful of his feelings, she merely straightened and eased out of his grip.

"Hey, Mare...uh, Mary Rose," Geoff corrected himself, "what's with you? You ought to be feeling on top of the world."

She smiled, this time spontaneously. "I'd settle for being on top of a hill, Geoff," she said lightly, knowing he couldn't dream that that was exactly where she intended to be before too much longer. "A beautiful green hill, with the wind blowing the grass and maybe a doe and her fawn on the horizon."

He shrugged. "Give me the bright lights every time," he said emphatically. "I've never been a nature lover." Then he added, "Say, have you given any more thought to setting up practice with me? I'll foot all the bills, you know. Or rather, Dad will. He's so proud of having a doctor in the family, he'll buy us nothing but the best in equipment, and he's already spotted several buildings that have suites we can rent until we can afford our own building."

Mary Rose's stomach began to tighten up. She couldn't tell Geoff what she had in mind before she told Sarah, yet she felt the pressure of his needs weighing upon her, and she wanted to let him down as easily as she could.

"Geoff, I just want to rest and take it easy for a while," she hedged. "Please...let's not worry about tomorrow right now."

"I don't ever worry about tomorrow when I'm with you, Mare...uh, Mary Rose." The romantic tone Geoff was striving for was spoiled somewhat by his hesitation over her name. He tried to cover it by reaching for her again.

She didn't mean to hurt him, but she couldn't help the spontaneous movement of her body away from his. She could see his face more clearly now, and caught the frown that appeared on his handsome face as a result of her movement.

"Hey, I know you've got some old-fashioned ideas about sex," he half joked, half grated. "And these days, I guess your values are coming back in vogue. But you've never minded my arm around you before ... or my kisses."

That was true, Mary Rose admitted honestly to herself. She had been curious.... But she'd never felt half the excitement Geoff obviously had during those kisses, which was why it had been easy to stop him from going any further.

"I'm just very tired," she said lamely.

"Aren't we all?" Geoff retorted. "Anybody who's ever been through medical training is exhausted. But, Mare," he added, slipping back easily into his old way of addressing her, "you must know how I feel about you. You know I don't just want you to go into practice with me because you're the best doctor of any of us who went through the program. I'm in love with you, honey. I have been since the first moment I saw those green eyes, that white-blond hair and that luscious body of yours."

Mary Rose didn't want to deal with this right now. But it wasn't fair to Geoff to refuse to deal with his feelings for her any longer.

"Geoff, I'm honored by your feelings for me," she said quietly, truthfully. "You're the answer to most women's dreams." And that was also true. He was intelligent, handsome, came from a wealthy family, was professionally competent and conscientious, and he was naturally kind. He just wasn't the man for her.

"What does that mean?" he asked, a tinge of harshness in his voice. "I don't care about most women. I want to be the answer to *your* dreams."

She rested her hands on either side of her, her head bent as she sat on the bench. This was hard... harder than she'd suspected, though she'd known it wasn't going to be easy.

"Geoff, you deserve a woman who does think of you as the answer to her dreams," she almost whispered. "But I... I can't be that woman."

"How can you know that?" he shot back. "I admit, we haven't had the time to be together as much as I've wanted to. But we seem to mesh when we are with each other. And when I kiss you, Mare..." He stopped, took a deep breath, then went on. "I'm sorry... you should have told me a long time ago you wanted to be called 'Mary Rose.'"

Yes, I should have, Mary Rose silently agreed. *And if I'd cared more, I would have insisted. But since I didn't love you, I let it pass.*

"Anyway," Geoff continued, "when I kiss you, it just about sends me off the deep end. I would have sworn you felt the same."

At that, Mary Rose looked up at him, wondering how he'd managed to convince himself she'd felt more than she had during their kisses. But maybe it was always like that with people. Hadn't Sarah managed to persuade herself that Mary Rose wanted the same things she did?

"I'm sorry, Geoff," she said softly. "I like you enormously... I respect you very much. But..."

"But you don't love me," he said grimly. "Well, I'm sorry, but I just can't accept that! We haven't spent enough time alone together for you to know yet how you feel about me! We've never even been to bed together!''

Mary Rose blinked at him, failing to understand his logic. Admittedly she'd been too busy pursuing her goal to gain any sexual experience. But surely it didn't work that way, did it? Going to bed with someone couldn't automatically make one fall in love.

"I...we have different goals, Geoff," she said, changing direction.

"And that's another thing," he declared vehemently. "What the hell are your goals? Whenever anybody tries to pin you down about what it is you want, you somehow manage not to answer! Well, I want an answer, Mare, and I want it now!"

Mary Rose held on to her patience. She had never loved anyone who didn't love her back. She'd never been in love period. So she had no firsthand experience of how it felt to be rejected. But instinct told her Geoff's anger was a defense against his pain.

"I want to be a good doctor," she said.

"All of us want that!" he responded impatiently. "That tells me nothing."

"All right," she acceded. "But perhaps we differ in our understanding of what makes a good doctor."

"Oh, for God's sake, Mare!" Geoff said angrily. "That sounds so self-righteous!"

Mary Rose sighed. "Yes, it does sound that way, doesn't it?" she replied helplessly. "I guess, Geoff, I'm not going to be able to explain what I mean until I get a few things settled with Aunt Sarah. When I've done that, I'll be able to explain things better to you."

He narrowed his eyes suspiciously. "Don't tell me you're thinking of joining the Peace Corps, or some fool idea like that!'' he said exasperatedly. "Get practical, Mare! It takes years to build up a good practice, and if you're away too long, gratifying your altruistic bent, you may never catch up!''

Her patience was slipping. She got to her feet, and Geoff got up, as well.

"Don't run away," he warned. "I want to get this settled. I've been panting after you long enough as it is, and I'll be damned if I'll trail around at your heels much longer! In case you don't know it, there are plenty of women who would gladly be in your shoes if they had the chance!''

At that Mary Rose's patience broke. "All right, we'll get things settled," she said tightly. "You had best go looking for one of those women, Geoff, because I have my own plans, and they don't include marriage for a long while, if ever!'' Turning away from him, she started walking back to the house.

He caught up with her and spun her around by the shoulder. Startled, she stumbled, then looked up at Geoff, astonishment written over her face.

He clasped her roughly around the waist and pulled her hard against him. "Let's see if you can keep up that indifference after this," he grated, then he kissed her, hard enough to bruise her lips, and kept on kissing her long after it became apparent he wasn't going to get the response he'd hoped for.

Finally he raised his head, and Mary Rose softened toward him when she saw the pain in his eyes.

"God, Mare, I didn't want to hurt you…I never want to hurt you," he muttered in shame. "I just thought if…''

But the look on Mary Rose's face—a combination of concern and warm pity—made the words die in his throat, and he was back to being angry.

"God, you're cold!" he snarled, and thrusting her away from him, he stalked off, every line of his body expressing his wounded dignity and his hurt.

Distressed, Mary Rose watched him go. She would have handled this better if only she'd known how. But Geoff was the only male she'd ever let get close enough to her to get hurt. Since she had known there was no point in getting seriously involved with anyone, she hadn't dated much at all during the past few years. By the time Geoff had come along, she had been curious and lonely. And she had made a big mistake.

She would have gone back to sit under the cherry tree, but Aunt Sarah poked her head out the back door and, spotting her, frowned and gestured imperiously. "What in the world are you doing out there?" Sarah demanded when Mary Rose had drawn close enough to hear her. "This party is for you, in case you've forgotten!"

"I just needed some air," Mary Rose said, and made to go past Sarah into the house.

Her aunt stopped her, however. "Geoff just came into the house looking as though he just witnessed the sinking of the *Titanic*," Sarah said irritably. "What have you done? I was thrilled that when you finally woke up and realized there was another sex in the world, you picked someone like him to fall for."

"I never fell for him, Sarah," Mary Rose said on a sigh. "I liked him, but—"

"Oh, for heaven's sake!" her aunt interrupted. Then someone came into the kitchen behind her, and Sarah couldn't say anymore for the moment. "Never mind," she whispered, trying to find the smile she'd lost. "We'll talk about this later."

"Yes, I want to talk to you." Mary Rose nodded and walked away before Sarah could ask what she wanted to talk about.

The rest of the evening passed in a blur. Mary Rose had long years of practice at hiding her thoughts, so she was able to laugh and talk fairly naturally with her friends. Geoff had left the party, and whenever someone noticed, she merely said he hadn't been feeling very well and had thought it best to go home.

When the last person had departed around midnight, her weariness had grown, but she still had the discussion with her aunt to get through. She went into the kitchen to fix the two of them a pot of tea.

Sarah followed her into the room. "Now what's all this nonsense about Geoff?" she demanded as she began to put glasses into the dishwasher. "He's a wonderful man, and if you can't see that—"

"I think he's wonderful, too, Aunt Sarah," Mary Rose broke in. Abruptly she decided not to beat around the bush. "But I can't picture him in Sweet Water, can you?"

It took a moment for the words to penetrate Sarah's brain, then she straightened and looked at her niece in astonishment.

Mary Rose flipped on the gas under the teapot, then turned and faced her aunt, her gaze level and unyielding. "Sarah, I'm going back to Sweet Water to practice medicine," she said with quiet conviction. "It's what I've always planned to do. I'm very grateful for everything you've done for me, and I'm aware you've done a lot, but I won't be dissuaded. I'm not going to marry Geoff, either. I may never marry at all, as a matter of fact. As you well know, there aren't many single men in Sweet Water, and the ones who do live there probably wouldn't want to marry a witch's daughter. That's what some of them used to call Ma, you know...a witch."

Sarah was stunned for the moment...too stunned to seize upon anything Mary Rose had said other than the least important thing. "Don't call Mary Violet 'Ma,'" she stuttered distractedly. "It sounds—"

"Backwoodsish?" Mary Rose interjected, smiling warmly at her aunt. "But that's what I am at heart, Aunt Sarah. No matter how you've tried to change me, basically I've always stayed true to my roots."

The teapot started to whistle and Mary Rose quickly turned off the flame under it. But she didn't start to make tea immediately. Instead she turned back to finish the confrontation.

"I hope you know that I love you, Aunt Sarah. That you'll always be welcome at the cabin. I'm not ungrateful for all you've done for me. It's just that I can't live the life you want for me. I always knew I couldn't. And I think you should have known it, as well," she added very gently.

Sarah got over her initial stunned reaction, and for the next week, as Mary Rose went about making preparations to go home, Sarah was at her heels, trying to change her mind. All to no avail.

On the day Mary Rose left on the bus—she had no car, and probably wouldn't be able to afford one for a while—Sarah was still unresigned.

"You'll come back," she vowed with a bitterness that had grown as the days passed. "You've forgotten what it's really like in that backwater. And when you find out, you won't be able to return here fast enough. But I'm not sure I'm going to welcome you as openheartedly as I did the last time, and it will be too late to re-capture Geoff. I hear he's already dating Linda Baer.''

As she had all week, Mary Rose let the words brush over her, the way a breeze might have. She never ar-gued and she never backed down. Now, as the bus pulled up, she took her aunt into her arms, despite Sarah's stiff-bodied lack of response.

"I love you," Mary Rose whispered into her aunt's ear. "I love you very much. And I thank you for every-thing. Come see me soon, please? Because you're right about one thing. I'll be missing you up in the cabin by myself. And I'll be thinking of you every day.''

At that, Sarah finally relented enough to give Mary Rose a faint squeeze with her arms.

Mary Rose had tears in her eyes as she walked to the bus and got in, but Sarah's eyes were dry. And they stayed dry until she was back in her house in Georgetown, safe from snooping noses and listening ears, standing in the doorway to her niece's empty bed-room.

"Damn you, Mary Rose!" she whispered, her fierce anger erupting. "How could you do this to me? You could have had it *all*!''

Striding into the room, she snatched up one by one the ornaments and trinkets Mary Rose had left behind and threw them against the walls. When there was nothing left to throw, she sank down on Mary Rose's bed and let her rage dissolve into racking sobs of futile, heartbroken disappointment.

Chapter Two

Caleb didn't realize he'd crossed into West Virginia until he saw the sign outside a small town that read Sweet Water, population 3,000. Well, that's big enough to have a store or two, he thought, smiling, and walked down the paved street to a sign that read Butler's General Store. Thinking he likely would be able to buy everything he needed in such a place, he went in and was immediately enchanted.

The interior was dark and gloomy, but there was light enough to see that groceries were situated on one side, clothes sat on racks and tables in the middle, and sundries were stacked on shelves stretching to the ceiling on the other side.

It didn't take long for Caleb to pick out a couple of pairs of thick socks, as well as some ointment and bandages for the cuts and scratches he was always getting. Then, as he was turning away, his eyes fell on a pile of old-fashioned school tablets—the kind small children used.

Caleb hesitated. As he'd tramped along the backpacking trails of the Appalachians for the past two weeks, an idea for a book had started to come to him in trickles and vague presentiments. But the premise hadn't jelled enough as yet for him to put anything down on paper. Normally he typed his books rather than wrote them in longhand, anyway. But what if something came to him that needed to be written down before it was forgotten?

Feeling a little foolish, he slid three of the tablets off the stack, along with a half-dozen No. 2 school pencils and the most basic pencil sharpener, and headed for the grocery section of the store.

He was getting damned tired of his freeze-dried food and was starved for fresh fruit, so he bagged some apples and oranges before reaching for a jar of instant coffee. And he couldn't bypass the basket of fresh eggs. He grabbed up a half-dozen of those, a pound of bacon and a loaf of bread, as well.

A woman a little past middle age stood at an ancient cash register at the back of the store. Her brown-gray hair was pulled back in a bun and she wore a rather shapeless dress.

"Howdy, mister," she said to him pleasantly as he brought his purchases to her to be rung up. "I reckon yore hikin' the trails?"

"Yes, ma'am," Caleb answered, smiling at her.

"We git lots of you folks this time of year," the woman said as she began to ring up the items. "Cain't see the attraction of walkin' blisters on a body's heels and sleepin' out in the rain myself, but I guess it takes all kinds."

Caleb merely smiled again.

"Where you headed next?" the woman asked as she began bagging up.

"I'm not sure I'm headed anywhere," Caleb responded with the simple truth. "I suppose I'm going vaguely south, but if I see something in another direction I want to explore, I'm flexible enough to change.''

Ina Butler shook her head and gave him a disapproving glance. "Wal, it must be nice not to have to go to work ever' day like normal folks," she sniffed. "That'll be seven dollars even, mister," she added, "and don't be givin' me no big bills. I cain't change 'em.''

Caleb fished a small bill out of his pocket and handed it to her.

"Thankee," Ina said, adding, "you be keerful now. There's still a few big animals back in them mountains, not to mention some good-for-nuthin' human critters that tries to hunt out of season and cain't hit the side of a barn even with a shotgun, so you watch out.''

"I certainly will," Caleb promised as he picked up the bag containing his purchases. "Good day to you, ma'am," and he smiled as he turned and walked toward the front door.

"Well, ya got manners, I'll say that for ya," Ina called out after him. "And that smile of your'n probly makes the young gals' hearts flutter, don't it?''

Caleb paused, grinning as he looked back over his shoulder. "I wouldn't know how my smile affects the girls anymore," he bantered. "I haven't seen any in too long to remember.''

"Pshaw," Ina scoffed. "Them city girls hike them trails just like the men do these days, and if you ain't run into any of 'em, it's cause you ducked off the trail when you seen 'em comin'.''

Her comment was too close to the truth for him to risk responding, because he had had a problem or two at the beginning of his trek shaking off the company of hiking females who seemed to want to join him after he'd made the mistake of stopping to chat with them. So he merely smiled, raised a hand in a casual wave of farewell and left the store.

After strolling through Sweet Water to the outskirts of the small town, Caleb started looking for a place to camp. It was getting close to evening and he was hungry. By the time he'd cooked and eaten his supper, it would be time to settle down for the night.

Eventually he saw a small, unpaved lane leading uphill, and he took it. After climbing for about two miles, he came to a clearing, in the middle of which was a picturesque old cabin. He hesitated, not wanting to trespass.

"I guess I could ask if it's all right with the owners to camp," he muttered to himself. He was tired and it was starting to look like a downpour was coming. So he walked to the cabin, stepped onto the porch and knocked at the door.

No one answered. And there was a deserted feeling about the place that made Caleb think no one lived there anymore. Feeling a little self-conscious, he turned the doorknob. The door opened easily and he stuck his head inside. "Anybody home?" he called. But it was just a formality. He could tell no one had been home for a long time. There was dust on the floor and the kitchen table, and the atmosphere had an empty feel to it.

A distant rumble of thunder made Caleb turn his head away from the interior of the cabin to look up at the dark, ominous clouds overhead. Then the first spatters of rain began to fall.

He didn't mind sleeping out under the sky when the weather was good, but he'd about had his fill of trying to sleep in a downpour, so the cabin was tempting. A flash of lightning and another loud crash of thunder made his decision for him.

To hell with it, he thought as he turned back and stepped through the door of the cabin. I'll leave some money if it looks like anyone normally inhabits the place.

He made a tour, which didn't take long, because the cabin was small. There was a living room, two bedrooms and a kitchen, all sparsely furnished with old-fashioned pieces that appeared handmade, but much to his regret there was no bathroom. Looking out a back window, he spotted a privy not far away and hoped the rain would stop before he had to use it. Then he returned to the kitchen.

The stove was wood burning and Caleb remembered seeing a small stack of cut wood beside the cabin. Shrugging out of his heavy backpack, he dashed outside to retrieve a supply from the middle of the bundle where the rain hadn't reached. Back in the kitchen, he stuffed a few of the logs in the stove, then got a large box of matches from a shelf nearby. The storm was making it dark inside the cabin, so he also lit an old kerosene lamp, still half-full of fuel.

Then he turned his attention to the dust-covered kitchen table. Using a pair of his socks with holes in the toes, he wiped the surface and a chair free of grime. He tossed his folded sleeping bag aside for the moment, then unloaded his backpack onto the table. After getting a skillet of bacon cooking, Caleb went to the sink to see if the old hand pump still worked. It squeaked at first, but eventually produced a stream of water. He filled his small pot and set it on the stove beside the skillet so he would have hot water for coffee.

As he worked and the delicious smell of bacon began to scent the air, Caleb gradually became aware that he was filled with an unusually intense sense of well-being. He paused in the act of turning the bacon, wondering if the feeling was due to the emotional cleansing he'd experienced over the past couple of weeks, or if this old cabin had a happy history that had left an aura behind it. He'd never believed or disbelieved the theory that houses picked up the atmosphere of their owners. But if the theory was true, he thought the former inhabitants of this place must have been benevolent, loving people, because he felt welcome here…and in some strange way sheltered from more than just the storm outside.

Caleb couldn't remember a meal ever tasting so good. He ate three eggs, half the bacon and half the loaf of bread, plus an apple and an orange. Afterward he stretched lazily, feeling drowsy. It was fully dark outside now, and this was the kind of night to curl up in bed and read. But the lantern was too low on fuel to last long enough for much reading.

After cleaning up, he took the lantern and wandered through the cabin, looking for a place to put his sleeping bag. There were two bedrooms, both with unsheeted mattresses on the beds, but the roof was leaking over the bed in one of them and from the condition of the mattress it looked like the roof had been leaking for years, so he turned away from that room and decided to sleep in the other.

Later, in the dark, wrapped in the warm cocoon of his sleeping bag, Caleb smiled sleepily, thinking what a stroke of luck he'd had to find shelter on a night like this. Then he fell asleep.

The next morning, after breakfast, it was still drizzling, and that was enough to convince him to delay getting back on the road. He had a strange reluctance to leave this place, anyway. He felt comfortable here . . . almost as though this were home. He did, however, set out clad in his slicker to explore the surrounding area.

Even in the gray drizzle Caleb appreciated the site of the cabin and thought the view must be outstanding on clear days. He could look out to the east and see the vague shapes of mountains. On the west there were woods. It was while wandering on the periphery of the woods that he spotted a small clearing in the trees within which lay a family cemetery.

Some of the graves were very old, and the only way he could halfway sense what had been carved on the wooden markers was to stoop and run his fingers over the indentations. One of the graves was covered with wildflowers, and the handmade cross that had been placed at the head of it had fallen. Caleb picked up the wooden cross and stuck it upright where it had once been. It was an unconscious act of respect as much as a desire to tidy the small, private enclave, which was by no means a sad place. Rather, it was peaceful and emitted a sense of continuity missing from the modern cemetery where Caleb's parents were buried.

He stared unseeingly at the cross for a moment while he wondered if he would have gotten so off track had his parents been alive when he'd sold his first book. If he'd had them to caution him about the temptations accompanying sudden fame and fortune, would he have gotten so out of control? He didn't know. And he didn't want to think about it right now. He wanted to recap-

ture the sense of peace he'd felt before such thoughts
had intruded upon his explorations.

Back in the cabin, he poured himself a cup of coffee
and sat down at the table. He didn't feel bored or anxious to get on his way. And as he sat and drank, the
book he'd begun thinking about on the trail began to
come clearer.

The next thing he knew, he'd dragged one of the
school tablets out of his backpack and was sharpening
one of his new pencils. He started writing, and the next
time he surfaced to the world around him, it was getting dark. He ate, went to bed and slept heavily.

When morning came, Caleb couldn't make himself
leave the cabin. All he wanted to do was sit back down
at the table and write. After thinking it over for a while,
he decided there was no reason he couldn't stay here for
as long as no one came along to run him off.

Staying meant buying more food as well as additional kerosene for the lamps and he didn't want the
woman at the general store to know he was still around,
in case she started asking where he was sleeping. He'd
noticed a supermarket on his walk through Sweet
Water, so he went there, instead. After stocking up, he
was back at the table, totally absorbed in his writing,
resentful even of having to get up to cook his supper.

It was like that for Caleb for days that stretched into
weeks. During the short times he surfaced from his
book enough to consider where he was, he prayed no
one would come along and order him off the place. He
began to have a superstitious feeling that if he had to
leave the cabin, the well of his imagination would dry
up and he would never finish the book that was flood-
ing from his mind with a force all its own.

That force was too valuable to lose. He hadn't felt it in far too long. And while the joy and excitement that were part of the force made his days pass in a blur and left him oblivious to his surroundings, they also made the days end more satisfyingly than they had in a long while. He went to bed each night feeling his exhaustion was earned. Sleep was no longer something he sought to blank his mind to his shame over wasting his time and talent.

Fortunately his luck held. No one came along before the book—which Caleb thought the best he'd ever written—was finished. There was nothing to keep him at the cabin any longer, and he needed to get the book typed and sent to his agent. But as he gathered his things, he did so lethargically. It was as though the cabin didn't want to let him go. Or was it the other way around?

Finally it dawned on him that if his book sold, he could buy the cabin, fix it up and have a place of refuge for the rest of his life. Excited impatience gripped him. He didn't necessarily have to send the manuscript to his agent in typed form, he realized. He could mail it in as is and ask his agent to get it typed for him if he thought the book merited the trouble.

Caleb counted the money he had left from the sale of his car. There was enough to keep him going for a while, considering how simple his needs would be if he continued to live at the cabin. And no one in Sweet Water would even need know he was around if he was careful. But first he had to call his agent about the book and mail the manuscript. He also needed to check the courthouse records to find out who owned the cabin. Surely whoever it was would be willing to sell him the place once he got the money to buy it. The owner obviously didn't want to live there himself.

A DAY LATER, Caleb was in a motel in the county seat, talking with his agent over the phone. After giving Ted Mayer a brief synopsis of his book, he was gratified when Ted seemed excited.

"Hell, yes, send it to me!" he responded heartily. "If it's as good as it sounds, I'll get it typed and submitted to a publisher."

Caleb laughed. "You may regret saying that when you see what you get in the mail," he predicted, looking over at the pile of school tablets he'd dumped on a table in the motel room.

"Nothing surprises me in this business," Ted snorted. "How do I get back to you?"

Caleb hesitated, then said, "I'll contact you, Ted. How long do you need before I should call back?"

"Give me a couple of weeks," he replied. "I'll read it as soon as I can after it arrives in my office, but considering mail service and such, two weeks ought to put us on the safe side."

"Fine," Caleb agreed. "And thanks, Ted. I know I haven't earned you your percentage in a long while, but maybe, if this one is as good as I think it is, that will soon change."

"I hope so," Ted said sincerely. "You've got the talent, Caleb. I've always known you'd come out of your slump sooner or later. If I hadn't thought that, I wouldn't be waiting with baited breath for what you're sending me. In fact, I'd probably tell you not to bother sending it at all. We may be friends, but facts are facts."

Caleb grinned. "You're the same old Ted."

"And I hope to God you're the same old Caleb," he responded. "Now I've got to go. I've got lunch with an editor . . . naturally."

"Naturally," Caleb echoed, grinning.

After visiting the post office to send off the tablets, he went to the courthouse, and with the help of an obliging clerk, he determined that a woman named Mary Rose Perkins owned the cabin and the twenty acres surrounding it. But it was a Sarah Zimmerman in Washington, D.C., who had been paying the taxes on the place for the past few years, and since hers was the only address available, he wrote it down.

Back in his motel room after dinner, Caleb picked up the phone and dialed Information to obtain Sarah Zimmerman's telephone number. A few moments later, he was explaining the purpose of his call.

"You can ask Mary Rose yourself about the cabin for all the good it will do you," Sarah Zimmerman responded harshly. "She's decided to move back to Sweet Water. But you'll never get her to sell you the place. She has some misguided idea about playing doctor among the poor, backward natives."

"I beg your pardon?" Caleb responded. Not only was he bitterly disappointed to hear that the owner of the cabin was returning to it, he was also confused.

"She just completed her medical training, Mr. Anderson," Sarah said bitterly. "But that doesn't means she's intelligent. If she was, you'd have a chance of getting the cabin. But as things are, my advice is not to waste your time with her. Now if you'll excuse me, I have some tests to grade. Goodbye."

At first Caleb felt despair. Damn, he wanted that place! But after the despair had waned somewhat, he thought long and hard. If this Mary Rose Perkins was just starting out as a doctor, her idealism might be the kind that many people felt before they got a taste of the real world. Over time, and considering the realities of life in a small backwater where her practice couldn't be very large or interesting, perhaps that idealism would dissipate.

Since he didn't have enough money to buy the place at present, anyway, Caleb had time himself. And if Mary Rose was as idealistic as her aunt had described her, might she not be willing to allow a struggling writer to camp out on a portion of those twenty acres she owned? Especially if he offered to fix the place up for her in order to pay for his campsite. There was plenty of work, after all. The roof leaked, for one thing.

Slowly Caleb began to smile. He wouldn't tell Mary Rose Perkins he wanted the cabin. That might scare her off. He would merely offer to help out...and while he was helping out, he would be waiting to see what happened with his book, as well as hoping Dr. Perkins was getting disillusioned.

Of course, his book might not sell and Mary Rose might never get tired of life in Sweet Water. But those were things Caleb refused to dwell on. He was feeling the same optimism and energy he'd felt in his younger days, when he'd been convinced that he would one day be published and life would fall his way. He would overcome this minor setback. He had a goal in mind and faith that he could reach it. And when you got right down to the basics of life, that was all any man needed to claim his dreams.

AS THE BUS ROLLED into Sweet Water, Mary Rose was astonished at the changes. For one thing, Main Street was paved now. There was a modern supermarket and other shops, in addition to Butler's General Store. They had rebuilt the school, too. And there were three churches instead of just one.

As she climbed down off the bus at a new gas station and waited for the driver to haul her suitcases out of the hold, Mary Rose looked around wide-eyed and smiled delightedly.

"Here you go, miss," the bus driver said after depositing the large box containing her medical supplies near her luggage.

"Thank you," Mary Rose replied.

"You're welcome." The driver touched his cap with a finger, then climbed back into his bus, shut the door and pulled away.

Now there was just one small problem. How was she going to get the things she had with her, as well as the groceries and cleaning supplies she needed to buy, two miles up a steep hill to the cabin?

Pivoting, she headed for the office of the gas station. Though he looked vaguely familiar, she didn't recognize the young man who stood up to meet her, but she had complete faith that before too much time had passed, she would again know every inhabitant of Sweet Water.

"May I help you, ma'am?" the young man asked.

"I hope so," Mary Rose said. "What's your name?"

"Why, I'm Jake Whittaker's youngest boy," he answered, peering at her as though trying to remember something. "My name's Todd. And if you don't mind my saying so, miss, you look sort of familiar, but I can't place you. Are you from around these parts?"

She grinned. "Yes, I am. I'm Mary Rose Perkins, and I was born in Sweet Water. I was in school with your elder brother, Jake, Jr., until I was fourteen and moved away.''

''Why, you don't say!'' Todd Whittaker responded, looking pleased.

''What's Jake, Jr. doing now?'' Mary Rose asked interestedly.

''Ah, he went off to Charleston and got himself married,'' Todd answered, shrugging nonchalantly. ''He runs a gas station there and has a couple of kids now.''

''How nice for him,'' Mary Rose said.

''You back on a visit or somethin'?'' Todd asked, his eyes running over her sophisticated clothing.

''No, I'm not visiting,'' she explained. ''I just completed my medical training and I've come back to set up a practice here and live in the cabin up the road. I still own it, you know.''

Todd's eyes were bugging out by the time she finished her explanation. ''You?'' he said wonderingly. ''Are you sayin' you're a *doctor*, ma'am?''

Mary Rose wondered if Todd was a young male chauvinist. ''That's right,'' she said amiably. ''Are there any other doctors in town now?''

Todd looked even more astonished and shook his head. ''Hell, ah, I mean, heck, no, ma'am! We still all go over to the county seat if it's somethin' minor, and to Charleston if it's major.''

Mary Rose was pleased by the news. Even after its spurt of growth, she was pretty sure Sweet Water couldn't support more than one physician.

''Well, then,'' she said, smiling cheerfully, ''it's about time Sweet Water had its own doctor, don't you think?''

Todd looked uncertain. ''Well...I guess...'' he said hesitantly.

"You don't sound very sure," Mary Rose said. "Is it because I'm a woman?"

Now Todd looked decidedly uncomfortable. But he was an honest lad, and he answered honestly. "Well, I might come to you for somethin' like a cut or a vaccination," he admitted, "but I don't reckon I'd want a woman doctor for nothin' too...ah...personal, if you know what I mean."

Mary Rose nodded, showing no concern. But she could hardly believe such an attitude still existed. Hopefully the women in town wouldn't show the same prejudice against a woman doctor, though, and if she could win them over as patients, maybe they'd be able to convince their husbands and sons to give her a try, as well.

"I see," she said, and then gave Todd her best smile. She was gratified to see her smile had the power to make him sit up and take notice. "Well, listen, I have a problem myself right now you might be able to help me with."

"Yes, ma'am!" he responded quickly. "Anything I kin do for you, why you just ask!"

"Well, as you can see, I have a lot of luggage, but I haven't any transportation to get my things up to my cabin."

"I've got a pickup!" he immediately exclaimed. "I can take you right now."

"Well, actually, I need to buy some groceries and cleaning supplies first," Mary Rose demurred. "No one's lived in the cabin for years, so I expect it needs a good cleaning, don't you?"

"I expect so," Todd agreed, looking somewhat disappointed at having to slow his headlong pace to oblige her.

"Could you take me after I've done my shopping?" she asked. "I'd be willing to pay you for—"

"No, ma'am!" Todd said sternly, and when Mary Rose looked confused, he hastened to explain. "That is, yes, ma'am, I'm willin' to wait to take you till you get your shoppin' done, but I ain't gonna take no money for it."

"Oh," she responded with relief. Then she gave him another one of her best smiles. "Thank you, Todd. That's very gentlemanly of you."

"Hell, I know my manners!" he said indignantly. Then he blushed and added, "Excuse the profanity, ma'am. I forgot myself."

"That's perfectly all right, Todd," Mary Rose assured him, thinking of all the profanity she'd heard from the doctors, male and female, she'd worked with over the past few years. "All right, then. I'll go down to the general store. Does Ina Butler still run it?"

"Yes, ma'am," Todd answered, and again he looked uncomfortable. "But if you don't mind a little advice, you'll get a better price and a better selection at the new supermarket. Ina charges a pretty steep ticket for her stuff."

But Ina can be a valuable ally in getting my practice started, Mary Rose thought. *She knows everyone in the county.*

Aloud she said, "Probably so, but Ina's an old friend, and I'd like to say hello to her. So I'll do my shopping there this time."

Todd shrugged. "You do your shoppin' there this time, you better be prepared to do it there from now on. Ina got her dander up somethin' fierce when the supermarket got built, and she takes it personal when she sees anybody so much as set foot in the rival store, even if she ain't got what it is you want. She wouldn't speak to my daddy for six weeks once when he bought some dog food for our coon hounds at the supermarket 'cause Ina was out, anyway, and charges six prices for what she's got when she's got it. But you do what you want, ma'am." He finished his little speech with a righteous expression. "Just don't say I didn't warn ya."

"I consider myself warned, Todd. And thank you for trying to help. But it just wouldn't be right to ignore Ina when I knew her all my life up until the time I left here, would it?"

Todd apparently decided it wouldn't be wise to offer any more opinions on the subject. He just shrugged.

"Well, I'll be going then," Mary Rose said, smiling as she began to walk toward the door. "When I've got everything, I'll come back here. If I have too much to carry, can we stop by Ina's to pick up my groceries?"

"Yes, ma'am," Todd agreed. He came to join her at the door to the office. "I'll go ahead and put your luggage in the back of my pickup, if that's all right?"

"It's perfect. Thank you, Todd."

"Yes, ma'am," he said, and a moment later, he had grabbed up the box containing her medical supplies and carried it to his pickup truck, which was parked nearby.

Mary Rose started walking toward the general store.

Chapter Three

The store hadn't changed all that much and neither had Ina. Except for the habitual sharp look in her eyes, she had never been a vivid-looking woman, and now she just seemed a little more faded than she had before.

"Hello, Ina," Mary Rose greeted the woman who was peering at her over the old cash register in the same puzzled fashion Todd Whittaker had before she'd introduced herself. "I'm Mary Rose...don't you recognize me?"

At that Ina's sharp eyes widened as she gave her customer a second once-over. "Why, land sakes, Mary Rose!" she finally exclaimed. "You look like one of the movie stars or magazine models! Who'd ever a thought it?"

Mary Rose decided to turn a blind eye to the back-handedness of the compliment. "Why, thank you, Ina," she said warmly. "And how have you been all these years? You look just the same."

But Ina wasn't interested in herself at the present, and she ignored the question and comment to concentrate on extracting information. "What you doin' back here?" she asked as she came out from behind the counter and circled Mary Rose, inspecting every inch of her. "I know you never sold the cabin, but I shore never expected you'd show up in Sweet Water again. You fixin' to sell that cabin now?"

Mary Rose remained unruffled by the scrutiny. "No," she said simply, turning her head to follow Ina's progress. "I never plan to sell the cabin. I've come back to live in it, as a matter of fact."

That stopped Ina cold, which was just as well, since she had completed her circuit and now stood in front of Mary Rose. "Live in it!" she exclaimed. "Why, you ain't got the sense God gave a gnat! That old place must be rottin' where it stands! It ain't been used in years!"

Mary Rose shrugged. "I expect it probably does need a little work," she said mildly. "But it was very well built, Ina, so I doubt it's actually rotting."

"Well, but even so!" Ina protested. "What the sam hill do you want to live there for? And how you plannin' to make a livin' in this town?"

"Because it's home to me. I plan to make a living as a doctor, Ina—I have a medical degree now. And don't you think it's about time Sweet Water had a physician of its own?" Mary Rose said, answering each question in turn.

Ina's eyes bugged out exactly the way Todd's had. "You?" she responded disbelievingly. "How'd you get to be a doctor?"

Mary Rose was a little insulted by Ina's tone, but she answered with polite patience. "I went to college and medical school, then through a residency program in a Washington, D.C., hospital, where I specialized in internal medicine," she answered factually.

Ina still looked a little shell-shocked. "I don't never remember seein' a *woman* doctor," she said faintly.

"Well, it sort of runs in the family," Mary Rose said with a shrug. "If you remember, Ma doctored people."

"Wal...I don't know if you'd call it real doctorin'," Ina hedged.

"The people she helped might disagree with you," Mary Rose said. "And speaking of people she helped, is Grandma Bolling still around?"

"'Course not!" Ina snorted. "She died mor'n ten year ago."

"I'm sorry to hear it," Mary Rose replied, but she wasn't surprised.

Ina shrugged. "She were a hundred years old," she said simply.

Mary Rose supposed that was sufficient explanation for anyone's demise. Then she decided it was getting late, and if she wanted to have time to make the cabin even minimally habitable before dark, she'd better get on with things. She would talk to Ina another day about getting word out that there was now a physician living in Sweet Water. After all, the West Virginia State Board of Medicine hadn't finished processing her application for a license to practice medicine in the state, and she couldn't treat anyone here until it did.

"Ina, I need all the basic groceries and cleaning supplies," she said, turning to look around at the interior of the store, "and it's getting late, so I'd better get busy. Is everything pretty much in the same place?" She crossed to pick up a metal hand basket, which she expected to have to refill several times—Ina didn't have full-size grocery carts.

Ina perked up at the prospect of making a sale, and she scurried to help. As she and Mary Rose filled and emptied the basket repeatedly, her mood brightened considerably. She hadn't sold this much at one time since the new supermarket had opened for business.

"That'll be $105.75," she announced with a great deal of satisfaction when the totaling was done. After Mary Rose had paid her, Ina asked, "You got a car to get all this stuff up the hill?"

"Todd Whittaker has offered to drive me up in his pickup," she explained. "As soon as we get all these bags carried to the front of the store, I'll walk down to the gas station and fetch him."

"Humph!" Ina sniffed. "His daddy ain't gonna like Todd closin' up the gas station to tote you home."

Mary Rose felt concerned. "I offered to pay him," she said, "but he refused to take anything."

"'Course he did," Ina said approvingly. "Todd's a good boy. Wish I could say the same for his daddy," she added a little grimly. "That old man probably still has the first dollar he ever made!"

Mary Rose looked away to hide a smile. She'd just remembered what Todd had said about Ina refusing to speak to his dad because of his disloyalty in buying at the supermarket. She also thought that if Mr. Whittaker still had his first dollar, Ina probably still had hers, too.

"Thank you, Ina," she said when the last bag had been deposited at the front of the store. "I'll go get Todd now so I can get some things done up at the cabin before dark."

Ina nodded. "Good thing you bought some kerosene for your lamps," she said forebodingly. "I bet it gets dark as Satan up there when the sun goes down."

"Yes, it does." She smiled. "Well, thanks again."

"Yore welcome," Ina said.

Mary Rose fetched Todd, who promptly locked up the gas station and gallantly opened the passenger door of the pickup for her. Then he drove to the general store and loaded the groceries into the back of the vehicle.

As they were on their way up the hill, Mary Rose's expression revealed the eagerness she felt to catch the first glimpse of the cabin she hadn't seen in far too many years. Todd glanced over at her and shook his head. "It shore is lonely up here, ma'am," he commented.

Mary Rose didn't respond. She was sitting forward in her seat, and the moment the cabin came into view, she pointed at it. "There it is, Todd!" she said eagerly. "There's my home!"

This time Todd didn't respond. He was afraid that if he said anything, he might hurt her feelings, because to his eyes, the cabin didn't look like anything anybody should get excited over. It was just an old, kind of run-down dwelling that appeared too small to be comfortable. A few minutes later, as he was carrying in groceries and realized the place had a hand pump at the sink and no bathroom, his puzzlement over why Mary Rose was touching things so gently and gazing at everything with such a loving expression in her pretty green eyes grew stronger.

"Ma'am," he finally asked as he glanced around him. "I don't mean to say nothin' out of turn, but just what is it about this place you like so much? It don't seem too...ah...comfortable to me."

Mary Rose's smile was luminous as she looked at Todd. "It isn't anything most people could understand," she answered quietly. "I know how it must seem to someone who wasn't born within these walls and to whom it was never home. I realize the cabin is too run-down, small and primitive for most people to want to bother with, and the land around it probably looks pretty ordinary to you. But there's more to certain places in this world than can be seen with the naked eye, Todd, and this is one of them. To me, God must have smiled and blessed this one spot for reasons I can't comprehend and don't really need to know. I just know what I feel when I'm here—peace and comfort and a sense of well-being that I've never felt anywhere else—and I know that this is where I belong."

Todd stood staring openmouthed at her for a long moment, then closed his mouth, shuffled his feet and finally shrugged. He was somewhat bewildered, but more than half-convinced.

Mary Rose smiled at him. "Are you sure you won't let me pay you for bringing me and my things home, Todd?" she asked.

He swallowed a sudden, youthfully male reaction to that smile and shook his head. "No, ma'am," he said firmly. "And if you need anything else, you be sure and get in touch with me."

Mary Rose had a sudden thought. "You wouldn't happen to know if anybody in town has a motorcycle for sale, would you?" she asked. "Or failing that, a bicycle? I can't afford a car yet, and I'm going to need some sort of transportation."

Todd was obviously shocked. "A motorcycle?" he exclaimed. "Ma'am, you ain't got no business on one of those! Them's dangerous!"

She shrugged. "Well, maybe so, but if you happen to hear of anybody with a motorcycle or a bicycle to sell, will you tell me? I have to have something to get around on."

"Shore thang," Todd said reluctantly, still looking troubled by her mention of a motorcycle. "Well, I reckon I'll get on back to the station," he added, putting one foot across the threshold.

"Thank you for your help," Mary Rose said warmly.

Todd nodded and left. When he'd gone, she turned to gaze at her home again, a soft smile of pleasure curving her mouth.

The cabin was dirty, but not nearly as dirty as she had expected to find it. Underneath the dirt, though, the place was exactly as she remembered it. She was elated about that. Sometimes childhood memories played tricks on one, but hers hadn't, and she was grateful.

There was no time to explore outside the cabin if she wanted a decent supper and a clean bed for the night, so she dug in immediately with broom and mop, cleaning solution and rags, humming happily as she worked.

There were only two things bothering Mary Rose at present. One was the odd sense of another presence around her—a feeling that someone had been in the cabin recently, perhaps had even lived there awhile.

"Well, perhaps a hiker or somebody spent a night or two here to get out of the rain," she muttered with a shrug.

The other was how much money it was going to take to modernize the cabin enough to make it suitable as a medical office, as well as a home. A telephone, electricity and modern plumbing must come first. They were essential.

But with the cabin and land as collateral and her medical degree as assurance that she could make a living, Mary Rose thought it wouldn't be too hard to get a bank loan. Meanwhile, while she waited for her West Virginia license, she could take a much needed vacation... in the best spot on earth.

CALEB STOOD just within the trees bordering the cleared space surrounding the cabin, and as he looked at the warm light spilling from the windows, he felt an odd mixture of emotions.

There was a feeling of resentment that someone else was inside the cabin he had come to think of as his own, even though he knew that seeing the present inhabitant as an intruder was inappropriate. No matter how possessively he viewed the cabin, legally it belonged to the person in it, not to him.

And there was a feeling of longing to be back inside those warm, sheltering walls, sitting at the scarred table, eating a meal he'd cooked on the old wood stove, because despite the fact that it was June, it was chilly outside. Fortunately, it didn't look like rain, though. Caleb didn't know if he could have stood lying in a soaked sleeping bag in the middle of a downpour with his beloved cabin so close, yet unavailable to him.

So he was hungry and chilled, resentful... and jealous. He hoped Mary Rose Perkins turned out to be a likable sort. Otherwise it was going to be even harder for him to accept her presence in *his* cabin while he was banned from enjoying it temporarily. But he couldn't tell a thing about her so far. He hadn't seen her arrive, and right now she was just a shadow who crossed the illumined windows from time to time.

"Ah, hell, Caleb," he finally said aloud resignedly. "Get yourself something to eat and then curl up in your sleeping bag. The sooner the night's over, the sooner you can begin to get back what's yours."

Without a thought this time to the oddness of his thinking in referring to the cabin as "his," he melted back through the trees to a relatively clear spot where he could have a fire to warm himself by and cook on and make him feel less lonely.

It was six in the morning and barely light, and Mary Rose was clad in her flannel nightgown, warm, fuzzy robe and a pair of rubber boots with fluff on the inside when she slipped out the cabin door to go to the privy. But her eyes displayed no sign of sleepiness. She was used to rising early, and her eyes were open and eager as she gazed around her at old beloved sights while walking to her destination.

She wasn't even watching what she was doing when she reached for the handle on the privy door. She had her head turned to the east and was looking at the sunrise as she tried to pull the door open. But she looked back quickly enough when, after pulling the door open perhaps six inches, it was abruptly pulled closed again from the inside, and she distinctly heard the simple, rusty hook jammed into the metal fastening.

"What the...?" she said, sounding as puzzled as she felt.

"Wait your turn!" a cheerful male voice responded from the interior of the privy. "I would have hooked the door, but I didn't think you'd be up this early."

Upon hearing the first word Caleb spoke, Mary Rose had dropped the handle of the door as though it was burning hot and taken three quick steps backward. But by the time Caleb's last word was spoken, she had stopped staring at the privy door with an expression of shock, and was now looking both indignant and plainly bewildered.

"Who *are* you?" she called out, her voice echoing the expression on her face.

"Could we leave the introductions until later?" Caleb suggested. "I'm in sort of a delicate position to make your acquaintance right now," he added apologetically.

He was barely controlling his half embarrassed, half amused laughter. This wasn't by any means the way he would have chosen to come to Mary Rose Perkins's attention. But he should have anticipated that Murphy's Law operated even out here in the backwoods.

Mary Rose pressed her lips together and narrowed her eyes. She was not in the least amused. She was flabbergasted and definitely irritated.

It occurred to her that perhaps over the years, hikers had found the cabin and, realizing that it was uninhabited, had made it a way station for themselves. If that was the case, though it went against her normally hospitable instincts she would have to post No Trespassing signs for a while until such people took her property off their list of stopping places. It was too dangerous living here alone to allow people freedom to come and go as they pleased. Because while most people were probably harmless and pleasant, it would only take one of the other sort to put her in serious trouble.

Without saying anything further, Mary Rose pivoted on her heel and retraced her steps to the cabin. She wanted to be dressed before she confronted the occupant of her privy. Actually, she wished he would just leave so she wouldn't have to say anything at all to him. If he ever showed up here again, she would have signs posted.

Through a crack in the privy wall, Caleb watched her stomp away, his gaze speculative. He hadn't seen her face because she had turned and stalked off before he had had a chance. But he found the white-blond of the braid hanging down her back intriguing. He couldn't remember ever seeing that color hair before, except on a few towheaded youngsters. And even though she walked with stiff-legged anger, and was clad in a bulky robe, he could tell she was gracefully slender.

Sighing, Caleb hoped the smile the woman in the general store had commented on would serve him well over the next half hour. Because he'd already made a bad impression on Mary Rose Perkins, and if something didn't rescue the situation—his smile or his charm or Dr. Perkins's innate goodwill—his plans were obviously going to come to a slamming halt before he could even begin to set them in motion.

AFTER DRESSING, Mary Rose went to the kitchen and poured herself a cup of the coffee she'd put on the stove before leaving the cabin. Then she walked over to the window from which she could see the privy, curious to know if her unwelcome visitor was going to go away or come to the cabin to speak to her.

She had just reached the window and had the cup to her lips, when a knock sounded on the door and made her jump in startlement, which made her spill coffee down the front of her sweatshirt. As a result, her already irritable mood nosedived further.

As she stomped to the door, she set her dripping cup of coffee down on the table and picked up a rag she'd left there the night before. She was dabbing at her shirt with the rag when she flung the door open and glared at the man standing outside it.

Caleb was taken aback by the glare. But he was also enchanted by the fiery green eyes. And then he saw what she was doing and realized why she looked so irritated.

"I'm sorry," he said simply, his eyes moving to follow Mary Rose's hand. As she dabbed, pushing the cloth of her sweatshirt close to her body, he realized she wasn't wearing a bra. He was even more enchanted. "Did you burn yourself?" he asked absently.

"Yes, I did," Mary Rose responded with a firm lack of truthfulness. "But never mind about that. What were you doing in my privy?"

The absurdity of the question made Caleb return his eyes to her face and smile. And suddenly she took in his appearance for the first time.

Dressed in faded jeans, a good brand of hiking boots and a gray, unlabeled sweatshirt with the sleeves pushed up, he was tall, well built, probably in his thirties, and engagingly attractive. His hair was a thick, somewhat overlong blondish brown, his eyes were a warm light brown and the bone structure of his face was strong and full of character. He had a firm chin and a nice, generous mouth.

Mary Rose liked firm chins and well-shaped mouths. And she liked the smile that was on this particular mouth. It was warm, humorous, generous . . . nothing phony about it.

"Do you really want me to answer that question the way it was put?" Caleb inquired, a mild note of teasing in his voice.

"What?" Mary Rose said absently. She was still taking inventory and was distracted.

Caleb's spirits lifted a little. Apparently the woman in the general store was right about his smile. It seemed to have had the effect of reducing Mary Rose Perkins's irritability several degrees at any rate.

"Never mind," he said. "Just let me apologize for startling you the way I did. If I'd realized you were such an early riser, I would have asked permission to use your facilities. As it was, I didn't mean to do any harm.''

Mary Rose wavered. This man was certainly well spoken, but who exactly was he? He wasn't wearing a backpack, so he must not be a hiker, but why else would he just pop up out of the blue at six o'clock in the morning?

''Who *are* you?'' she asked, putting her thoughts into words as she frowned at him. But it was a puzzled, rather than an angry frown.

''Forgive me,'' he said. ''My name is Caleb Anderson. And may I know yours?''

''Mary Rose Perkins,'' she said. ''Knowing your name, though, doesn't tell me who you are, does it?''

Caleb shrugged. ''Do you want the short version or the long version?'' he asked amiably.

She sighed. ''The short version will do for now,'' she allowed.

''Well, then, the short version is that I'm an out-of-work writer who's been hiking the Appalachians to try to clear his mind. But I'd be delighted to tell you the long version if you'll invite me in for some fresh coffee, because from where I stand, it smells delicious.''

Mary Rose eyed him warily. ''If you're a hiker, where's your backpack?'' she asked, a slight hint of suspicion in her tone.

''Over there in the woods,'' Caleb said, gesturing in the direction he'd come from.

She frowned again. ''You slept over there last night? Without asking my permission?'' she accused.

He thought fast. ''I got lost and it was too dark to see where else to go, and I was afraid that if I asked for permission, you'd tell me no. Then what would I have done? I might have broken a leg trying to get back down that hill in the dark. So I decided not to ask, and I apologize for my negligence."

Mary Rose stared consideringly at him, thinking he was a bit glib. On the other hand, if she was any judge of character, he wasn't a dangerous criminal or even a petty thief. She decided to give him the benefit of the doubt and stepped back.

"Come in and have some coffee," she invited wryly, and earned herself another one of those smiles she was beginning to like very much.

"Thank you," Caleb said warmly, and he looked around him as he walked into the kitchen. He immediately spotted how clean it now was and saw that the open shelves were well stocked with food and cleaning supplies. He wouldn't have thought it possible, but Mary Rose's brief occupation of the cabin had increased the welcoming atmosphere rather than detracted from it, and he warmed to her.

A moment later he was sitting at the table with a cup in front of him, studying her face as she poured his coffee, and he decided that she was definitely attractive. Her beauty wasn't blatant, but it certainly wasn't commonplace, either. She was unique.

The uncommon color of her hair was matched by the unusual clarity of her green eyes, which were framed enchantingly with long, dark lashes. Her skin was a pale, translucent cream without a blemish to mar it, her bone structure was delicate but firmly carved, and her figure was trimly feminine.

"Don't stare at me," Mary Rose said as she raised her eyes to his after she'd finished pouring his coffee. "For all you know, I might be cursed with an inferiority complex, and you could be making me feel very uncomfortable."

Caleb was startled. And then he was amused. He shook his head. "You don't have an inferiority complex," he said with certainty.

"Then maybe I have a superiority complex, instead?" She smiled mischievously.

Again he shook his head. "No, you don't have that, either," he said just as certainly. "You're very balanced."

"And you make snap judgments," Mary Rose told him dryly as she went to put the coffeepot back on the stove. "I'll be back in a minute," she announced, and headed for the front door.

"Where are you going?" he asked, alarmed, half-afraid she was going off to fetch the sheriff to get him tossed off her land.

Mary Rose gave him a mildly annoyed look as she opened the door. "Where I was headed before I found out it was already occupied," she informed him tartly.

Caleb grinned and she stepped outside the cabin. A moment later, however, she was back. He looked at her in surprise, but she didn't deign to speak to him. She merely went to a nearby shelf, retrieved a roll of toilet paper and headed for the door again.

"I left some in there," he commented, trying to sound merely informative. But he was unable to keep his amusement from leaking into his voice.

"Thanks," Mary Rose retorted, but she didn't put the paper back, and an instant later she was gone again.

Caleb took advantage of her absence to have a quick look around. It didn't take long to discover that the floors had all been mopped and the furniture dusted, and the bed he had used now boasted sheets and blankets. It was unmade, but Caleb figured it wouldn't stay that way long. Mary Rose seemed possessed of tidy habits.

He was a little chagrined when he glanced into the other bedroom, because it was obvious that this was the room Mary Rose intended to use as her medical office. An open box containing medical supplies was on the bureau, the stained, moisture-ruined mattress was rolled up on the bedsprings and a white lab coat hung on a hook behind the door.

The effect on Caleb was odd. He felt excluded. It was only then that he realized he'd been half hoping that if Mary Rose hired him as her handyman, she would let him stay in the spare bedroom. But that was ridiculous. No single woman with any sense would let a strange man share her house. And if she did, in a community as traditional as Sweet Water, the townspeople might brand her with a scarlet *A*.

"So it's back to the great outdoors for me," he muttered, feeling temporarily dispirited.

He was back at the kitchen table with a fresh cup of coffee by the time Mary Rose returned. She washed her hands at the hand pump, poured herself another cup of coffee, then seated herself at the table across from him and looked him over with frank curiosity.

He was definitely the type of man to catch a woman's eye and make her heart race a little, she decided...even a woman like her, who, since she had seldom noticed men in a romantic way, found it rather disconcerting to be doing so now with a total stranger.

"Where are you headed from here?" she asked.

Caleb hesitated, then shrugged. "Actually, I'm out of money," he lied, and felt surprisingly uncomfortable over having done so. Maybe it was the honesty in Mary Rose's gaze that made him feel so guilty about being less than straight with her. "I'm hoping to get some work so I can last through the winter," he added.

Mary Rose felt sympathetic. Money was a problem for her, too. "What kind of work?" she asked. "You said you were a writer—do you plan to try to work for a small newspaper or something?"

Caleb shook his head and smiled. "I'm not a journalist," he explained. "I write novels. No, I'm pretty good with my hands." Another lie. The most he had done in the way of handiwork had been an attempt to change a lightbulb. But surely, if one had a modicum of common sense, one could figure out how to repair something.

"I was hoping to find people who needed repairs done on their houses," he went on, injecting a hopeful note into his voice. He watched Mary Rose's face closely to gauge her reaction.

"I'm going to need some work done on this place," she responded, looking around her. "But I'll have to wait until I get a bank loan in order to fix this place up for my medical practice so I can start seeing patients here."

"Patients?" Caleb said, remembering to sound curious.

Mary Rose returned her clear gaze to his face. "Yes. I'm a doctor...an internist. Actually, I'm just starting out. This will be my first practice."

Caleb looked suitably impressed. "Congratulations," he said.

"Thank you." She smiled, pleased.

"But will you make much money in a town this small?" he asked, dubious.

Mary Rose shrugged. "I'm not in medicine for the money," she said simply. "I was born and grew up here, and I love this place."

Caleb didn't want to hear that, but he kept his expression from showing what he felt.

"I came back here because Sweet Water is my home and the town has never had its own doctor," Mary Rose continued. "And though I won't ever become wealthy practicing here, it will give me the opportunity to do some research on the healing properties of various plants that grow in the area. My mother used to treat people with potions she made up from the plants, and she taught me what she knew. I wrote it all down so I wouldn't forget. Now I'm going to continue her work."

Caleb was alarmed by her intention. But if he said anything discouraging at this point, it would sound odd, so he took another tack.

"You said you didn't have much money yet," he remarked casually. "Do you have enough to at least buy the materials to fix your roof? I noticed it's in pretty bad shape. If you can afford the supplies, I'd be willing to do the work for room and board."

Mary Rose blinked at him in puzzlement. "Now why would you do that?" she asked bluntly. "It wouldn't earn you enough to get through the winter. And though I could feed you, I couldn't give you a room. Surely you understand why."

Caleb did understand, and he remained silent for a moment, thinking. Finally he decided to risk a modicum of honesty. "I guess I'm willing because there's something about this place that strongly appeals to me," he said sincerely. "I feel comfortable here...as though I belong."

Mary Rose opened her eyes wide and held Caleb's gaze. "You really feel that?" she asked wonderingly, thinking that if he meant what he said, he must be pretty special. Very few people reacted to the unique atmosphere of the cabin and the land around it. Even Sarah, who had grown up here, had apparently never felt the almost supernatural pull of the place. Quite the opposite, in fact. She had been repelled rather than embraced by her former home.

"Yes, I do," Caleb said earnestly. "And as far as having a place to stay, as long as the weather is good I can stay outside. I have a sleeping bag, of course. Maybe by the time the weather started changing, I'd have your roof done. You really shouldn't put it off, you know. From what I could see from the outside, one spot seems to have leaked for a long time."

She nodded absently. The condition of the mattress in the bedroom testified to the truth of Caleb's words. And she did have enough ready cash to afford roofing materials. It just seemed odd that he would be willing to do it for her with nothing more than a few meals as pay for his labor...unless, as he said, her home was gaining the kind of hold on him it already had on her. Yet why should that be so?

Sensing her doubt over his motives, Caleb smiled his most winning grin at her. "I'm a free spirit," he said, shrugging. "Money doesn't mean all that much to me, either. I've discovered that other things are more important."

He was telling the truth. He'd discovered firsthand the dangers of coming into a great deal of money very fast and letting material things get in the way of his work. But he did, of course, want to earn enough again to allow him to buy this cabin.

"And there's another thing," he added, trying to sweeten the pot. "I know it's a little late in the season, but wouldn't you like to have a garden? Some tomatoes and cucumbers, maybe?"

Mary Rose smiled reminiscently. "Yes, I would," she admitted. "But it is late. What's planted now might not grow."

Caleb shrugged. "We could always give it a try and see what happens," he suggested. "I saw an area where there used to be a garden, and it wouldn't be that much trouble to spade it and stick in plants. If they grow, fine. If they don't, so what?"

Mary Rose eyed him in a puzzled, but believing fashion. "You seem very determined to stick around here," she commented musingly. "Does this place really call to you that strongly?"

Caleb spoke in a firmer tone than was perhaps wise for his purposes. "Yes, it does. It does, indeed. Maybe I'm crazy, but I've never felt so drawn to a place in my entire life."

It was hard for Mary Rose to believe that her home could produce that feeling in someone other than herself, especially a complete stranger. But wouldn't it be interesting to test Caleb Anderson and see if he was telling the truth? Of course, if he was being honest, there was the danger that he might never want to leave here, and they couldn't both own this place. Unless...

On that thought Mary Rose felt a faint blush warm her skin, and she decided she was an idiot to speculate about such things after only having just met Caleb Anderson. It might be true that she found him more attractive than she could ever remember finding any other man. He was very easy to be with, too. Otherwise she would never have allowed the conversation they

were having to get this far. But at this point in their acquaintance, she didn't know him nearly well enough to
be thinking of him as other than a particularly attractive stranger.

"Well," she finally said, "I suppose I'd be an idiot
to turn down an offer as generous as yours, wouldn't
I?" She smiled at Caleb in what she hoped was merely
a friendly manner. She didn't want him thinking she
was looking for anything other than getting her roof
repaired.

As the tension ebbed from his body, Caleb felt weary,
as though he'd just run the two miles uphill from Sweet
Water to the cabin at a headlong dash. "Thank you,"
he said, flashing his most brilliant smile at Mary Rose.

His smile made Mary Rose's heartbeat speed up momentarily... enough to make her wonder, somewhat
warily, if, in letting Caleb stay around, she wasn't biting off more than she could wisely chew, considering
her lack of experience in romance. But she didn't back
down.

"You're welcome," she replied, unable to tear her
gaze away from Caleb's smile.

He noticed her attraction to him and was not only
pleased by his effect on her, but responded with a cor-
responding sexual interest of his own. But the part of
him that wanted the cabin cautioned restraint. A short-
term affair wasn't his goal here, and could possibly keep
him from gaining his objective.

"Are you hungry?" Mary Rose asked Caleb as she
got up from her chair.

"Starved," he responded, and his eyes involuntarily
settled on her trim figure. Then he made himself look
away and cautioned himself again about having those
kind of thoughts.

Mary Rose saw Caleb's look and interpreted it correctly. Then she quickly turned away to keep him from knowing she had. "Fine...then you're about to receive your first wages," she said. And as she reached for a skillet in which to fry some bacon, she was trying very hard not to feel more pleased about the admiring, mutedly sensual way he had looked at her than the situation probably warranted.

Chapter Four

"I don't recall," Mary Rose said as she and Caleb walked downhill to town, "that there's anywhere in Sweet Water to buy roofing materials. But the place has gotten bigger and more modern than it was when I lived here as a child, so maybe we won't have to go over to the county seat. And that's just as well, since we don't have any way to get there except by bus."

Caleb was in too good a mood to worry about such minor details. Things were going well. Instead of kicking him off her property, Mary Rose had hired him to work for her as he'd hoped she would. And he genuinely liked her, which made the delay in obtaining the cabin for himself a lot easier to bear.

Of course, he hadn't counted on being sexually attracted to the cabin's owner, and since he was pretty sure she was attracted to him, as well, things could get tricky if he didn't watch his step. However, if he just kept his eye on his objective and refused to encourage such feelings in either of them, things should work out for the best, not only for him, but for her, too. He was more than willing to believe Mary Rose would eventually be happier practicing medicine somewhere else, because it suited his purposes to think that.

"I guess the thing to do," Mary Rose went on, "is stop by the gas station and talk to Todd. He'll know if there's anyplace in town to buy what we need, and if there is, I'm sure he'll be willing to haul the stuff up to the cabin for us in his pickup."

"Sounds good to me," Caleb agreed. He was relieved that she wasn't going to have them go to the general store, where the woman who'd waited on him his first day in Sweet Water might remember him and ask what he was doing back in the area.

In the office of the gas station, Todd was sitting in a roller chair behind a battered desk, upon which he'd placed his cowboy-boot-clad feet. He was reading a comic book and listening to a radio playing very loud rock music. But the moment he saw Mary Rose step through the door accompanied by a strange man, the feet came down to the floor with a loud thump and the radio was switched off like magic.

"Howdy, ma'am," he said as he quickly stood, touching his fingers to the baseball cap on his head. Then his bright blue eyes slid to Caleb and made a covert inspection before returning to Mary Rose.

"Good morning, Todd. This is Caleb Anderson."

"I'm pleased to meet you," Caleb said, smiling at the young man as he stepped forward and held out his hand.

"Pleased to meet 'cha," Todd echoed as he took Caleb's hand and shook it firmly.

"Todd, Caleb is a writer who's been hiking the Appalachians to, ah, clear his mind," Mary Rose explained, and hoped the concept wasn't too far outside Todd's experience for him to understand it, considering the comic book now lying on the desk. "He camped out near the cabin last night, and this morning we met up. He pointed out my roof needs fixing, which I discovered for myself last night when I got a look at one of the mattresses that had been sitting under a leak. He likes it around here and has offered to fix my roof for me, and of course I gladly accepted, because he isn't going to charge me anything but his meals.''

From the way Todd looked at him during Mary Rose's explanation, Caleb had a pretty good idea what the young man was thinking. He couldn't blame the boy for being suspicious. He was a stranger and Mary Rose was a beautiful woman living alone. She also had the sort of quality that aroused a decent male's protective instincts. Todd's were obviously operating full blast.

Blithely unaware of Todd's reaction to Caleb, Mary Rose was saying, ''Is there someplace in town to buy materials to fix the roof? I know there didn't used to be and you had to go to the county seat, but things have changed a lot since I used to live here.''

''There's a new hardware store over where the old mill used to be,'' Todd answered. ''I reckon they'll have what you want.'' He spoke grudgingly as he imparted the information, and continued to look hard at Caleb.

''Oh, good!'' Mary Rose said. ''I'm so glad we won't have to take the bus to the county seat and back. As you know, Todd, I don't have any transportation. Caleb doesn't either.''

Caleb noted that Todd looked as though he well believed that a hiker who could spin what was probably a tall tale about being a writer in order to hang around a woman as attractive as Mary Rose wouldn't have a minor thing like a car.

''I guess I kin take the stuff up to the cabin for you,'' Todd said, but he didn't sound the least enthusiastic. And he was still gazing at Caleb as though he thought this stranger were nothing but a conman out to take advantage of a gullible female.

Mary Rose was surprised by Todd's tone. Then, as she saw how he was looking at Caleb, she realized what was on her young friend's mind. "Oh, Todd," she scoffed, but not in a demeaning way, "surely you don't think Caleb is untrustworthy."

Todd reddened, but he didn't protest her conclusion.

Mary Rose was amused by his protectiveness. "Todd, I'm an excellent judge of character," she said firmly, "and if I thought Caleb was the sort of man who couldn't be trusted, I wouldn't have agreed to let him stay on my land and fix my roof."

Caleb could see Todd wasn't at all convinced that Mary Rose's judgment of men was as infallible as she apparently believed it was. He decided it was time to have a man-to-man talk. "Mary Rose," he said smoothly, getting her attention, "why don't you go on over to the hardware store and talk to someone about the supplies we'll need?"

She gave him a puzzled, disgruntled look. "But what good will it do for *me* to find out?" she asked. "Surely you're the one who needs to ask the questions?"

"Oh, I'll be over there as quickly as I can," Caleb assured her. "I just want to talk to Todd for a moment before I join you."

Mary Rose looked from Caleb to Todd, and since it was obvious from Todd's expression that her defense of Caleb hadn't impressed him, she sighed and decided to do as Caleb had suggested. Maybe he could reassure Todd. She certainly hoped so.

"All right," she said wryly. "Todd can tell you where the hardware store is. I need another kerosene lamp, anyway, so I can use the extra time to get one. But I'm going to let you do the talking about the roof.''

She said goodbye to Todd and left the office.

Caleb waited until she was out of earshot, then turned to the young man, a smile on his lips. Todd didn't smile back.

"She must be a very intelligent woman to have gotten through medical school," Caleb said companionably, "and God knows, she's lovely. But she's a little too trusting where men are concerned, isn't she?"

Todd made a grunting noise by way of reply and continued to stare at Caleb suspiciously.

"Do you read, Todd?" Caleb asked.

Todd scowled. "'Course I do! I bin to school!" he said sarcastically.

Caleb hastened to smooth his ruffled feathers. "No, I meant, do you read for pleasure? Some people don't, of course. They'd rather watch television than read."

Todd shrugged. "I read sometimes," he admitted grudgingly, his eyes sliding to the comic book on the desk and away again. "Mostly when I'm stuck here on a slow day and ain't got nothin' better to do."

Caleb saw where Todd's eyes had rested momentarily, but he wasn't necessarily discouraged by what the boy had chosen to read. He didn't look as though he'd been out of high school all that long, and it was likely he'd had to read meatier volumes in school than he preferred to read these days.

"Have you ever heard of a book entitled *A Man's Tale*?" It had been on the best-seller list four years back, but Caleb wasn't sure teachers would have recommended it to their students due to some of its adult content.

Todd frowned and looked thoughtful. "Seems like I have..." he muttered. He looked up at Caleb, still frowning. "Was it about a guy sorta comin' of age? His first time with a woman and thangs like that?"

Caleb nodded, smiling, thinking that that part of the book, if nothing else, should have interested a young fellow.

Todd's eyes suddenly widened. "Caleb Anderson...hey are you sayin' you wrote that?"

Caleb nodded. "And *Perry's Folly*, as well," he said.

"Well, hey..." Todd stammered. "If Mary Rose knows that, then I can see why..."

But Caleb was shaking his head. "I'm not sure she does," he said ruefully. "At least, she hasn't indicated she does. I think her trust in me is instinctive. And she's right that I don't intend to attack her some night when lust overcomes my good sense," he added wryly.

Todd was frowning in a puzzled fashion again. "But if you can write stuff like that, how come you're wantin' to fix Mary Rose's roof?" he demanded. "Looks like if you're famous, you'd be rich, too!"

Caleb shrugged. "I haven't sold a book in a couple of years, Todd," he admitted. "And while it's true that I made a good deal of money on the two books I did sell, I went through it pretty quickly. There are a lot of temptations in New York City, and I yielded to most of them."

"Well, yeah...if I had me a fortune, I'd do some fast spendin' myself," he said. "But still..."

Caleb sighed. "I was pretty young and stupid when the fame and money came my way, Todd. I'm afraid I didn't handle either very sensibly. In fact, I got so involved in other things besides writing, I eventually found myself unable to write at all anymore. That's why

I haven't sold anything in two years. But I'm trying to get the writing back now.''

Todd was looking more sympathetic and less suspicious now, but he still seemed puzzled about Caleb's wanting to fix Mary Rose's roof.

''Look,'' Caleb began, trying to explain, ''writing is a highly personal thing. Some writers can write no matter what their circumstances or environment, but apparently I'm not one of them. I need the *right* place to write . . . the perfect atmosphere. And there's something about Mary Rose's place that's right for me. I can't really explain it to myself, much less to anyone else. But the fact is, it's the cabin and the area around it that make me want to stay here for a while . . . not Mary Rose. And if I have to fix her roof in order to stick around, that's what I plan to do.''

Todd's eyes opened wider. ''She told me her place affected her like that . . . not as far as writin' goes, a' course, but as far as it bein' the right place for her. Seemed downright spooky to me when she told me about it, and I only half believed her. But there must be somethin' to it if you feel the same.''

Caleb frowned. Todd's statement made him feel uneasy . . . guilty almost. He didn't want to feel as though he would be taking what he wanted from Mary Rose when she felt she needed the cabin just as much as he did. He much preferred to believe it would be in her best interest to sell the place to him.

Todd was shaking his head. ''Sorry I misjudged ya, Mr. Anderson,'' he said, holding out his hand.

Caleb took it and, smiling, said, ''Call me 'Caleb.' ''

'' 'Caleb,' it is,'' Todd replied. Then he shook his head again. ''You know, though, don't cha,'' he added, ''that if the rest of the folks around here find out you're stayin' up there with the doc, they might think the same thing I did—that you've got somethin' on your mind besides fixin' her roof."

Caleb sighed. This whole business was getting too damned complicated. Maybe he should have gone someplace else to wait out Mary Rose. But there wasn't anyplace else he wanted to be. "Got any ideas on how to keep people from thinking that?" he asked.

Todd shook his head. "Damned if I know," he said simply. "But if any gossip does start up, I'll put in a good word for you. I cain't guarantee anybody'll believe me, though."

Caleb grimaced ruefully. "Thanks," he said, his voice dry. "Well, I guess I'd better get over to the hardware store," he added, and he shook Todd's hand again. "Thanks for your help."

"Like I said," Todd reiterated, "if ya'll need help gettin' the roofin' stuff up the hill, let me know. I might not be able to leave the station to haul it for you myself, but you can borry my pickup if you need it."

"Thanks again," Caleb responded with a warm smile. "We may take you up on that. I could drive the stuff up the hill, unload it, then bring your pickup here and walk back."

"Feel free." He gave Caleb directions to the hardware store and was back with his feet up on the desk and his radio blaring by the time Caleb was out the door.

As Caleb walked to the hardware store, he was aware he faced an ethical dilemma. While he wanted Mary Rose to leave Sweet Water and sell him the cabin, he had been counting on her own disillusionment to accomplish his purpose. He hadn't planned on ruining her reputation to gain what he wanted. But he didn't want to leave here, either.

He was still frowning over the problem when he entered the hardware store and spotted her talking to its lone occupant, a burly man in his fifties.

"Oh, there you are," she said when he joined the two of them. "Mr. Phipps, this is Caleb Anderson. He's the one who's going to fix my roof."

Mr. Phipps looked Caleb over, a doubtful expression on his face. "You know much about roofin', young feller?" he asked.

Caleb thoughtlessly told the truth. "Actually, I don't," he admitted, "and I'd appreciate any advice you can give me. Or if you have any written material on the subject, maybe you could steer me to it?"

Mary Rose frowned over Caleb's admission. When he'd told her he was good with his hands and offered to fix her roof, she'd assumed he'd fixed a roof before. But then she gave a mental shrug. He could probably figure out how to fix her roof without too much trouble, and even if he didn't do an expert job, anything he did would probably help stop the leaks. After all, he wasn't going to charge her for his work, so it wasn't as though he'd set out to cheat her.

Mr. Phipps sighed long-sufferingly and muttered something under his breath that sounded like "These days, everybody and his brother thinks he's a handyman." But he rummaged through some papers under the counter until he found a pamphlet and handed it to Caleb. "Maybe that'll get you started," he said dryly, and then he steered Caleb and Mary Rose over to a section of the store that had a representative selection of roofing shingles. "You pick what you want," he said, "and I'll order it. It'll take maybe two days to get 'em here. And you'll need some roofin' tar and nails and such, too. If you ain't got a hammer, better get yourself one. I'll have that stuff ready for you same time's the shingles get here.''

"Thank you, Mr. Phipps," Mary Rose said absently. She was already involved in looking over the selection.

Caleb would have stayed out of the selection process, but Mary Rose kept asking his advice, and since he eventually intended to live under the new roof he was going to put on the cabin, he found himself responding. Finally they narrowed the choice to a type of shingle Mary Rose could afford and they both approved of and gave the order to Mr. Phipps.

When they left the hardware store, Mary Rose looked toward the new supermarket. "I wonder if Ina has spies posted," she mused. "I used up most of my cleaning liquid last night and I could use some more, but Ina sure charges a hefty price for the stuff."

"What?" Caleb asked, startled.

Mary Rose told him what Todd had said about Ina's jealousy over the new supermarket. "And I need Ina's goodwill," she finished. "She knows everybody and she's a focal point of information in this town, so if I get on her bad side, I might as well pack up my medical bag and leave Sweet Water for good."

However tempting such an idea was to Caleb, he knew better than to take Mary Rose seriously for the moment, so he offered to help.

"I need some writing paper, so I'll get you what you need, as well," he offered. "What brand of cleaning liquid do you want?"

She looked at him curiously. "I thought you didn't have any money," she said.

Caleb shrugged. "I'm not flat broke," he allowed. "Just close to it. I always make sure to keep enough to buy writing supplies, even if I don't eat."

Mary Rose could understand such thinking. If it came to eating or replacing some vital medical instrument she needed, she knew what her choice would be.

"Speaking of eating," she said as she handed Caleb some money, "get us some meat for supper. Since I don't have a refrigerator, I bought only enough food yesterday for dinner last night and breakfast this morning."

"Any preference?" Caleb asked. He felt like a heel for depleting Mary Rose's small finances, but she would think it strange if he offered to pay for anything other than his writing materials.

"I'm not picky." She shrugged. "Get what you like—chicken, pork chops, round steak... And if there's enough money left over, buy a can of salmon. I can do up patties tomorrow night and not have to make another trip to the store."

"Round steak?" Caleb asked. He wasn't familiar with cuts of meat and had never heard of that particular one.

"It's cheap, tough steak," Mary Rose informed him with a grin. "You pound it to tenderize it, dip it in flour or batter and fry it."

"Okay, sounds good."

"I'll meet you back at the cabin," she called over her shoulder as she started walking away. "I still have some housework to do and I want to look around. I didn't get the chance yesterday."

Caleb waved at her, then headed for the supermarket, fighting an urge to skulk because he didn't want to run into Ina, who might recognize him if she saw him again. Fortunately he didn't run into the woman, and in half an hour he was headed back to the cabin, with some tomato plants and packages of vegetable seed added to his purchases.

After finishing her housework, Mary Rose headed for the family cemetery to say hello to her mother. On the way she spotted Caleb's camping spot and frowned. The place was all right when the weather was fine, but what was he going to do during a storm? And how was she going to be able to sleep during such a storm while worrying about him drowning out here?

But she put the matter out of her mind for the time being when she arrived at her mother's grave. Her eyes lit with pleasure over how the wildflowers she'd planted had survived and now formed a living carpet of beauty over the site. It also seemed a very good sign to her that the redbud cross she'd made was still standing upright. That was something of a miracle, considering how much time had passed.

Mary Rose supposed she ought to replace the redbud cross with something more permanent. In fact, there was room to plant a redbud tree where the cross now stood, which she considered would be an even more fitting monument to her mother than anything man-made.

"Maybe in the fall," she murmured as she knelt by the grave. "Would you like that, Ma? Would you like a tree for a headstone rather than something granite or marble?"

But she knew the answer. Of course her mother would rather have a living monument than a dead one, and that settled the matter. In the fall Mary Rose would plant the tree where the homemade cross now stood.

As she plucked weeds from among the wildflowers, she talked to her mother as though she were just back from a short trip away from home and Mary Violet had been waiting to hear all about it.

"I'm not sure how easy it's going to be for people around here to accept me as a doctor, Ma," she said. "Mostly I guess they're not used to a woman being a doctor. But maybe they still think of you as a witch and me as the witch's daughter."

She grinned, remembering how she and her mother had laughed about such superstitious nonsense, which had reared its head after Mary Violet's potions had helped some people doctors hadn't been able to heal.

"I guess we can't blame the folk around here too much, Ma," she commented humorously. "Even most of the physicians I've met, while they didn't term you a witch, dismissed out of hand the idea that anything you concocted worked where a doctor's medical skills hadn't. When I tried to tell some of them about it, they looked at me pityingly and told me that whatever healing occurred had nothing to do with your potions. They understood even less than the people around here did about your gift."

As Mary Rose went on talking to her mother, she was unaware that Caleb stood listening a short distance away. Upon arriving back at the cabin, he'd taken his packages inside and, not finding Mary Rose there, had set out to find her to ask where she kept her gardening spade. He didn't recall seeing one when he'd been living at the cabin. But when he'd come upon her kneeling by one of the graves, talking, he'd hesitated to barge in on what he'd thought at first was prayer. Then, when he'd realized she wasn't praying but was talking to her mother as though the woman were still alive, he'd felt awkward about making his presence known.

"Well, Ma," Mary Rose was saying now, "all I can do is try. I do seem to have your gift for healing. And I'm pretty positive God wants me to use my talents here. Aunt Sarah thinks I'm wasted up here, but she's thinking in terms of money and professional recognition, whereas I'm thinking in terms of people. There are folk here who need medical attention just as much as people do in a big city, and where else can I get the chance to experiment with the plants? Besides—" she smiled with satisfaction as she got to the heart of the matter "—this is home. This is where I'm happiest. This is where I belong."

Troubled at hearing those words, Caleb melted away from his eavesdropping. Obviously Mary Rose felt the same way about the cabin and the surrounding area as he did. So did he really have any right to this place?

But, damn it, he wanted it, too! Maybe he wouldn't be saving lives with his books—no one's other than his own—but he couldn't help how he felt about this place any more than Mary Rose could! The thought of going back to the way he'd been before he'd found it terrified him.

He went into the cabin and started a pot of coffee, thinking all the while. But for all his thinking, all he could come up with was his original plan. If he did nothing overt to make Mary Rose leave the cabin and sell it, but instead waited for her to become discouraged and leave of her own free will, then his conscience would be clean.

Much against his will, he also concluded that doing nothing overt included protecting Mary Rose's reputation. So after dinner that night, he supposed he'd better tell her about his conversation with Todd and ask her if there was someplace in town where he could pitch his sleeping bag. That way, maybe the two of them could stop any gossip from springing up.

It would be a sacrifice on Caleb's part to sleep elsewhere, but he thought a clean conscience might be worth it. Besides feeling like home, there was something about this place that made him want to adhere to his finer instincts, rather than to his baser ones. He had an uneasy sense that if he behaved too selfishly, the cabin might cease to shelter him...and benefit his writing as...generously as it had before. The risk wasn't worth it.

WHEN MARY ROSE RETURNED, Caleb asked her where the spade was, and she got a key off a high shelf and took him to the east side of the cabin, where an old wooden box fastened with a padlock rested under an overhang of the roof.

The lock was stiff and Caleb finally had to take the key from Mary Rose and exert pressure to open it.

"It probably seems strange to you that I locked these things up," she said as she rummaged among the tools inside the box, "since it wouldn't cost much to replace them and I didn't think anyone around here would take them. But these were my daddy's tools, and I didn't want to take a chance that a stranger might come by and walk off with them."

Caleb remembered that the door to the cabin had been unlocked. "But you didn't feel the same about the things inside the cabin?" he asked, surprised.

Mary Rose gave him a funny look. "How did you know I hadn't locked the cabin up?" she inquired.

Caleb regretted his mistake instantly. "Oh, I just assumed you hadn't," he said lamely. "People in these parts don't, do they?"

His answer satisfied Mary Rose. "Well," she said, "while it's true I didn't want to lose the stuff inside the cabin, either—my grandpa made most of the furniture—my ma taught me it was a duty to offer shelter to strangers."

Caleb said nothing for a moment. He realized that if the cabin had been locked, he wouldn't have broken in no matter how hard it had rained the night he had first seen it. He might have taken what shelter he could get on the porch, but he wouldn't have broken a lock to get in.

"I think your mother must have been a very wise and good woman," he finally said as Mary Rose stood up with the garden spade in her hands.

She gave him a brilliant smile as a reward for his compliment to her mother. "Yes, she was," she agreed. Then she laughed. "Although some people thought she was a witch, most people understood that her gifts came from God, not the Devil."

"Why did some people think she was a witch?" he asked good-humoredly, although he already knew the answer from listening to Mary Rose's conversation at her mother's graveside.

She shrugged and handed him the spade. "I told you about her making medicines from some of the local plants," she said matter-of-factly. "And they worked, usually. So that led to a certain amount of superstition concerning her abilities."

"Is she the reason you became a doctor?" Caleb asked as he accompanied her to the front of the cabin.

Mary Rose hesitated. "Yes and no," she finally answered. "The idea of becoming a doctor didn't really occur to me until after Ma died, and if she hadn't died, I imagine I would just have stayed here, taking care of her and doing what I'd always done. But when she did pass on and I knew I would have to go live with my Aunt Sarah—and knowing what store she set on book knowledge—I figured if I was going to learn, anyway, I might as well study what interested me. And what fascinated me was helping cure people of their ills. At the end of Ma's life, when the cancer developed, she taught me all she knew so I could make the medicines that were helping people but that she could no longer make herself. And I loved doing it."

"I'm surprised you didn't study pharmacology then," Caleb commented. They were standing on the porch now, but he intended to spade the garden, so he made no move to go inside.

"I did—that is, I took as many courses in botany and chemistry as I could, while still taking everything I needed to become a doctor," Mary Rose said. "But I just somehow knew being a doctor was what I was meant to do."

At one time Caleb wouldn't have accepted such a statement as valid. But since discovering the cabin, he was a great deal more willing to take such feelings without a customary grain of salt.

"Don't try to do all the spading at once," Mary Rose said, grinning. "If you're not used to that kind of work, I think you're going to find it's a lot harder than it looks. And I don't have a pair of gloves to give you to keep the blisters away."

Caleb looked at her consideringly. "I take it you've done this kind of work yourself?" he asked.

"Sure," she said matter-of-factly. "From the age of seven to fourteen, I spaded the garden every year myself. My daddy was killed when I was six in the same accident that resulted in Ma becoming paralyzed, so there wasn't anyone to make a garden but me, and we needed it."

Caleb felt both pity and admiration for Mary Rose, but he sensed she wouldn't appreciate the pity at all, and he was afraid she might take his admiration the wrong way. So he spoke teasingly instead of expressing his real feelings.

"Are you of the opinion," he asked, raising one eyebrow, "that a seven-year-old girl could spade a garden easily, while I would find it difficult?"

Mary Rose snorted. "There was nothing easy about it, Caleb Anderson," she advised him in a tone of warning. "When I first started, it took me a solid week to get the whole garden spaded, and I had blisters on both palms the size of eggs. So I'll be very surprised if you feel quite as macho, when I call you in to eat supper, as you feel right now. But go see for yourself. I'm a firm believer in the value of personal experience in teaching a lesson."

On that note she entered the cabin and shut the door behind her, leaving Caleb standing with a slightly amused look on his face.

Spading the garden turned out to be neither as hard as Mary Rose had predicted, nor as easy as Caleb had assumed it would be. By suppertime his back felt mildly crippled and he was sporting the expected blisters on both hands. But the garden was spaded, and as he looked over his work, he felt such a strong sense of gratification, he was willing to credit the notion that working on the land was emotionally therapeutic.

When he entered the cabin, dinner was on the table, but when Mary Rose saw him wince as he washed his hands, she insisted on treating his blisters before they ate.

"You're my first patient in Sweet Water," she said with a great deal of satisfaction as she smeared ointment over the blisters.

"Glad to be of service," Caleb said dryly, then he winced again.

Mary Rose chuckled. "You don't sound sincere," she mocked.

"It's hard to be sincere when I'm in this much pain," he informed her, and he winced still again as she secured a gauze pad over one palm with surgical tape.

"I'm told I have a gentle touch." She smiled somewhat evilly as she pressed the pad tightly to Caleb's palm.

"Who told you that?" he grunted. "Some male patient who endured your sadism in the hope that if he didn't scream too loudly, you'd go out on a date with him?"

Mary Rose gave him a chiding look. "I got the message from all kinds of patients," she replied. "Men, women and children." And with one last less-than-gentle pat on his bandaged hand, she picked up her medicaments and set them aside. "Let's eat," she said, sitting down on the other side of the table. "All this is getting cold."

Caleb would have been glad to eat if he could have managed spooning the delicious-looking food onto his plate. But Mary Rose had bound the bandages so tightly around his palms he could barely hold on to his utensils.

"Want some help?" she inquired in a bland tone.

"If you don't mind."

Mary Rose took his plate, loaded it with mashed potatoes, chicken-fried steak—she made a big issue out of cutting up his meat for him—pan gravy and creamed corn, then plunked it back in front of him.

"Thanks," he said, and picked up his fork the best he could, intending to take a bite. Spading the garden had given him an enormous appetite.

"Wait for the blessing," Mary Rose instructed in the tone of a severe schoolmarm, and when Caleb looked up in surprise, he saw she had her head bowed and her hands folded. "Lord, we thank You for this food and all our other blessings," she prayed. "And we ask for Your guidance and blessings in the future. Amen."

The blessing was uttered so quickly Caleb didn't have time to bow his head, and he couldn't possibly have folded his hands in their present condition, so he merely fumbled his fork into his fingers as best he could and began eating.

"How much did you get done?" Mary Rose asked a moment later.

"I'm finished," he informed her with a certain smugness. "If I hadn't gotten started so late, I'd have done the planting, as well."

"Hmm," Mary Rose said, and shrugged nonchalantly.

"Is that all you've got to say?" Caleb demanded. "No praise...no well dones?"

"Well done," she answered obligingly.

Caleb sighed and shook his head. "Despite all that big talk you were giving me earlier about how you were spading gardens from the age of seven, I think you've forgotten what it's like. Otherwise I'd be getting a little more appreciation for my labors."

"You're getting paid," Mary Rose reminded him, and pointed her fork at his plate meaningfully.

"Well, I have to admit, right now this seems like pretty good pay, but an hour ago, I wasn't so sure."

Mary Rose just grinned and took another bite of chicken-fried steak.

A little later, Caleb told her about his conversation with Todd concerning the gossip that could start up in town because of his presence at the cabin. He was careful to speak matter-of-factly so Mary Rose wouldn't think he had plans to give credence to any gossip.

"So where in Sweet Water can I pitch my sleeping bag?" he finished. "I'm obviously going to have to sleep elsewhere if we're to keep your reputation spotless."

Mary Rose grimaced. She felt more annoyed than she should have about the idea of Caleb having to sleep elsewhere to keep people from gossiping. "I haven't the faintest idea," she said. "And I'd hate to think that if you picked the wrong place, you might be arrested and end up in jail."

Caleb looked up, startled. "I wouldn't like that much myself," he agreed.

"And if it rains, where would you go for shelter?" she pointed out.

Caleb shrugged. "If it comes to that, where would I go if I remained here? You've already told me I can't stay in the cabin. And I don't blame you for that," he added quickly.

Mary Rose hesitated. "Let me think about it," she said at last, and she stayed silent for a long while, debating the problem. It dismayed her that she felt extremely reluctant to have Caleb leave the property every evening. Why should she care? she wondered uneasily.

She'd only just met him. And it *would* be harder to establish her medical practice if Todd was right and people began gossiping about her and Caleb. But at the same time, why should she let the residents of Sweet Water run her life for her? She'd spent long enough doing things the way other people wanted.

Finally she knew she was going to opt for independence, regardless of what it might cost her. And it had nothing to do with wanting Caleb close at night. Nothing at all.

"Well, I guess I'm just going to have to take a chance with my reputation," she said aloud.

Caleb quickly looked up at her, surprised by her words.

"I admit," she added jokingly, "it would be better to get people accustomed to me as a doctor before hitting them with the idea that I might be a fallen woman. If they were used to coming to me for their medical needs, they might overlook a fancied moral lapse or two. But since I can't think of anyplace else for you to sleep and I know I'd never be able to stand thinking of you out in the rain, I guess I might as well have the people of Sweet Water know right from the beginning that I'm my own woman."

Caleb's conscience began bothering him immediately. "But Mary Rose—" he started to protest.

She cut him off. "I'm used to being considered a little odd," she said with simple acceptance. "When I was growing up, so many people viewed my mother as a witch that they thought I must be a little strange, as well. And even when I got out into the big wide world, I was considered different from the norm. So it won't bother me at all if it continues."

"It bothers me, though," Caleb said soberly, and surprisingly, it did. He wondered uneasily if he was beginning to feel just a little too protective of Mary Rose, in view of his objective.

She gave him a sweet smile. "Thanks, Caleb," she said with such sincerity that his conscience was pricked anew. "But as long as I know and *you* know that we're behaving with complete circumspection, maybe the townspeople will sense our innocence."

Caleb looked down at his plate. "Maybe," he said quietly, but he didn't really believe any such thing. And as he raised his eyes to Mary Rose's and took in her soft beauty, enhanced by the warm glow from the kerosene lamp burning nearby, he wondered uneasily if he would always be able to behave as circumspectly as she apparently thought he would, and as he knew he should. Looking at her lovely smile and clear green eyes, he acknowledged that the temptation she represented was pretty powerful.

Caleb's conscience demanded that if he was going to take Mary Rose's cabin one day, he should leave the rest of her alone. Common sense demanded the same thing. An affair with her might spoil everything. But for the moment, his body wasn't listening very hard to either his conscience or his head. And from the look in Mary Rose's eyes as she met his gaze briefly before hastily getting up from the table to take her plate to the sink, her body wasn't any smarter than his.

Chapter Five

I never figured you'd turn out to be a hypocrite, Mary Rose Perkins, she thought to herself as she washed the supper dishes. *Especially over a man you don't know from Adam!*

But a hypocrite was exactly what she felt like at the moment. Oh, she had fooled herself there for a while that she was willing to risk the good opinion of the residents of Sweet Water just for the sake of being her own woman. But that look she'd exchanged with Caleb at the end of her self-righteous little speech had put the lie to her words. She wasn't risking her reputation for any goal so noble as establishing her independence! She was risking it for nothing nobler than sheer lust!

Mary Rose paused in her dishwashing and shook her head. She felt thoroughly bewildered by her own behavior. She had worked so hard and so single-mindedly for years to reach a goal now within her grasp, and all that time she had had no real trouble sublimating the normal emotions and desires most females began satisfying in their teens. Why, then, was she risking her good name now for a man she barely knew?

Maybe the answer was that she shouldn't have sublimated all those emotions and desires for so long.

Maybe, after being suppressed for all these years, they had reached boiling point and were ready to bubble over whether the rational part of her liked it or not.

Or maybe Caleb Anderson was just the sort of man almost any woman would risk things for. If that was the case, Mary Rose didn't appreciate God's timing in allowing someone like him to come into her life at this particular moment. A couple of years down the road, when the rest of her life was in order, would have been far preferable.

Thanks a lot, God, Mary Rose grumbled half humorously, half glumly. But she knew deep down that it wasn't God she should be blaming. All she had to do to get herself out of the situation was send Caleb on his way. Yet she wasn't even willing to send him as far as Sweet Water to sleep!

WHILE MARY ROSE washed dishes, Caleb went out onto the porch and sat on the steps to enjoy the evening. The June night breeze felt pleasantly caressing against his skin, and the scents it carried created a sense of vague longing inside him. He was experiencing a late bout of spring fever, no doubt, he told himself firmly.

Then he heard Mary Rose open the screen door, and as she came out to join him, he knew damned well he wasn't suffering from spring fever—or if he was, the object of his longing wasn't vague at all. She was sitting down beside him right now.

Once again he cautioned himself to keep a tight hold on his baser inclinations. This was not the time to be thinking about casual pleasures. She was not a casual sort of woman, anyway.

Beside him, Mary Rose sighed with a combination of healthy fatigue and delight at her surroundings.

"Ma and I used to sit out here on summer nights," she reminisced. "I've missed being able to do this."

"You said your mother was paralyzed," Caleb began, trying to ignore the brush of her arm against his. There was no skin contact because he was wearing long sleeves, but in his present mood and in this sort of atmosphere, it didn't take much to set his senses off.

Mary Rose nodded. "Daddy, Ma and I were going to town in the wagon one day when I was six. We couldn't afford a car. A fox jumped out in front of the mules and scared them. They bolted and the wagon turned over. Daddy was killed and Ma's legs were paralyzed, but I wasn't hurt."

Caleb shook his head, thinking how easy it was for someone's whole life to be changed in the space of a few moments. But it hadn't taken much longer after he'd discovered the cabin for him to undergo a startling change of his own—though it was far from the tragedy Mary Rose had spoken of.

"Ma had to stay in a wheelchair after that," she went on. "It was one of those old-fashioned wooden ones with the high back. I broke it up with an ax after she died and burned most of it in the stove."

Caleb was a little startled. "Why did you do that?"

Mary Rose shrugged. "It was painful to look at it," she said simply.

Caleb shook his head again. "It must have been a sad life for her," he said quietly.

Mary Rose smiled. "Most people would probably think so, and if Ma had ever made it seem as though she was suffering, I might have thought so more than I did at the time. But she was always cheerful. She never complained, even that last year of her life when the cancer caused her so much pain. And she always kept her eye on what was happening outside, either through the big window in the cabin or out here on the porch. She made my childhood a joy, Caleb. I wish every little girl had such a mother.''

Caleb remained silent. He felt a little humbled by the picture of her mother Mary Rose had painted. The woman had had so little, but apparently had been contented and happy. He, on the other hand, had had so much at one time, yet couldn't remember ever feeling particularly contented or happy except when he was writing, which was the major reason he was determined to have this cabin. It represented happiness to him now.

"Tell me about yourself, Caleb," Mary Rose invited, trying not to sound as curious about him as she felt. She might be lusting after him, but if she could keep him from knowing this, maybe nothing would come of it. Anyway, lust was one thing...falling in love was quite another. For her, it was frightening, an unknown territory she wasn't sure she was quite ready to explore.

"Oh, I had a fairly normal childhood," he said, smiling. "I was an only child, and though I often wished I had a brother, the lack of one didn't really bother me. We lived in a fairly large town in upstate New York, and I played Little League ball and went to school like all the other boys."

"When did you decide to be a writer?" she asked.

"In high school," he answered. "I had an English class where the teacher encouraged her students to write essays and short stories. I seemed to have a talent for writing, and I enjoyed doing it enormously. After that I just took it for granted that I would one day be a full-time writer."

"Did you go to college?"

"Yes."

"Have you ever sold anything?"

Caleb hesitated. It piqued his ego a little that Mary Rose didn't recognize his name. "Yes, I've sold two books," he said quietly.

"Really!" Mary Rose was delighted for him. "What were they?"

He told her the names and when they'd come out, but she didn't recognize them.

"I'm afraid that was when I had a medical text in my hands almost twenty-four hours a day," she said ruefully. "I had very little time to read novels."

Caleb shrugged and waited for the inevitable question—the one where Mary Rose asked why he was now almost flat broke.

She frowned. "But Caleb," she said, "if you've already been published, why—"

"Why am I now a bum?" he interrupted, his tone dry.

"You're not a bum," Mary Rose chided him.

"Maybe not," he allowed. "But I probably deserve to be."

"How so?" she asked curiously.

He rested his forearms on his thighs and looked down at his bandaged hands. To his surprise, he wasn't feeling reluctant to disclose his past foolishness to Mary Rose. Instead he welcomed the chance to be honest with her for a change.

"My first book earned me a great deal of money," he said simply, "and it also brought me into a circle of people who liked to live fast and hard. I was young and full of myself and it was easy for me to fall in with their life-style. I did manage to write one more book worth publishing before the drinking, the women and the late nights took their toll. But after that . . .'' He shrugged. ''When the money began to run out, I tried to replace it by writing another book. But whatever talent I'd had seemed to have disappeared.''

Mary Rose was staring at his profile, admiring it on some level, even though she was totally caught up in his story. Caleb's past life was so drastically different from her own she was fascinated.

''What did you do then?'' she asked.

''I panicked,'' Caleb admitted. ''I couldn't face going back to the way I'd had to live when I first started writing. So I got myself engaged to a rich young woman who was willing to subsidize me because she thought I would eventually be a rich and famous writer again.''

''But it didn't work out?'' Mary Rose kept her voice soft and unobtrusive.

Caleb shook his head. ''I finally woke up and realized that if I ever wanted to get my self-respect—and my writing—back, I had to walk away from her. So I did. She probably doesn't realize yet how lucky she is that I did, but I think she will one day.''

Was that a warning to me? Mary Rose wondered uneasily. Aloud she asked, ''And have you gotten your self-respect and your writing back?''

''I've written one book since then,'' Caleb answered, avoiding the part of Mary Rose's question concerning his self-respect. He'd thought he'd gotten it back at the same time he gotten back his writing. But he wondered now if he could keep it should he do anything to harm Mary Rose. ''I haven't heard anything on it yet,'' he added.

She thought Caleb's self-respect was so tied up in his writing that he'd answered both parts of her question.

"Well, I wish you luck," she said sincerely. And because of his admission at the hardware store that he wasn't as good a handyman as he'd made himself out to be but had merely been desperate for work, she added teasingly, "If your book does sell, you won't be needing to do any more repair work, right?"

"Right," Caleb responded wryly. All of a sudden he felt like a cheat. While he still wanted the cabin very badly, he was beginning to wonder if it hadn't been a mistake to come back to the place and get to know Mary Rose this well. He didn't like the guilty feelings he was starting to have about fooling her.

"Are you working on anything else now?" she asked.

"Not at the present," Caleb said, but even as he said it, he became aware that an idea for a novel was beginning to niggle his subconscious—a novel with a heroine like Mary Rose.

Suddenly that was the last sort of idea he wanted to have, and he stood up abruptly, startling Mary Rose.

"I'm tired after all that spading," he said casually, trying to dispel the impression he must have made on Mary Rose with his abrupt movement. "I think I'll visit your privy, then go crawl in my sleeping bag."

Without getting to her feet, Mary Rose looked up at the clear night sky dotted with thousands of stars. "Well, I don't think you'll have to worry about rain tonight," she said, and was dismayed with herself when she realized she was wishing it would rain so he would stay with her in the cabin.

"Yeah," Caleb agreed, sounding almost grim. He had a pretty good idea of what would happen when it did rain and he was forced to take shelter in the cabin with Mary Rose, and he wondered if his self-respect would survive the encounter.

"Good night, Caleb," she said, doing her best to sound merely friendly and not as disappointed as she felt because he was leaving.

"Good night," Caleb echoed. "Sleep well." And he walked into the dark.

Mary Rose sat outside awhile longer, trying to clear her mind of everything except appreciation for the soft, scented air, the quiet broken only by the sounds of crickets and frogs, and the way the stars were so much more brilliant away from city lights. But she wasn't entirely successful. A longing for something more than what the cabin and Sweet Water had always represented to her had settled in her heart, and she couldn't seem to banish that longing no matter how hard she tried.

CALEB COULDN'T GET the idea for a new book that had started as a brief thought out of his mind, even though he didn't want to write a book about Mary Rose—or her mother, either, since the character that was forming in his mind seemed to be a composite of the two women.

At last, he stopped fighting against it and set about constructing the plot in his head, trying to concentrate on the practical rather than the emotional side of the story. The emotional undertones seemed somehow too dangerous to concentrate on for the present.

Before he'd gotten very far, however, he fell into a sound sleep. And in the morning, he wondered if his capitulation—his cessation of mental struggle—was what whoever or whatever had put the idea for the book into his mind in the first place had wanted.

That possibility made him laugh at himself, and he decided that the atmosphere here, while it certainly stirred his creative juices, might also stir fantasies too wild to countenance. If he didn't watch it, he told himself humorously, once he lived here full-time he might come to be viewed as a warlock...the way Mary Rose's mother had come to be viewed as a witch.

"ARE YOU GOING to come out and supervise the way I plant?" Caleb asked as he speared another bite of scrambled egg with his fork.

Mary Rose finished munching her crisp bacon before she answered. "Well, actually, we ought to check an almanac before we plant," she said.

Caleb looked up, startled.

She smiled unrepentantly at him. "But since it's so late and I don't have a current issue of one, we'll just stick the seeds in and hope for the best."

"You're not serious," Caleb said uncertainly, "about using an almanac, I mean. Isn't that what tells what sign of the moon to plant under and all that?"

"Yep. And you bet I'm serious. Ma and I always used one to time our planting, and it never failed us. You can't argue with experience, Caleb." She shrugged, a twinkle in her green eyes.

She had encountered skeptics like Caleb over the years and was used to their negative attitude toward anything from the past. If it was new, it had to be better. But that was a philosophy Mary Rose didn't necessarily subscribe to. She preferred to take whatever worked from both the old and the new.

"I know you're the hired hand," she added, and was amused when Caleb gave her a slightly disgruntled look, "but do you mind if I actually help you plant the seeds? I always enjoyed doing it, and I haven't had a chance to get my hands in some rich soil for years."

"You're the boss," he said with a shrug. "All you
have to do is threaten not to give me lunch or dinner,
and I'll be putty in your hands."

Mary Rose snorted. "Said like a true menial laborer
under the whip of a heartless capitalist overlord," she
responded. "So I wonder why it is I don't believe a
word."

Caleb smiled. "Well, I have to admit," he said
mildly, "I have wondered upon occasion if there might
be a rebellious streak in my nature."

"Oh, I doubt it." She shook her head, her expression a little too serious to be believed.

"You do?"

She nodded. "Yes, I think it would probably be more
accurate to say that there's a streak of complete an-
archy in your nature."

Caleb considered that idea with the sober contem-
plation it merited . . . or at least he gave the appearance
of doing so.

"No," he finally said. "I'm willing to admit some
control has to be tolerated. Let's just say I favor an independent frame of mind."

Mary Rose rolled her eyes. "So, okay, Mr.
Independent," she said with exaggerated patience, "do
I have your permission to help plant my own garden or
not?"

"Suit yourself," Caleb responded mildly.

"Thanks—I will." Her tone was dry. "Do you want
some more coffee?" she asked.

"Yes, thank you," Caleb responded almost primly,
making Mary Rose roll her eyes again.

Shortly thereafter the two of them were on their knees
in the dirt, arguing about how deeply to plant the corn
seeds.

"You're pushing them in too far," she protested.

"The rain will wash them away if I don't," Caleb said, scowling.

"Have you ever planted corn before?" Mary Rose demanded, scowling back at him.

"No, but common sense..." He started to defend his position, but she brushed his defense away with a wave of her hand.

"Well, I have," she stated emphatically, and reached in and got the two corn seeds Caleb had pushed so far into the soil they were almost out of sight. She mounded some dirt under them, then replanted them.

"I thought you came out here merely to help," Caleb muttered darkly.

"Maybe my instincts were telling me you needed more than help," Mary Rose complained. "*Direction* is what you need, Mr. City Slicker, so hush up and learn."

The wrangling continued—more or less good-naturedly, depending upon how strongly one or the other of them felt about his or her position at any given moment in time—until the whole garden was planted.

Then they stood back and admired their handiwork.

"Maybe we ought to put our names on sticks and place them where we each planted," Caleb drawled. "Then we can see who was right and who was wrong."

Mary Rose turned an innocent smile in his direction. "I would never humiliate you like that," she said sweetly.

"'Pride goeth before a fall,'" Caleb warned.

"And fools tread where angels don't dare," Mary Rose returned smartly. Then she quickly changed the subject. "Listen, Caleb, I need a bath, so you'll have to stay away from the cabin awhile."

Before he gave himself time to think that it might be inappropriate to respond naturally, Caleb answered with a leer. "Want me to fill the tin tub for you, then wash your back?"

Mary Rose blushed a little and turned away so he wouldn't notice. "No, but you can drag the tub into the kitchen for me," she said before pivoting on her heel to return to the cabin.

When Caleb caught up with her, she was in control again, and announced, "After I have my bath, I'm going to go see Ina."

"Why?" Caleb asked, feeling a little alarmed. He hoped Mary Rose wasn't going to insist he go with her.

"I need to enlist her help in spreading word around that I'm putting up my shingle after my West Virginia medical license is approved and I get the cabin into shape to see patients here," she explained. "Which reminds me," she added with a grimace, "I need to get over to a bank at the county seat soon and put in for a loan."

Then, not looking at him, she said, "And I think I'd better introduce you to Ina and explain what you're doing here. It won't do if she finds out about you on her own. She'll resent having any news of that sort kept from her, and I need her goodwill too much to risk making her mad."

Caleb stopped walking. Mary Rose continued on a few steps before she paused and looked warily back at him.

"Are you really that innocent," he asked dryly. "Just because you tell Ina I'm staying here to fix your roof and for no other reason doesn't mean she's going to believe you."

Mary Rose shrugged. "Maybe not. But having her find out from someone else just isn't a good idea. And you're charming and believable. Maybe if you tell her straight out you have no designs on my virtue, she'll believe you."

Rather than volunteering to do as she suggested, Caleb remained silent. He simply looked at Mary Rose in a way that made her heart rate speed up and brought another blush to her pale cheeks.

After the moment of silence had stretched out between them, she awkwardly said, "Well, maybe it won't come to actually swearing anything. Maybe Ina will believe us without—" She stopped and bit her lip, and try as she might, she couldn't look away from the male challenge in Caleb's eyes.

He continued to stare at her for another long moment, and though he felt vaguely guilty about creating the sexual tension that was rising between them, he couldn't seem to make himself stop building upon it. Finally, however, he had to say something.

"I'll do the best I can, Mary Rose," he promised softly. "But I would prefer not to have to swear anything."

He left it at that, and Mary Rose was just as glad he did. She wasn't sure she was ready yet for anything more conclusive to be said between the two of them. She swallowed, nodded, then turned sharply on her heel and walked into the cabin.

After checking the pan she'd put on the stove before going out to work in the garden and finding that the water was boiling, Mary Rose went into her bedroom to gather up clean clothing and try to regain her equilibrium. A glance in the mirror above the old dresser disclosed two dabs of color on her cheeks, and she grimaced. Caleb would have to be blind not to have seen them.

"Grow up, Mary Rose," she muttered under her breath. "Caleb's technique may be a lot more subtle than that of some of the men who have propositioned you in the past, but you don't have to fall for it."

But she had to admit that she apparently was a lot more susceptible to subtlety than she was to blatancy...at least where Caleb Anderson was concerned. Or maybe it was his looks, personality, sense of humor, or the aura of self-contained maleness he exuded that she was sensitive to.

Mary Rose sighed. "That's an awful lot to be attracted to," she told herself. "What else is left?"

She shook her head. "Just relax," she told herself firmly. "Caleb won't do anything you don't invite, so you're still in control of what happens. Remember that."

The admonition to herself should have been comforting. Except that it wasn't remembering who was in control that worried her. Refusing to exercise the control she held could very well turn out to be the real problem.

CALEB WANDERED the clearing while Mary Rose bathed, and tried very hard not to let any images connected with what she was doing enter his mind. But he wasn't successful.

"It's not like she's a nun, completely off limits," he muttered to himself as he scowled in the direction of the mountains to the east. "She's single and over twenty-one. And while it's true that it would be wiser and more honorable not to act on what you're thinking, there's surely no harm in the thinking itself."

He tried to hide his awareness of her when, fully dressed, she came out to tell him it was his turn to wash. Her hair was still wet and she'd braided it. Caleb suddenly found himself wondering what her hair would look like loose.

"If you want a bath yourself, I've got another pan of water heating on the stove, but it's not quite hot enough yet," she said. Then she added innocently, "But by the time you've emptied the tub of my bathwater, your hot water should be ready."

"I beg your pardon?" he said, distrusting her innocent look and tone of voice. "Did you say by the time *I* empty your water?"

"Well—" Mary Rose stepped up the intensity of her innocent look "—the tub is too heavy for me to dump. I used to empty the water into the sink a bucketful at a time. But that takes a while. So I just thought that if you wanted to hurry things up, you could drag the tub to the porch and tip it over the side."

Caleb was unable to keep a long-suffering tone out of his sigh. "Wouldn't it be simpler if I just used your water to bathe in?" he asked.

Mary Rose looked doubtful. "I was pretty dirty," she murmured, turning her gaze somewhere other than Caleb's face. It was stupid, but his using her water seemed such an intimate thing to do.

"Yes, you were," he agreed untactfully.

She decided to remind him who was paying his wages. "The salmon patties I'm going to make for supper are exceptionally good," she said to no one in particular, "and I plan to have mashed potatoes again. A certain person I know seemed to have liked mashed potatoes, if the amount he ate last night was any indication. And if we pick up a bag of ice in town, we could have iced tea. I also noticed that Ina had fresh peaches and angel food cake and Cool Whip for sale at the store, so I might even manage to fix a dessert tonight.''

Caleb was already walking toward the cabin before Mary Rose even got to the part about dessert, but she raised her voice slightly to make sure he heard that part, too.

Half an hour later, when he began dragging the tin tub out of the cabin for the second time to empty it and Mary Rose saw that he had on the same clothes he was wearing before he bathed, she frowned.

"Don't you have anything clean to put on?" she asked as he tipped the tub over the edge of the porch.

"Nope," he said simply. "I don't have many clothes with me, and the ones I do have are all dirty right now."

It was Mary Rose's turn to sigh. "Where are your dirty clothes?" she asked resignedly.

When Caleb turned, he had a mischievous smile of satisfaction on his face. "I thought you'd never ask," he teased, and before the two of them set off for Sweet Water a while later, his dirty clothes were soaking in a pan of soapy water in Mary Rose's kitchen sink.

"You obviously need more clothes," she groused as they walked. "Can you afford some underwear and an additional shirt or two, at least?"

"Maybe," Caleb allowed.

"I suggest you make a few purchases from Ina," Mary Rose proposed dryly. And then she smiled. "It might even help our cause. It's hard for Ina to condemn people who spend money in her store."

"Right," Caleb agreed, and he only hoped she was right about Ina. But his main concern at the moment was whether Ina might recognize him and say something about his having been in Sweet Water previously.

He decided it might be wise to make a small confession before he got caught flat out.

"Mary Rose," he said casually, "I met Ina once before."

Startled, she looked over at him. "When?"

"Oh, a while ago when I first came through this area. That's when I first saw your cabin."

Mary Rose stopped walking and stared hard at him as something clicked in her mind. "Caleb, did you stay in the cabin then?" she asked.

He hadn't meant to go quite that far with his confession, but he decided to admit at least part of the truth.

"Yes. That's how I knew you didn't lock the door when you left . . . and how I knew about the leak in the roof."

Mary Rose stared at him, feeling somehow very let down that he hadn't told her the truth before.

Her look prodded him into making a few other hasty explanations. "It was raining cats and dogs, Mary Rose," he protested. "Surely you don't mind that I used your cabin to get out of the storm."

"No, that's not what I mind," she said slowly. "What I mind is your waiting until now to tell me."

Caleb shrugged and wondered irritably why he felt so damned guilty! It wasn't as if he'd stolen anything from her. And it wasn't as if he intended to steal anything from her. He was perfectly willing to pay her a more than fair price for the cabin when the time came.

"At first I didn't say anything because I was afraid you'd be angry with me. Then, by the time I realized you wouldn't be angry, it seemed awkward not to have mentioned it in the beginning. So I just . . . let it go," he explained sheepishly.

Mary Rose was frowning at him. While the matter they were discussing was not all that serious, it bothered her that Caleb hadn't been aboveboard.

"You mentioned," she said thoughtfully, "that there was something about the cabin that drew you strongly. Is that why you came back this way?"

Caleb hesitated. "The cabin drew me," he responded in a manner that would allow him to get out of telling an out-and-out lie. "It still does."

Mary Rose nodded absently. "I felt someone had been there," she murmured. She studied Caleb's face, subconsciously looking for any indication that he couldn't be trusted. But all she saw were the same strong, rugged features that had spelled character to her upon first meeting him, and still did.

"Caleb," she said almost awkwardly, "I know this may sound awfully petty, but it bothers me that you didn't tell me the truth from the start. It isn't a big deal, I know, and I suppose you didn't actually lie to me, but..."

That "but" and something about the way Mary Rose looked and sounded almost made Caleb tell her the whole truth. But they had reached the bottom of the hill, and at that moment Todd Whittaker came skidding to a stop in front of them in his pickup. He opened the passenger door and stood up on the running board to gaze at them over the top of the cab.

"Hey, guys, I'm not working right now. You need me to tote your roofing shingles up to the cabin?"

"Thank you, Todd, but we haven't got them yet." Mary Rose smiled at him. "They're supposed to be in at the hardware store tomorrow."

Todd grimaced. "I gotta work tomorrow," he explained. "But I told Caleb he could borry my truck to haul that stuff uphill for you."

"Thanks . . . I'll come by the station in the morning," Caleb said, smiling appreciatively.

"Sure thang." Todd shrugged, popped back in the cab of his pickup and took off to the sound of burning rubber.

"Todd's a great boy," Mary Rose said fondly.

Caleb glanced at her. "He's not a boy," he pointed out. "He's a young man. If you paid attention to the way he looks at you, you'd realize that."

"Well, he seems like a boy to me," she said.

There wasn't time now to finish the conversation they'd started about the cabin and Caleb felt relieved, but he also felt uneasy. It apparently had mattered a great deal to Mary Rose that he hadn't told her the truth. He suspected it would matter a great deal more to her if he continued to hold back the fact that he'd stayed there as long as he had. But if he confessed everything to her, would she be angry enough to refuse to sell the cabin to him when the time came?

His thoughts on the subject dissipated as they entered the general store. Ina was restocking shelves near the front, and she greeted Mary Rose in a friendly manner, then looked at Caleb with dawning surprise on her homely features.

"Well, hello, young feller," she said as she put the box of shoelaces in her hand down on one of the tables that held men's shirts. "What you doin' back here?"

Caleb smiled. "I liked this place and wanted to see it again," he said.

Ina glanced from Mary Rose to Caleb and back again. "How'd you two meet up?" she asked bluntly.

Caleb was glad that Mary Rose took the burden of explanations upon herself. And he wasn't really surprised when he saw that Ina didn't appear completely convinced after Mary Rose finished. However, he was surprised when the older woman merely shrugged.

"Well, honey," she said to Mary Rose, "in my day, if a pretty single woman and a handsome single man was livin' that close to each other, there'd have been hell to pay. And there'll probably be some gossip about you two even the way things are now. But your business is your business, and I ain't gonna stick my nose in it."

Mary Rose's smile lit up her face like sunlight after the rain, and when she glanced at Caleb with a twinkle in her green eyes, he had difficulty tearing his gaze from her face. Then she turned back to Ina and quickly went on to another subject.

"There's something else I wanted to tell you, Ina," she said. "I took the liberty of giving your address as the place to send my license to practice medicine in the state. So if you'd keep an eye out for it, I'd appreciate it. And if you'd pass the word around town that I'm going to be setting up here as a doctor soon, I'd appreciate that, too. As I told you before, I'm trained as an internist, so people can come to me with just about any problem. If it's something I can't handle, I'll refer them to another specialist."

"Sure, honey," Ina said. "I already told a bunch of people about you, but I'll keep gittin' the word out."

"Thanks, Ina," Mary Rose said sincerely.

Caleb looked down at the palms of his hands. They were unbandaged now after his bath, and though they looked pretty repulsive, Mary Rose had advised him to leave them open to the air unless he was going to be doing something that might expose them to infection.

"You mean you were practicing medicine on me without a license?" he asked teasingly.

Ina peered at his weeping palms and grimaced. "How'd you get them blisters, young feller?" she asked.

"I spaded a garden for Mary Rose," Caleb replied.

Ina clucked her tongue in sympathy. "That'll do it to you," she agreed. "It's kinda' late to be makin' a garden, but maybe you'll get somethin' out of it."

"I didn't practice medicine without a license." Mary Rose gave Caleb a mock scowl. "I'm licensed in Maryland, Virginia and Washington, D.C."

"Okay, okay." He grinned at her as he backed off.

While Mary Rose and Ina were getting groceries, Caleb walked to the table with men's shirts. He picked out a couple he liked, as well as two pairs of underwear and some more socks.

Later, as Ina was ringing up their purchases she said to Mary Rose, "You remember that potion your ma always made up for Grandma Bolling's arthritis?"

Mary Rose nodded. "I remember," she said. "I know how to make it, too."

"You do?" Ina brightened. "Well, that's good news, 'cause I'm startin' to be bothered by a touch of the rheumatiz myself."

"I'm sorry to hear it," Mary Rose responded. "Would you like to try the potion and see if it helps?"

"Don't mind if I do," Ina promptly agreed. "Grandma Bolling always swore by it. How soon you think you can make it up?"

"I'll do it this evening. We have to come into town tomorrow, anyway, to pick up the roofing shingles, and I'll drop off a jar of it then."

"Why, thankee, Mary Rose," Ina said, obviously pleased. "Sure hope it works. Some mornin's when I get up out of bed, it feels more like I'm eighty than sixty."

That reminded Mary Rose of Ina's husband, who had always complained of poor health, and of Ina's father, who had been elderly when Mary Rose had left Sweet Water to go live with her Aunt Sarah.

"Ina," she said, chagrined by her lack of manners, "I haven't asked you how Jasper or your father are doing. Are they well?"

Ina immediately adopted a woebegone expression. "Naw, honey, they've both passed on. Daddy went about the same time Grandma Bolling did, and Jasper died three years ago."

"Oh, I'm so sorry," Mary Rose said sympathetically.

Ina merely shrugged. "I'm gittin' used to doin' without 'em now," she said in a practical tone of voice. "But I missed 'em pretty good there for a long while."

"I'm sure you did."

Ina walked them to the front of the store. "I'll tell everybody we're gonna have us a doctor in town soon," she told Mary Rose as they stepped out the door.

"Thank you, Ina. I hope it won't be too long before I get my license and have the cabin fixed up to practice medicine there."

"That old place could use some help," Ina agreed. She waved goodbye as Mary Rose and Caleb walked toward the post office.

"I hope this post office has boxes to rent," Mary Rose said as they neared the very small building with the American flag atop it.

"Surely they have rural mail service if it doesn't," Caleb said.

"I imagine they do," Mary Rose agreed, "but if things are like they used to be, whoever delivers the rural mail takes his time and sets his own schedule, and I'd like a little more reliability than that."

Electing not to subject himself to another long explanation about who he was and what he was doing in Sweet Water, Caleb said, "I'll stay outside while you go in."

"Okay, I won't be long."

"Glad you come back here," June Waverly, the postmistress, declared. "We've lost people before 'cause it took so long to get 'em to the county seat for doctorin'."

"Yes, I remember a few of those cases," Mary Rose told her.

"First time I need somethin'," June declared, "I'll be along up the road to see ya—you can count on that."

Mary Rose smiled because June looked so spankingly healthy. She thanked her old friend, took the key to the box she'd rented, then rejoined Caleb.

Back at the cabin, Mary Rose would have washed Caleb's clothes, but he gently moved her aside from the sink and did his own washing, despite the sting of the water and soap on his palms.

His consideration made Mary Rose warm to him further. In fact, she became soberly aware that if he kept doing things to make her like him too much, her feelings might one day slip over the line to love. But what about Caleb's feelings? How seriously should she take that exchange they'd had after planting the garden?

It was too soon to tell.

Chapter Six

Caleb grimaced as he looked into the pan on the stove. Pieces of what he would have sworn were bark floated in an ugly yellow broth of gently boiling water.

"Do people actually drink this stuff?" he asked Mary Rose. "It looks lethal."

She pushed a strand of white-blond hair off her damp forehead as she moved from the sink, where she'd been washing dishes, and looked into the pot. "It tastes pretty bad," she admitted, "but it's definitely not lethal. But a lot of medicines that come from plants are poisonous and have to be processed before they can be used."

Caleb shook his head. "I think I prefer capsules and pills, or even a shot, to having to drink something like this."

Mary Rose smiled as she went back to her dishes. "I guess if you ever got arthritis, you'd rather have the potato treatment then," she remarked drolly.

"I beg your pardon?" Caleb thought he hadn't heard her right.

"It's an old remedy. You boil two quarts of potatoes and bathe the affected joints with the hot liquid twice a day."

"Hmm," Caleb said noncommittally.

"The thing that bothers me," Mary Rose went on, warming to her subject, "is all the potential medicines we're losing every day."

"How so?" he asked absently as he stuck a finger in the container of Cool Whip and lifted a bite of the delicious creamy substance to his mouth.

"Stop that!" She scowled at him. "You've had your dessert already, and anyway, your manners are atrocious!"

Caleb gave her an innocent look. "I was merely being thrifty," he informed her virtuously. "Surely this stuff will spoil by tomorrow."

"Well, at least use a spoon," she instructed. "To answer your question, it has to do with the rain forests."

Caleb, who had immediately taken Mary Rose at her word and was dipping up Cool Whip with a spoon now, glanced at her in a puzzled fashion.

"Rain forests?" he repeated.

She nodded. "There are thousands and thousands of plants growing in the rain forests that haven't been tested for their potential medicinal qualities yet and that could possibly provide a cure for a disease like cancer. But many of those plants are becoming extinct before they've been tested because people are moving into the rain forests and cutting and clearing everything in their paths."

"But if it's a choice between survival for people who are living now and the discovery of something we're not even sure exists..." Caleb didn't finish, merely shrugged.

"You can't look at it like that," Mary Rose said. "For one thing, the soil in the rain forests is so poor that it can't support crops or animals for more than a few short years, and then the people have to move on. What they leave behind is devastation where once there was something marvelous... something with the potential to save many thousands of lives. For another thing, the rain forests affect the weather over the entire earth. Without them we're all in trouble."

"But aren't governments doing anything to stop this devastation?" Caleb asked, frowning.

"Very little," Mary Rose said with a sigh. "There are a few things happening, though, that will help. For instance, some concerned people have bought up part of the debt of various countries in exchange for having the governments keep vast tracts of rain forest exempt from settlement. And there are ethno-botanists who are racing against time to rescue what they can. They're handicapped by the sheer variety of plants, many of which won't be of any use. So they've started using Indian medicine men to direct them to plants already proven to be of use as cures."

"By whom?" Caleb asked, startled.

"By the medicine men," Mary Rose answered, looking at him in surprise. Then she smiled. "Oh, I see. You're accustomed to thinking of medicine men as witch doctor charlatans. Well, you're wrong. Many of them know cures we, with all our sophisticated equipment and knowledge, haven't discovered yet. For example, did you know that athlete's foot can't be cured, only suppressed?"

"No, I didn't know." Caleb smiled, thankful he didn't suffer from that particular ailment.

"Well, many South American medicine men are able to treat such fungal infections a lot more successfully than we are," she informed him dryly. "Rather humbling, isn't it?"

"I guess it is," he allowed.

Mary Rose could tell, however, that he was actually skeptical. She sighed, but wasn't surprised. It was hard, she realized, for those who had been brought up thinking one particular way to change their minds easily. Then she got a mischievous look in her eyes.

"Say, Caleb," she said innocently, "sleeping outside in the damp the way you do, you might turn up with a cold sometime. Maybe I should make you up a bag of asafetida to wear around your neck to keep you healthy. After all, I want you in good shape to work on my roof."

Caleb gave her a very skeptical look. "You have a homemade cure for the common cold?" he asked, dubious.

"Not a cure. Just something that wards off colds."

Mary Rose's manner made Caleb suspicious. "Okay," he drawled, "what's the catch?"

"The catch?" Mary Rose repeated innocently.

"The catch," Caleb repeated firmly.

Mary Rose's glance slid away from his, making him even more suspicious.

"Well," she said in the tone of one merely passing along a rumor, not a fact, "some people say they'd prefer a cold to the odor of the asafetida, but I think that's very shortsighted, don't you?"

"I doubt it," Caleb said dryly. "Never having smelled asafetida, I can't say for sure, of course, but if you don't mind, I think I'll forgo testing the matter."

"Suit yourself," she said lightly. Then, after a momentary pause, she added, "How about a black ribbon around your neck?"

"I beg your pardon?" Again Caleb was certain he hadn't heard her correctly.

"A black ribbon around one's neck is supposed to cure croup," Mary Rose explained, trying to sound suitably serious.

Caleb sighed. "Why don't we just wait until I get the croup before we try that," he said, attempting to match Mary Rose's serious tone.

"Suit yourself," she responded again. "Of course, we could always rub some kerosene on your chest and put a flannel over it. That's good for a chest cold."

"Sounds like it's also good for a bonfire, if one happens to run out of wood and doesn't particularly like the person with the chest cold," Caleb muttered.

"What was that?" she inquired brightly.

"Never mind," he said in a louder voice.

"And if the chest cold should develop into pneumonia," Mary Rose went on as though there had been no interruption, "we can use yellow axle grease and turpentine on you."

"Penicillin's out of fashion, I suppose," Caleb mumbled. Then he raised his voice and said, "If you don't mind, since I'm going to have to continue sleeping outdoors, I'd just as soon not discuss all the dire things that could happen to me as a result."

Mary Rose merely smiled and changed direction. "Oh, I just thought of something else," she said cheerily. "Are your blisters stinging?"

They were a little, but by this time Caleb thought it might be safer not to say so. "My hands are fine," he replied firmly.

"Oh. Well, if they start hurting, or if you get a burn while you're here, I'll just mix up some vinegar and flour, and I guarantee you, the pain will disappear like magic.''

Caleb sighed, dropped the now empty Cool Whip container and his spoon into Mary Rose's dishwater and headed for the door.

"Where are you going?" she inquired in a tone too innocently surprised to be believed.

"I think it's time I myself disappeared," he informed her dryly. "Like magic." And he vanished out the door, the sounds of Mary Rose's laughter trailing him like a ghost.

THE NEXT MORNING at breakfast, Mary Rose asked Caleb if he'd studied the pamphlet on roofing they'd gotten from Mr. Phipps.

"Not yet," he admitted, "but I have it in my pocket."

"We're picking up the shingles today," she reminded him.

Caleb eyed her sternly. "Was that a nag?" he asked.

She grimaced. "I was trying really hard not to make it sound like one. I guess I didn't succeed, huh?"

He chuckled and shook his head. "I don't think you'll ever make a genuine capitalist pig overlord," he said with satisfaction. "You just don't have that streak of iron desire to exploit and bully that's required for the position."

"Humph!" she said sulkily. "I bet if I really worked on it—"

"Please don't," Caleb interrupted her hastily. "I work better for softies than bullies."

"Is that a promise?" she asked, directing an innocent green gaze his way.

"Yes," he said with a sigh, "that's a promise. Now hush and let me read in peace, boss," he added as he dug the pamphlet out of the back pocket of his jeans. "I can't concentrate when I'm being nagged."

Mary Rose clamped her lips firmly together and kept them that way as Caleb finished his breakfast and read his pamphlet. But when he looked up at last, she quickly found her tongue. "Think you're going to have any problems?"

He adopted the look of the superior male. "Of course not," he drawled. "Any reasonably intelligent twelve-year-old could follow these instructions."

"Uh-oh," Mary Rose responded gloomily.

Caleb glared at her. "Bite your tongue, woman," he ordered as he got to his feet. "Or at least wait until I've screwed up before you start predicting doom."

"Let me see that," she countered, grabbing for the pamphlet.

Caleb quickly held it out of her reach. "Leave the roofing to the men," he growled as he circled the table and headed for the door. "Women know nothing of such manly arts."

"Some men don't, either," Mary Rose muttered as Caleb disappeared out the door to check the old ladder propped against the cabin beside the formerly pad-locked toolbox.

After she finished washing the breakfast dishes, Mary Rose went outside to see what Caleb was up to. She found him nailing back one of the wooden rungs that had come loose from the ladder . . . or at least attempting to. She wasn't encouraged by the sloppy job he was making of it.

"Are you sure that will hold?" she asked doubtfully.

He scowled up at her. "This ladder is unsafe," he pronounced in a tone resembling that of a disgruntled OSHA inspector.

"You think what you're doing will make it any safer?" Mary Rose inquired mildly. "We could probably borrow a ladder from somebody—"

"I'll handle it," Caleb interjected firmly. "My ladder repairs may not *look* very pretty, but I'm sure they'll be effective."

"Well, it's your neck," Mary Rose murmured, "but I think you ought to know I don't have a lick of home owners' insurance in case you fall."

"Ah, but you're a doctor," Caleb reminded her lightly, "and you can fix my neck free if I fall."

"Some necks aren't fixable," Mary Rose muttered warningly as she turned to go back in the cabin. "Especially *stiff* ones," she added under her breath, referring to his macho pride.

She didn't think she'd spoken loudly enough for Caleb to hear, but he called, "I resent that defamation of my character!"

Mary Rose paused and threw him a glowering look over her shoulder. "That's not all you're going to resent if my roof still leaks after you're done with it," she predicted dourly, and then she continued on her way, ignoring his laughter.

When she had completed her housekeeping tasks and Caleb had finished mangling the ladder, they set off to deliver Ina's potion, then pick up the roofing supplies at the hardware store.

"You know, Mary Rose," Caleb said conversationally, "I don't want to tell you your business, but it seems to me a doctor ought to have a telephone."

She gave him an enigmatic look. "I bet that according to most of the women in America," she pointed out, "I have a God-given right to have hot and cold running water, an indoor bathroom, electricity and a refrigerator, too. However, those things, as well as the telephone, are going to have to wait until I get a loan and can afford them."

Caleb gave her a pitying look. "Come to think of it, you *are* a bit underprivileged, aren't you?" he commented sadly.

"No more than you," she disagreed, unconcerned. "Want to compare bank accounts?"

Caleb wisely chose not to answer.

"No, really," Mary Rose said, and sighed dramatically. "The truth is, I'm just a simple girl, a back-to-nature type who's decided not to risk being called a greedy American overconsumer."

"But you're going to consume when you get the money, right?" Caleb asked with a smile.

"You bet!" She laughed.

"Ah, then there's hope that you'll fit in with the prevalent culture in America yet." Caleb grinned.

They stopped by the gas station to borrow Todd's pickup, then drove to the general store, where Mary Rose ran in to take Ina the potion she'd made. Turning a blind eye to any inroads inflation might have made on the price of such things, Ina handed Mary Rose a crinkled one dollar bill in payment for the jar of murky-looking water and bark.

Then Mary Rose and Caleb went to the hardware store to pick up the roofing shingles and the paraphernalia that went with them. Caleb drove back to the cabin and Mary Rose helped him unload everything

134

before he returned the pickup to the gas station and walked back to the cabin.

"Sure is nice to have friends, isn't it?" Mary Rose said, grinning, as Caleb joined her on the porch for a brief rest.

"I beg your pardon?" He was panting a little from the climb.

"Well, how would you have liked to come up that hill carrying all that?" Mary Rose asked, pointing to the pile of shingles.

"I think I would have quit my job first," Caleb said firmly.

"I wouldn't give you severance pay," she advised him.

"No supper?" Caleb pretended dismay.

"No lunch, either," she sniffed.

"Keep up that attitude and you'll turn into a filthy capitalist pig overlord yet," he predicted.

"I try." Mary Rose sighed. "But someone once told me I just don't have the iron streak of—"

"Never mind..." Caleb interrupted. "I wish we'd remembered to buy some ice," he said, changing subjects. "I'd like a glass of iced tea before I start being exploited."

"Wimp," Mary Rose said sadly. "Next thing I know, you'll be demanding weekends off, medical benefits and vacation pay."

"I think medical care is the only benefit I can realistically expect. If it's not too much to ask, may I at least have a glass of water to strengthen me for my task?"

"You know where it is."

After he'd gotten his glass of water, Caleb began toting shingles up to the roof via the sad-looking ladder he'd fixed.

Despite the banter, Mary Rose watched anxiously as he began to climb, hoping to goodness he wasn't going to come crashing through the rungs and land on his head. But Caleb had been right in predicting the ladder would hold him, because he didn't come crashing down. Mary Rose fully expected her roof to look every bit as bad as the ladder by the time he got done with it, but if it kept out the rain, she had no intention of quibbling over the minor matter of its appearance.

While Caleb was pounding on her roof, Mary Rose cleaned house, and as she tidied the spare bedroom, she looked forward to the day when it would be suitably outfitted as her medical office. Even then, it wouldn't bear much of a resemblance to what most doctors termed an adequate office, but she felt it would suit her wonderfully.

She made peanut butter sandwiches for lunch, but when she called Caleb and he appeared at the door, she blanched. He was absolutely filthy! Streaks of dirt and tar, in seemingly equal proportions, decorated him from head to foot.

"Let's eat out on the porch," she hastily proposed.

He looked down at himself and shrugged. "Maybe we'd better," he agreed. "But I'm going to have to come in and have a bath tonight...unless it rains, whereupon I think I'll just find a sheltered spot, strip and let the elements have their way with me."

Mary Rose had a sudden mental vision of Caleb nude, standing in the rain, followed by a vision of him asleep in the cabin because of the weather, and she was only half joking when she said, "I'll start praying for rain right after lunch."

"And what have you been doing while I've been slaving under your iron rule?" Caleb inquired as they

sat on the porch, eating. He asked the question to keep
Mary Rose from inquiring how the roof repairs were
going. The instructions Mr. Phipps had given him
weren't helping much. He still didn't know what the hell
he was doing. His only hope was that the mess he was
making up there would somehow miraculously result in
a waterproof roof.

"I've been cleaning out my future office," Mary Rose
answered. "And I've been daydreaming about how nice
it would be for me if, right when I'm ready to begin my
practice, a mild epidemic of flu swept through Sweet
Water. I could make my reputation as a successful
doctor in record time then."

"But there is no cure for flu is there?" Caleb asked.

"Not officially, but Ma used to make up capsules
with quinine, soda and asafetida in them along with an
Indian herb tablet that helped a lot of people," she said
with a grin.

This time Caleb didn't rise to the bait. Instead he
said, "Well, then, while you're praying for rain, I'll
pray for a mild epidemic of flu. But right now, what I
really wish is that you had a refrigerator. I'm dying for
a cold drink…and this peanut butter isn't helping." He
grimaced at the sandwich he was holding in his grimy
hands and ran his tongue around inside his gooey
mouth.

Mary Rose glanced over, and at seeing how dirty his
hands were, she frowned. "Caleb, you should wash
those hands and let me put ointment and a bandage on
them before you go back up to the roof. In fact, we
should have done that before you ever started."

Caleb shook his head. "I don't feel the pain anymore," he said in a martyrlike tone, then added much
more prosaically, "besides, the way you put bandages

on, I'd never be able to hold the hammer when you got done with me."

"I'll make them looser," Mary Rose promised. "No kidding, Caleb... you're liable to get an infection."

He grimaced again. "I'll give you a try," he agreed, "but the minute you drag out the vinegar and flour, or if I feel the circulation in my hands being cut off by your bandages, the deal's off."

Mary Rose jumped up and went inside to mix some of the hot water she always kept simmering on the stove with some cooler water from the pump. Then she went to her medical bag and got some antiseptic soap and the ointment she'd used before.

When she returned to the kitchen, he was waiting for her with his shirt off, and Mary Rose missed a step at the sight of his very masculine, very well-proportioned upper body.

"I decided to cut down on the risk of contaminating the kitchen and left my shirt outside," he said, grinning.

"Ha-ha." She struggled to keep from sounding as breathless as she felt and to hide the effect the sight of his bare chest was having on her. She wondered why it was that after seeing hundreds of completely nude male bodies during her medical training, one man's chest should affect her so strongly. But she knew the answer. This was *Caleb's* chest.

"Let's wash your hands first," she proposed as she went to the pan of warm water she'd prepared and poured some of the antiseptic soap into it.

Caleb winced as he put his hands into the water, and Mary Rose felt a tender concern for him that startled her.

Of course, she had to stand directly beside him to help clean his hands, and his bare arm brushed against her bare arm, and for a while, Mary Rose was so distracted by the contact that she was helping Caleb by sheer instinct, rather than conscious thought.

"Well, there's still tar on the fingers and the backs of your hands," she finally pronounced, hoping her voice wasn't giving away her inner turmoil, "but it's gone from your palms, which is all I'm concerned about at the moment, so let's dry you and get you slathered in ointment and bandaged."

Mary Rose reached for a towel and gently patted Caleb's hands dry, not daring to look directly at him for fear he would see how aware of him as a man she was. But when they sat down at the table so she could apply the ointment and bandages, their eyes met, and she felt as though she'd suddenly been deprived of all breath. The sober sensuality she saw in his light brown eyes and the sexual tension she could suddenly sense in his body were exactly as vivid as what she was feeling herself.

Caleb felt no surprise about what he was seeing in Mary Rose's clear green gaze, and he made no effort for the moment to hide what he was feeling himself. But there was a quality of innocence mingled with her feminine sexual awareness of him that made him wonder about the extent of her experience.

It seemed hardly credible that she really could be as innocent as she looked. On the other hand, there was a great deal about Mary Rose that didn't fit the norm. And if there was any chance whatsoever that he might be the first man for her, Caleb didn't want to deal with it. He already felt guilty about lying to her.

That kind of thinking gave him the will to look away from the gently burgeoning desire in her naked gaze.

"Time's passing," he said, and hearing the revealing huskiness in his voice, he wished he could do something about it, but he couldn't. "We'd better get on with this." He raised one of his hands in an awkward gesture, still not meeting Mary Rose's eyes.

She felt a great wave of disappointment sweep over her, followed by another, equally strong wave of embarrassment. Quickly she cleared her throat and took Caleb's hand. "These don't look as bad as I feared they would. You must heal quickly."

He didn't respond, and Mary Rose was too distracted by the thought that entered her mind on the heels of her last statement to notice. She was wondering if Caleb healed as quickly from wounds of the heart as he did from physical ones. She didn't know how long ago he'd broken off with his fiancée, but he obviously wasn't suffering over that broken engagement.

Then she began wondering how quickly she herself might heal from a broken heart. Considering that Caleb had just ignored what must have been a blatant invitation in her eyes, she didn't think she was in much danger of having to deal with a broken heart anytime in the near future. And maybe she should feel lucky that her education in such matters seemingly was going to be put off for a while.

But she didn't feel lucky as she gently smeared ointment on Caleb's palms, then covered them with bandages and taped the bandages loosely. She felt... cheated.

"There," she said, and she got to her feet and made sure she was turned away from Caleb while she gathered up her medicaments. "That should take care of things for a while."

"Aye-aye, boss," Caleb said as he stood. He was glad she was behaving normally, but he didn't fool himself that her manner was an accurate barometer of her mood. He'd felt her disappointment . . . and he felt like a heel.

Why couldn't he be either a complete villain or a complete hero? he wondered moodily as he went outside to begin work on the roof again. A complete villain would seduce Mary Rose, and all the time he was sleeping with her, he would be actively working to make her medical career here a failure. And when her career had failed, he would buy her cabin at the lowest price he could get away with and wave a cheerful goodbye to her as she went off to try again somewhere else.

On the other hand, a complete hero would have left here the moment he'd come to realize how much the cabin meant to her. And he wouldn't have made a mess of her roof. He would have admitted he didn't know what the hell he was doing, suggested she hire the services of a competent roofer, then disappeared into the sunset.

But Mary Rose couldn't afford the services of a competent roofer, and Caleb was no perfect hero. He still wanted the cabin. He just wanted it in a way that wouldn't hurt his conscience. And while he wasn't proud of himself for holding such an attitude, he wasn't sufficiently ashamed of himself to do the heroic thing, either.

When she was certain that Caleb had gone outside, Mary Rose returned to the kitchen and sat down at the table, studying her hands as she listened to what was going on inside her heart.

She had never had more than a mild crush on a boy during her adolescent years. Her inner goal had been too all-encompassing, driving her to work very hard at her studies. She'd had a social life; in fact, she'd been very popular. But her socializing had always been conducted on her own strict terms. Study came first, fun was reserved for what little time was left over, and she had been adamant about resisting any sexual exploration. She didn't want an unwanted pregnancy, and anyway she hadn't felt attracted enough to any of the boys she'd dated to make her dream fade from view.

It had been the same in college and medical school, except that she had put even more pressure on herself to do well academically in order to assure that the scholarships, which made her feel less dependent on Sarah, would keep coming. Even when she had dated Geoff, she had put him last and her career first, because he didn't inspire in her the sort of blind passion that could get in her way.

So, up until now, no man had ever made her feel the way Caleb did just by looking into her eyes with raw desire spilling forth from his gaze. True, she'd seen raw desire before, but it had never provoked a storm of response within her. Rather, the few times she'd felt anything at all, it had been only a gentle breeze of curiosity and very muted excitement. Caleb was the first man she had ever really wanted. Yet Caleb, though he'd obviously been feeling desire for her, apparently wasn't going to do anything about his feelings... or hers.

Mary Rose had no intention of making the first move. Even if she'd felt comfortable about approaching Caleb, when he'd turned away from her a few moments ago it had made her keenly aware of the hurt that could come her way if his response wasn't what she wanted it to be.

A huge sigh escaped from her throat as she got up and fetched her purse, then went outside. Caleb was working on the other side of the roof and didn't notice her start to walk downhill. By the time he did look up and see her, she was too far away to hear him call and ask where she was going.

Not wanting to talk to Ina or anyone else for the present, Mary Rose went to the new supermarket and bought some chops for supper and a bag of ice. When she left the store and headed for the cabin, however, she came upon a listless, overweight little girl leaning against a utility pole on the corner.

Something about the child's manner made Mary Rose pause and say hello.

"'lo," the little girl responded in a tired little voice. Her blue eyes held a mild curiosity, but it was as though she didn't have the energy to work up too much excitement about anything.

"What's your name?" Mary Rose asked.

"Beth Mullins," the child answered.

"It's nice to meet you, Beth," she said, "but you know what I'm wondering?" When that got her a surprised look from the child, she added, "I'm wondering what you've been doing today to make you so tired. Have you been playing hard?"

Beth Mullins's surprised look turned into a grimace. "I ain't been doin' nuthin'. I'm always tired."

Mary Rose studied the girl a moment longer, noting the dry-looking skin, the bloated appearance of her body and the way her throat bulged slightly. "Has your mom taken you to a doctor to find out why you always feel tired, Beth?" she asked.

The child, whose gaze was now on her shoes, shook her head. "She just tells me I was born lazy," she muttered. And then she looked toward the supermarket, straightened and took a step away. "I gotta go," she said. "Ma's through shoppin'."

Mary Rose frowned and looked down the street at the woman who'd just exited the supermarket. She had a professional desire to go speak to her about Beth. But the child was already walking away, and Mary Rose wasn't sure how Beth's mother would take it if a doctor approached her out of the blue about her daughter, so she walked on back to the cabin.

She used the time to think about how she should behave toward Caleb. It was going to be harder now to pretend she wasn't attracted to him.

Having hidden her real feelings from her Aunt Sarah for so many years, Mary Rose was an expert on the practice. Though she had come truly to love her aunt, she had also always felt a certain wariness of her, as well. It had been such a relief to be able to be honest with Sarah at last, even though the consequences of that act were as painful as Mary Rose had always suspected they would be. Therefore she didn't look forward to that same "watch-your-tongue" tension with Caleb that she'd employed with Sarah for so many years.

"I wish I could take back that look," she muttered irritably as she climbed the hill to the cabin. "Especially since it didn't accomplish anything."

But there was no way to close Pandora's box now that it had been opened. Having had a taste of the power of such feelings, Mary Rose knew she would now never be able to forget what was possible with the right man.

"No wonder the poets whine so much about unrequited love," she mumbled disgruntledly. "Or unrequited *lust*, whichever it is Caleb's managed to stir up in me. You can't get the stupid feelings out of your mind, no matter how hard you try!''

By the time the cabin came into sight, Mary Rose had fatalistically decided she had no choice other than just to act as though nothing had happened. There was something to be said for keeping up a good front, no matter how uncomfortable it made one feel inside. So she waved at Caleb up on the roof and smiled as naturally as though the sight of his bare torso didn't affect her. He waved back. Then she went inside the cabin.

Throughout dinner Mary Rose kept up a stream of inconsequential chatter that made it easy for Caleb to pretend things were the same between them. But later, as he bathed the sweat and tar and dirt off himself in the kitchen while she sat out in the yard and watched the day die, the truth kept nudging his conscience.

He admired Mary Rose's efforts of pretense, of course. He even admired his own. But the fact remained that all they were doing was pretending. The attraction between them was still there, and if he didn't get out of here soon, one or the other of them was sure to take the first step toward doing something about it.

Chapter Seven

The next morning, Caleb felt so stiff and sore it was an effort for him to climb out of his sleeping bag. This took him by surprise, because while he'd let himself get out of shape during the preceding two unproductive years, he'd thought the hiking he'd done had put him back in tip-top condition.

"You must be getting old," he muttered as he hobbled toward the privy. "Maybe you ought to ask Mary Rose for some of that foul-looking arthritis medicine she cooked up for Ina."

He had no real intention of doing any such thing, though. He'd as soon drink scummy pond water.

When he reported for breakfast, Mary Rose noticed the stiff way he walked and how gingerly he seated himself at the table. "What's wrong with you?" she asked bluntly as she set a cup of coffee in front of him and went back to the stove to turn the sausage.

Caleb cupped the mug of coffee and scowled. "Nothing," he said, and took a sip of coffee.

His reply sounded too defensive to Mary Rose's sensitive ears. Besides, it was obvious from the way he moved that he was lying through his teeth.

"Oh, I see," she said in a mildly wry tone. "You just turned into an old man overnight due to some spell cast on you. Funny, I never knew my woods were enchanted. What'd you do, kiss a magic frog, expecting it to turn into a princess, and just make it mad, instead?"

Caleb's scowl deepened. In his present mood, the way Mary Rose had referred to the woods as "hers" irritated him. It was true, of course...technically. But since he'd been sleeping out there, he'd begun to think of the surrounding property as his, just as much as he did the cabin. "I don't want to talk about it," he growled.

Mary Rose sighed. She knew very well what was bothering him, and what to do about it. But to work out his physical kinks, she would have to touch him, and even if he'd sit still for a massage, she was quite certain touching Caleb would be a mistake. Also, it would hurt her pride if she offered her help and he turned it down.

As they ate breakfast, Caleb maintained his surly silence. Mary Rose was silent, as well, because she was having a battle of conscience. It went against her nature to refuse to help someone for personal reasons, even when that someone was a bad-tempered grouch who didn't deserve her help.

Though she was as human as anyone else and there were certain patients she'd rather work with than others, she had long since learned to do her job without prejudice. So when Caleb had finished eating and dragged himself up from his chair, wincing all the while, Mary Rose told herself firmly that she could suppress positive feelings about a patient just as readily as she could suppress negative ones.

"Take off your shirt and go lie down on my bed," she ordered.

"What?" Caleb knew he sounded stupid, but what other reaction made any sense under the circumstances?

"I said," Mary Rose repeated with tight-lipped firmness as she set down her coffee cup, stood and faced him with a determined expression in her glinting eyes, "take off your shirt and go lie down on my bed. I'm not in the mood for any of your macho heroics this morning."

Caleb wasn't any clearer about what she had in mind than he had been before she'd given her so-called explanation.

"Why?"

"Because I had enough of them yesterday," Mary Rose groused as she came to him and rapidly, expertly, undid the buttons of his shirt, while he looked down at her fast-flying hands with a puzzled expression on his face. Mary Rose whipped the shirt off him, tossed it aside, then placed a hand on his bare shoulder and shoved him hard in the direction of her bedroom.

Caleb could tell she had meant business, so he didn't resist. But as he walked reluctantly in the direction Mary Rose obviously was determined he should go, he sighed.

"No...I meant, why am I going to your bedroom?" The way he'd phrased the question put an instant, and in some ways hilarious, vision into his head of Mary Rose attempting to violate his pristine body. He didn't know whether to burst out laughing or meet his fate by lying back and enjoying it without a murmur of protest.

"For a massage, of course." Mary Rose glared at him. "Do you think I'm a complete idiot? You hobble around and wince and can barely move, and I'm not supposed to put two and two together?"

After a brief hesitation, during which he didn't know whether he felt disappointed or relieved, he said, "Oh."

At that Mary Rose picked up on what he'd been thinking, and her face went red with temper and embarrassment. "Shut up and lie down!" she said fiercely, giving him another ungentle shove across the threshold of her bedroom. "And while you're lying there, see if you can clean up your mind."

Caleb opened his mouth to protest, but since he was guilty as accused, he closed it again and meekly stretched out facedown across her bed. But before she could begin her massage, he had a thought. "You will be gentle, won't you?" he asked, half teasing, half pleading.

"Why should I be?" Mary Rose was rolling up her sleeves, and the expression on her face indicated he didn't have a prayer of getting a "gentle" massage.

"Because I'm fragile," he said hopefully. When that didn't work, he added, "And because you're a doctor, sworn to help patients, not maim them."

That brought an unamused twist to Mary Rose's mouth. "Doctors are only human. They make mistakes just like everybody else," she said threateningly.

"But the consequences can be so much more disastrous," Caleb pointed out. "Usually for the patient."

"If you die, you die" was Mary Rose's terse reply before she climbed onto the bed, straddled his hips and placed her hands on his shoulders. "Lie flat!" she ordered.

"Yes, ma'am!" Caleb muttered somewhat resentfully. But that was the last thing he uttered, other than some yelps and moans and groans, for the next fifteen minutes until Mary Rose had finished inflicting her brand of torture upon him and climbed off his hips.

"Feel better?" she asked sweetly as he sat up, looking somewhat dazed and decidedly abused.

"Better?" he snorted. But even as he said it, he was flexing his arms and back and discovering that most of the soreness was gone. Still, he wasn't ready to admit that her rough handling was responsible for his relief. He started looking himself over, instead.

"Now what are you doing?" Mary Rose demanded, her hands on her hips and a scowl on her face.

"Looking for bruises," Caleb informed her nastily. "I want evidence when I report you to the American Medical Association."

Mary Rose curled her lip at him and turned smartly on her heel. "Look away," she called confidently over her shoulder. "You won't find anything. I know all the tricks."

She disappeared through the door and he was still staring morosely in that direction, when her head popped back around the opening. The smile on her lips was ominous. "Next time, I'll use the rubber hose," she promised, and then she was gone again, from the room and from the cabin, it seemed, for she wasn't in the kitchen when Caleb returned there to retrieve his shirt.

Mary Rose had made herself scarce because she wasn't sure how much longer she could keep up a good front. Now she was in the family cemetery, kneeling beside her mother's grave, absently pulling weeds and trying to calm herself.

Caleb had had some justification for thinking his massage was overly rough. It had been. And the reason was that from the first instant her hands had touched his bare, tanned, muscular shoulders, Mary Rose had known she was in serious trouble. Being rough was the only defense she had against the desire to stroke instead of pummel.

She wished now she'd told her medical ethics to go hang. Caleb would have gotten over being stiff and sore after a while. But, no, she thought, grimacing with self-disgust, she'd had to play Dr. Schweitzer and in the process discover that the feelings she'd had while exchanging that infamous look with Caleb the day before were small potatoes compared to what she felt while touching him so intimately.

Sitting back on her heels, she frowned and looked down at her mother's grave. "Ma, what do I do about this?" she asked plaintively.

And in her mind, she heard her mother's voice answer her. *Nothing. Everyone has to go through falling in love for the first time, whether it hurts or not.*

"But I don't want to fall in love right now," Mary Rose protested. "It will get in my way. And besides, Caleb's not cooperating." The last sentence was more of a complaint than a comment.

Love doesn't go by schedules, her mother's voice echoed in Mary Rose's head, sounding amused. *And if it were a prerequisite that the one loved always loves back, there wouldn't be any broken hearts, now would there? And broken hearts provide a great deal of grist for the mills of poetry, plays and literature, so they must be fairly common.*

Mary Rose sighed. She hadn't liked that answer much. Her mother's voice wouldn't let her alone, however.

You just told Caleb that doctors were people like everyone else and made mistakes. Well, you're a woman as well as a doctor, Mary Rose, and maybe it's time you were on the other end of the stick for a change. You've gotten off scot-free for a lot of years.

Mary Rose scowled. "I couldn't help it if I didn't fall in love with any of the fellows I dated," she muttered self-defensively.

And Caleb can't help it if he doesn't love you.

Now there was a dose of truth Mary Rose didn't care for at all. But because it was the truth, she made herself accept it eventually... after she wallowed in disappointment for a while.

Finally she gave a long, drawn-out sigh. "I don't think I care for this love business much," she murmured. But her tone was accepting now. "I guess it doesn't matter, though. I can't help what I feel. And Caleb can't help what he feels. He'll probably be gone soon, anyway, and I'll get on with my life. Maybe it's for the best that he doesn't seem to want to get involved with me. Like I said... now's not a very good time to have my attention diverted from what I need to do."

Feeling better, if not exactly spunky, Mary Rose got up and started to walk away. But after a couple of steps she stopped, turned around to face her mother's grave again and smiled.

"Thanks, Ma," she whispered.

You're welcome, honey, the voice in her mind replied.

Chapter Eight

Caleb was pounding on the roof and Mary Rose had just finished doing the breakfast dishes, when a knock sounded on the door.

Surprised, she dried her hands and went to answer it. She found Beth Mullins and her mother standing on the porch. A rusty, beat-up pickup was parked out on the lane.

"Hello," Mary Rose said, sounding as curious as she felt.

"Howdy. Are you Dr. Perkins?" the woman asked.

"Yes, I am," Mary Rose replied as she opened the screen door. "Won't you come in?"

"Okay," the woman said, and taking Beth's hand, she crossed the threshold, dragging her daughter with her.

"Have a seat," Mary Rose invited as she pulled a couple of chairs out from the table.

Mrs. Mullins and Beth sat down, and the woman boldly looked around at the kitchen.

Mary Rose sat down across from Mrs. Mullins, who was still gazing at everything as though she found it hard to believe anyone, especially a doctor, would actually live in such primitive conditions.

"I was born and grew up in this cabin," Mary Rose said matter-of-factly. "Well, actually, I just lived here until I was fourteen. My mother died then and I had to go live in Washington, D.C., with my aunt. But I always intended to come back, because I love it here. Once I get a bank loan, I'm going to modernize the place, though."

Her little speech had the effect of making her visitor relax. "Well, I was wonderin'," Mrs. Mullins admitted. "You don't see too many people livin' like this these days."

"True," Mary Rose agreed, smiling.

"That good-lookin' feller on the roof your old man?"

"Uh, my 'old man'?" Mary Rose thought she knew what Mrs. Mullins meant, but she decided she'd better make sure.

"Your hubby!" Mrs. Mullins explained somewhat impatiently.

"I'm not married," Mary Rose replied. "That's Caleb Anderson. He's just fixing my roof."

Mrs. Mullins raised an eyebrow. "Well, if I warn't married, I'd be out there a'flirtin' with that one. He's got a powerful set of shoulders on him, don't he?"

It wasn't really a question and Mary Rose didn't bother making a confirming comment. She preferred to find out why Mrs. Mullins and Beth had come to see her, rather than dwell on Caleb's shoulders.

"Mrs. Mullins, are you here to see me as a doctor or a neighbor?" she asked, glancing at Beth, who hadn't said a word since she and her mother had arrived but merely stared at her hands in her lap.

"As a doc," Mrs. Mullins promptly answered. "Ina Butler told me you was settin' up a practice here, and then my Beth said you asked her on the street yesterday whether I'd taken her to a doc to see about why she's so all-fired droopy most of the time. Well, I just always thought she was lazy. But if there's a chance she's got somethin' wrong with her, why let's get it fixed. I'd rather she was peppy than have to watch her lyin' around lookin' like she ain't got the energy to swat a fly three-fourths of the time."

Mary Rose glanced at Beth again and saw that the child's lips were curved down resentfully now. Then she returned her gaze to the child's mother.

"Mrs. Mullins," she said, "I just thought it curious that a child Beth's age should be so listless. And there are other signs that made me wonder if you've ever had her thyroid checked."

Mrs. Mullins frowned. "Her what?" she asked.

"Her thyroid," Mary Rose repeated. "It's a gland located in the neck."

Mrs. Mullins raised her hand to feel her own throat. "Naw," she said, "I ain't never had Beth to the doctor for much of nuthin'." Apparently finding nothing identifiable, she dropped her hand. "Beth's always been tolerable healthy, 'cept for the usual thangs like sore throats and earaches."

Mary Rose got up from her chair and came around to Beth. "Tilt your head back a little, honey," she said gently. And when the child had, Mary Rose ran her fingers over the bulge. "Can you see how her throat curves outward more than most people's?" she asked Mrs. Mullins.

The woman nodded. "Yeah...now that you mention it, it does," she agreed.

"Well, that's not necessarily a sign that there's anything wrong with your daughter's thyroid, but coupled with her dry skin and hair and her listlessness and weight gain, I think the indications are sufficient that you should have her checked for an underactive thyroid,'' Mary Rose suggested. "Do you have a doctor over in the county seat?''

Mrs. Mullins was beginning to look alarmed. "Wal, we seen one of them fellers over there a couple times,'' she said, "but I cain't 'member his name.'' Then she frowned. "But why should I go over there, anyways?'' she asked. "I brought Beth to you.''

Mary Rose patted Beth's shoulder, then returned to her chair. "Yes, but I haven't received the license that says it's legal for me to practice in West Virginia yet,'' she explained. "It should arrive any day now. I'm licensed elsewhere, but I can't treat anyone here until I've received authority from the state board. Besides,'' she added with a regretful shrug, "until I've modernized this cabin, it wouldn't even be a good idea for me to take a blood sample from Beth, unless I immediately took it to the county seat for analysis. I'm not set up to do anything like that yet. And a blood test might not be conclusive. She might need a test that has to be done in a hospital, and I can't present my credentials to the county hospital until I receive my license.''

"What kind of test?'' Mrs. Mullins asked anxiously. Beth was looking nervous, as well.

"Nothing painful or frightening,'' Mary Rose hastened to assure both of them. "And if Beth does have a problem with her thyroid, it's easily corrected with medication. She'll just have to take a pill every day. Do you have medical insurance?''

Mrs. Mullins nodded. "My old man works as a janitor for the school system in the county seat. We live over here 'cause it's cheaper. But that insurance don't cover everthang. Are we talkin' about a lot of money for these tests?''

"I don't know what your regular doctor charges for office visits,'' Mary Rose said, ''and you'll have to go through him to get Beth the tests she needs. But while your insurance may not cover the complete cost of everything, this sort of test is covered, I'm sure, and it's important that it be done, Mrs. Mullins. If Beth's thyroid ever stops functioning entirely and she goes too long without medication...'' She stopped, not wanting to alarm the child unduly. ''I think you should take Beth in as soon as possible,'' she said, instead.

"But I cain't remember that doctor's name,'' Mrs. Mullins complained. ''Seems like it was Jones or Jakes or Jensen...somethin' like that.''

"Do you have any bottles of medication he's prescribed for someone in the family in the past?'' Mary Rose asked. ''His name would be on the label.''

Mrs. Mullins brightened. ''Yeah, there's some penicillin left over from when little Jamie...that's Beth's little brother,'' she explained, ''had his last earache.''

"How long ago was that?''

"'Bout a year and a half, I reckon.''

"Well, after you've gotten your doctor's name off the label, I'd throw the remaining penicillin away,'' Mary Rose suggested as tactfully as she could. ''It's sometimes dangerous to take medications that have gotten old.''

"That so?'' Mrs. Mullins asked, sounding surprised and rather disappointed. Medicine cost money.

"Yes,'' Mary Rose confirmed.

"Well, if you think it's best to go to him again,'' Mrs. Mullins said regretfully, ''I guess that's what we'll do.

How long before we can start comin' to you, though, do you think?''

Mary Rose smiled, pleased that she seemed to have made a good impression.

"Suppose I let you know when I've gotten my license and have my office in order," she suggested. "Meanwhile, I strongly advise that you go ahead and take Beth over to the county seat. Agreed?"

"Agreed." Then Mrs. Mullins got up and pulled Beth up from her chair.

Mary Rose stood. "Thank you for coming here to talk to me," she said warmly as she escorted her visitors out.

Mrs. Mullins paused at the door. "Wal, we ain't never had a woman doctor before, but Ina vouched for you and you seem okay to me. Besides, I ain't never liked havin' to go all the way over to the county seat for our doctorin'. Don't do it lessn' I cain't hep it."

That remark made Mary Rose say, "I would like to know how the tests come out. Would you mind if I stopped by your house in a week or so to find out?"

"You would, huh?" Mrs. Mullins seemed pleased by Mary Rose's interest.

"Very much so," Mary Rose assured her.

"Wal, then stop on by. But you could phone just as well, couldn't ya?" she asked.

"No, I don't have a phone yet," Mary Rose said ruefully. "I've only been back here for a few days, and there hasn't been time to get one. So if you'll just tell me where you live, I'll come by one day soon."

"We live behind the hardware store. They tell me it used to be an old mill there."

"I know where that is," Mary Rose said.

"Okay. Wal, right now, I gotta pile of washin' to do, so me'n Beth better git goin'. You take care now, Doc,'' Mrs. Mullins said, and giving a little wave of her hand, she started walking toward her battered pickup, dragging Beth with her.

"Bye, Beth,'' Mary Rose called after the two of them.

Beth looked back shyly and lifted a hand in farewell.

Mary Rose watched her first potential patients in Sweet Water drive away and felt great. Then she frowned. She needed to get to the county seat herself and see about that loan. The work on the cabin might take a while, and the sooner it was started, the better.

After she'd finished her last chores inside, she went to check the garden, though it was too soon for anything to be showing. Of course nothing was and as she was coming back to the house, Caleb yelled to her from the roof.

She looked up and shaded her eyes from the sun. Seeing Caleb minus his shirt again, she could understand why Mrs. Mullins had commented so favorably on his shoulders. They were fine specimens, all right.

"What?'' she called back.

"I said, who was that woman?'' he hollered.

Mary Rose opened her mouth to answer, then decided it was too long a story to yell it out.

"I'll tell you at lunch,'' she called.

Caleb shrugged and went back to work.

Mary Rose would very much have liked to climb up to the roof and see for herself how good a job he was doing, but something stopped her...probably the memory of the ladder he'd fixed and his irrational touchiness about the quality of his work. If the roof looked as bad as she suspected, she knew she wouldn't be able to keep from commenting. And if she didn't keep her opinion to herself, Caleb might walk off the job, leaving her with no roof at all. She didn't need that expense, as well as all the others she could see coming her way.

Shaking her head, she went into the cabin and collected a basket, then headed for the woods to gather plants to dry.

LUNCH WAS cold sausage sandwiches. Caleb had never had such a sandwich before and he skeptically lifted the top slice of bread.

"We had sausage left over from breakfast, and I didn't want to be wasteful," Mary Rose said, daring him with a look to comment. "Don't knock it until you've tried it. When I was a little girl, I used to take this kind of sandwich to school for lunch a lot."

Remembering the temper she had displayed that morning, Caleb elected not to say anything. He merely took a bite of sandwich, chewed it and nodded. "It's okay," he said, delivering his verdict in a neutral tone.

"It'd be better on cold biscuits," Mary Rose remarked, relenting slightly, "but since I didn't make any this morning, store bread will have to do."

Caleb looked at her in a puzzled fashion as he chewed. "Why do you call it 'store bread'?" he asked.

"It comes from a long time ago, when farmers' wives did most of their own baking," she explained. "They only bought bread at the store once in a while, when they came into town to shop, and it was considered a treat. To distinguish it from regular old home-baked bread, biscuits or corn bread, they called it 'store bread' or sometimes 'white bread.'"

"Interesting," Caleb said, studying her face. When Mary Rose was relaxed and smiling, the way she was now, he thought her gently beautiful. Then he remembered the way she'd been that morning and "gentle" was in no way the appropriate adjective for her. "Fiery," "vindictive" and "sadistic" came to mind, instead.

Noting how he was staring at her, Mary Rose spoke without taking time to consider the consequences. "What are you thinking?" she asked curiously. "And why are you staring at me like that?"

Caleb swallowed the food in his mouth and shrugged. "I was just thinking you never bore me," he responded lamely. It was the most tactful way of expressing his thoughts.

On the other hand, at seeing the pleasure his remark brought into her sparkling green eyes, he realized what he'd said was absolutely true. Mary Rose *didn't* bore him.

"What a nice thing to say," she remarked in a pleased tone. "You don't bore me, either, Caleb," she said, returning the compliment.

He was as inordinately pleased by her compliment, as she had been by his. For a moment they looked at each other with shared, unabashed, mutual pleasure. Then Caleb wondered what the hell he was doing, sitting here smiling like an idiot over such a simple thing, and he changed the subject to hide his annoyance with himself.

"Who was the woman who came by?" he asked.

Mary Rose explained the situation.

"You could tell that just by looking at the little girl?" Caleb asked curiously.

"Not positively," Mary Rose said. "It's just a possibility. We'll have to wait for the tests for confirmation. As for telling by looking, when you go to the doctor, don't you notice that he looks you over all the time he's talking to you?''

Caleb thought a minute. "I haven't been to a doctor in so long, I've forgotten," he admitted.

"You're pretty healthy, huh?" she asked, and for the moment was able to run her eyes over him in a professional, rather than a personal way... despite his bare shoulders.

"Yes, and don't look at me like you're trying to find something wrong," Caleb complained. "Earn your fees on somebody else."

"Ha!" Mary Rose retorted as she got up to go fill her glass with water from the hand pump. "You couldn't afford my fee, anyway."

"True," he acknowledged. "So please don't find anything wrong until I can afford to have whatever it is treated."

"There's nothing wrong with you to find," she declared. "You look disgustingly healthy."

"What's disgusting about being healthy?" Caleb countered.

Mary Rose sighed.

"Got you, didn't I?" he crowed.

She thought for a moment, searching for some way to regain lost ground. "On the other hand, looks can be deceiving," she said politely. "There are those who seem perfectly healthy but whose mental condition is, well, shall we say 'less than perfect'?"

Caleb just looked at her and chewed his sausage sandwich.

Mary Rose smiled sweetly, innocently, back at him.

But Caleb had the last word. "One has to be a little crazy to write books," he informed her loftily. "It's an asset." On that note, he drained his glass of water, got up and strolled in triumph out of the cabin.

As Caleb hauled himself back onto the roof, he paused a moment to look up at the sky, wondering why the light seemed dimmer now than it had that morning. Then he frowned. It looked like rain.

Lowering his head, he gazed gloomily at the part of the roof over the spare bedroom. Because the holes there had been large, he'd fixed them first. Using the term 'fixed' loosely, of course.

"Oh, hell," he muttered grimly. "Rain. Just what Mary Rose and I need right now."

He resumed hammering shingles, pounding a great deal harder than he had before the prospect of sleeping in the cabin with Mary Rose had come up.

Mary Rose stood at the screen door, gazing up at the sky and frowning. It looked like rain!

"You shouldn't have offered," she muttered. But she had, and she couldn't blame Caleb if he took her up on the offer. Who in his right mind would stay out in the rain in a sleeping bag when he could be under a roof...even a roof that was no doubt being very inexpertly repaired.

"There'd better not be any leaks," she grumbled. But of course, a leaking roof was the least of what worried her at the moment. What concerned her was the prospect of temptation and possible rejection that suddenly loomed on her horizon as threateningly as the rain clouds.

A moment later she left the cabin and headed for Sweet Water to get more ice. This time she intended to buy a picnic cooler, as well. She was getting darned tired of trudging back and forth to town for ice every day just because her wimpy roofer wanted his tea cold!

Chapter Nine

Mary Rose managed to cadge a ride from Todd back up the hill, which was a relief, because the picnic cooler was heavy.

When Caleb saw the pickup coming toward the cabin, he dearly hoped Todd wasn't going to insist on climbing up on the roof to inspect his progress. Todd might be young, but growing up in these parts, he probably had all kinds of handyman skills, and would recognize at a glance that Caleb had no idea what he was doing.

He wasn't pleased when the young man killed the motor and climbed out of the truck. "Howdy, Caleb!" Todd called to him.

"Hello!" Caleb called down, hoping he didn't sound as unwelcoming as he felt.

Mary Rose thought it was time she repaid Todd for all his help. "Say, Todd," she said with a smile, "how would you like to have dinner with Caleb and me?"

Todd blushed, and though he hesitated before answering, he was obviously pleased by the invitation.

"Ah, come on," she coaxed him. "I'm a pretty good cook, and we're having fried chicken."

Caleb could barely hear the conversation, but what he did hear alarmed him. If Todd stayed for dinner, he was bound to climb up on the roof and see how the repair job was coming along.

"I imagine Todd's got a date, Mary Rose," he quickly called.

That hadn't occurred to her. She looked at Todd curiously. "Do you?" she asked.

"Ah...no, ma'am, I don't," he answered, much to Caleb's disappointment. "There's just a bunch of us that usually show up at a club over at the county seat when we got a free evenin'."

Caleb brightened.

"But don't you have supper before you meet your friends?" Mary Rose persisted.

"Yes, ma'am."

Caleb's face fell.

"Well, then?"

Mary Rose was smiling again, and Caleb had a feeling Todd was pretty well defenseless when it came to her smile. When it turned out he was right, Caleb scowled.

"Well, thankee," Todd said awkwardly. "I'll be glad to have supper with ya."

Then Caleb's worst fears came to pass.

"I'll just climb up thar and see if'n I can give Caleb a hand," he said, and headed for the ladder. When he reached it, he paused, stared in a puzzled fashion at the so-called repaired rungs, shook his head, then started climbing.

There was nothing Caleb could do to stop him, and he tried to get his expression to look a little more welcoming. He was glad Mary Rose had disappeared inside the cabin so she couldn't hear Todd's evaluation of the repairs.

When Todd stepped onto the roof, he started to say something, but then his eyes opened wider as he noted the quality of the work.

Caleb sighed inwardly. There was nothing to do but confess and try to enlist Todd's silence. "As you can see, I'm not very good at this sort of thing," he said with dry humor.

It was clear Todd didn't know how to reply without seeming rude and critical.

"You know anything about roofing?" Caleb asked in a more or less casual fashion.

Todd found something interesting to look at on the horizon and shrugged. "A little," he admitted.

Caleb thought that probably meant Todd knew a lot about roofing.

"Would you mind giving me a demonstration then?" he asked.

Todd took his attention off the horizon and looked at Caleb in surprise. "You serious?" he inquired.

"Never more so," he said ruefully. "I need all the help I can get."

Todd nodded absently as he looked around him. It was clear he agreed with Caleb's assessment.

"Well, in the first place..." he began, taking the hammer from Caleb.

By the time Mary Rose called them in to supper, a great deal of the damage Caleb had managed to inflict on the roof had been rectified. After receiving the dinner call, Caleb looked at Todd with appreciative respect and whispered, "Thanks. It's probably going to rain tonight, and if you hadn't come along to help, I bet Mary Rose would have been drowning in her bed by morning."

Todd grinned. "I guess you don't want me mentionin' to Mar...uh, Doc Perkins...that you wasn't doin' too good up here before I come along."

Caleb grimaced. "I'd put it a little stronger than that," he admitted. "It's more like, if you could find it in your heart to keep your mouth shut, I'd be grateful enough to pay you any sort of bribe you named...if I ever get the money to be worth blackmailing, that is."

Todd snickered and held out his grimy hand. "You got my word on it," he vowed, and laughing, the two men climbed down from the roof to wash up for supper.

MARY ROSE STOOD on the porch beside Caleb, watching Todd drive away after supper. Her nervousness over the prospect of Caleb sleeping in the cabin that night was growing. And the fact her nervousness would probably all be for nothing because Caleb most likely wouldn't do anything more exciting than snore that night, anyway, made her feel irritable.

"I guess you'd better get your sleeping bag," she said in the tone of one suggesting her companion might as well go get dressed for an approaching funeral where the deceased hadn't been well thought of.

The prospect of sleeping so close to Mary Rose, yet not being able to touch her had Caleb feeling irritated. Her unenthusiastic proposal increased his irritation, even though he thought he understood the reason for it.

"I don't recall ever receiving a more gracious invitation," he responded in a slightly resentful tone.

Mary Rose cast a baleful glance in his direction. "If you'd rather sleep out in the rain because my invitation wasn't engraved at the best printing shop, suit yourself!" she said shortly, then she turned on her heel, pulled open the screen door, stomped across the threshold and let the door slam behind her.

Caleb glared after her. "I might just do that!" he yelled to her back.

Mary Rose returned to the doorway. Caleb thought she might be going to apologize and reoffer the shelter of her cabin in a more civilized manner. If she did, he intended to be more civil himself about accepting. He had no desire to sleep out in a downpour, even if the next few hours did test his willpower to its limits.

Glaring, Mary Rose slammed the inner door in his face!

Caleb cursed under his breath and vowed to endure the coming deluge even if it gave him pneumonia. Turning, he stalked down the steps and headed for his outdoor bedroom.

He lasted thirty minutes before, dripping and shivering, he was back, pounding on the cabin door.

Mary Rose flung open the door, still glaring. "What do you want?" she demanded.

Presented with the irrefutable evidence that she had not mellowed in the least, Caleb lost his temper. "Oh, for God's sake!" he yelled as he jerked open the screen door with a violent motion that made Mary Rose step back. He crossed the threshold and came into the kitchen. "Look at me! What do you think someone as soaked as I am wants?"

Mary Rose had stepped back, but she was undaunted. "I do not appreciate your attitude," she said coldly.

Caleb gritted his teeth. "And I don't appreciate being made to feel like somebody's least favorite poor relation come to stay for the duration!" he retorted as he

threw his wet sleeping bag on the floor and started unbuttoning his dripping shirt.

"Very well," she said stiffly. Turning away from
Caleb, she began to fill the coffeepot with water, not
even noticing that she was pumping so hard the water
was coming out in a gush rather than a stream. "You
are welcome to come in out of the rain, Mr. Anderson.
Please don't think you have to be a gracious guest,
though—having come to know you a little, I certainly
don't expect thanks for saving you from certain
drowning."

That did it as far as Caleb was concerned. He'd been
starting to regret yelling at her, but every one of his finer
instincts died aborning. Narrowing his eyes, he began
to undo his jeans in much the same way he might have
drawn off his glove had this been another age and he'd
just been insulted by a worthy male opponent whom he
intended to slap across the face and challenge to a duel.

Since she had her back to Caleb, Mary Rose felt safe
in grimacing over her overflowing coffeepot. Hoping he
hadn't noticed, she poured some of the water out and,
still without turning, prepared the pot to make coffee.
As she was doing so, she became aware of some curious rustling noises coming from his vicinity, and she
began to grow alarmed.

After placing the pot on the stove, she had no more
excuse not to look at him. So, bracing herself, she
turned . . . and promptly let out a small, half-stifled
scream. He was stark naked!

Caleb smiled benignly, very satisfied by the effect
he'd had on her. His revenge accomplished, he took his
sopping clothes and headed for the living room, where
he'd left his backpack with his clean clothing because he
always bathed in the cabin.

For a moment Mary Rose could do no more than stare, openmouthed and eyes popping, after him. But when he was out of sight, she closed her mouth with a snap and was furious to feel her face heating up in a blush.

"Why, you...you..." she sputtered under her breath. When she couldn't think of anything sufficiently scathing to call him, she resorted to a simple "That's not fair!"

"Did you say something?" Caleb called out from the living room. His tone was too innocent to be believed.

Mary Rose certainly didn't believe it. "No, I did not!" she yelled back furiously.

There was silence from the living room, and the quiet only increased her fury. She began looking around the kitchen for a weapon. Nothing that, when applied in her present state, would result in a fatal blow, of course. But something that would let Caleb Anderson feel the weight of her temper!

In the living room Caleb was chuckling to himself. The look on Mary Rose's face when she'd seen him standing there starkers had put him in a delightful mood. The snickering stopped, however, when he began to realize that she'd have had the same effect on him if he'd seen her nude.

Grimacing, he began to try to think of some way to get his mind off what he couldn't—or at least *shouldn't*—do and onto something safer. Then he remembered the fresh tablets of paper in his backpack, and felt relieved. It was still early, and instead of sitting at the kitchen table lusting after Mary Rose, he could sit at the table and write.

He didn't suspect a thing as, dry and dressed in his last set of clean clothing, he walked back into the kitchen. Fortunately his reflexes were quick, for once he realized what was about to happen—about the time the water left the bucket Mary Rose was holding—he was able to pivot and shield his precious writing tablets with his body before the water hit.

He could picture how satisfied she must be over her revenge, because he could hear her snickering in the background. Straightening, he held out his tablets, and at learning they were dry, he managed to recoup his good humor. Turning, he ignored the water dripping down his back and smiled. "Feel better?" he inquired in his most patronizing tone.

"Oh, yes," Mary Rose snorted happily. Her snickers had turned to full-blown laughter. "Much better!"

Caleb rolled his eyes to the ceiling and shook his head before heading for the towel draped on the sink. Setting the tablets down, he began unbuttoning his shirt. Behind him, Mary Rose was howling with laughter. When he had his shirt off, Caleb dried himself. Then, after wringing his shirt out over the sink, he turned and placed the garment over the back of a chair to dry. She was still laughing.

The laughter stopped abruptly, however, when Caleb, a pleasant smile on his lips, his gaze directly on Mary Rose's laughter-teared eyes, put his hands on the top button of his jeans.

"Hold it!" she gasped. Before he could go any further, she darted out of the room.

Caleb's smile broadened momentarily, then faded. He'd had his fun, and he'd really had no intention of undressing in front of her a second time. But he didn't look forward to sitting around in a pair of wet jeans, either.

Before he could decide what to do, Mary Rose was back with a large towel in her hands. She threw it at him and he caught it in one hand. She was already backing away, her expression surprisingly sober for one who'd been lost in the throes of hysterical mirth only a moment earlier.

"Uncle," she capitulated in the meek tone of one who knows she's met her match. Then she turned around and waited while Caleb climbed out of his wet jeans and wrapped the towel around his hips.

He didn't say anything until he'd retrieved his tablets, found a couple of pencils and sat down at the table. And all the while he was preparing to write, he knew deep down in his soul that writing wasn't what he wanted to be doing right now. The look on Mary Rose's face when she'd cried "uncle" had made him want to go to her, take her in his arms and hold her tightly in vivid acknowledgment that he'd been wanting to hold her like that almost from the moment he'd met her. And then he wanted to kiss her, slowly and deeply, and feel her kiss him back, and then . . .

"I'm decent now," he said quickly before any more pictures could take over his mind and heat up his body.

Mary Rose turned around, and was relieved to see Caleb seated at the table. His torso was bare, of course, and that was bad enough, but at least she couldn't see his hips and start imagining . . .

"I'll see if the coffee's ready," she said, hastily diverting the thought in her mind. "Oh, are you going to write?" she babbled as she passed the table and saw the tablets and pencils. "That's a good idea. With the rain and everything, it's a perfect night for . . . writing." To cover the revealing hesitation, she continued, "Of course, I'm not a writer, so I don't really know, but it would seem to me—''

"Mary Rose."

She stood at the stove, staring blindly at the coffee-pot, and didn't look around. "Yes?" Then she bit her lip. Her voice had trembled on that one word.

"I'm sorry I was . . . rude."

Caleb wasn't looking at her. But he could feel her presence so acutely it was almost as though he were touching her. And he could smell the faint fragrance of the scented soap she bathed in. The scent made him ache inside.

Mary Rose took a deep breath. She didn't intend for her voice to tremble this time. "I'm sorry for what I did, too," she said quietly, then added, "I think the coffee's ready. Would you like a cup?"

"Yes . . . thank you."

As Mary Rose got cups down from the cabinet and went about pouring coffee, Caleb forced himself to open the tablet, take up a pencil and try to get his mind on something other than the woman moving so softly around the kitchen. Despite her quietness he felt her physical presence as strongly as if she were in his arms.

After pouring the coffee, she set his cup down in front of him, then started toward the door to the living room, taking her coffee with her.

"Where are you going?" Caleb asked before he could stop himself.

Mary Rose paused and looked at him hesitantly over her shoulder. "I thought I'd go into the living room and read one of my medical books," she said.

Caleb hesitated, and just when Mary Rose had decided he wasn't going to say anything else, he added, "Why don't you read in here. I'd like the company."

Though he immediately bent his head over his tablet and pretended to write something, apparently not waiting for a reply, Mary Rose suddenly felt as though the stones in her stomach had been replaced with pleasantly fluttering butterflies. Without a word she went to get the medical book she wanted, then returned to the kitchen to sit down across from Caleb.

For two hours she read and he wrote. Mary Rose was surprised that she was actually able to concentrate. Caleb was surprised that he was actually able to write. The rain pattered companionably on the roof, but it was the only disturbance that impinged on their activities, except for when Mary Rose would get up to replenish their cups of coffee.

Finally she yawned and looked up. Caleb had looked up a couple of minutes earlier, intending to tell Mary Rose he was ready to go to bed. Instead he'd been caught by the lovely picture she made with the flickering light from the kerosene lamp shifting across her delicate features, catching the golden highlights in her pale hair . . . and now creating a glow in her green eyes.

"It's getting late," she said, speaking slowly because of the expression on Caleb's face. He hadn't looked away when she'd raised her head. And he wasn't pretending not to be enchanted by what he was seeing. "I . . . the coffee's all gone, too," Mary Rose stammered. "So . . . I guess . . ." She forgot what she'd been about to say. As had happened before, she was too caught in Caleb's gaze to think about anything else.

He fought a brief battle with himself. What would one kiss matter? he thought with wistful hunger. Except that if he ever touched Mary Rose, he knew he could never be satisfied with just one kiss. So, though it was one of the hardest things he'd ever done, he looked away. "Yes...I guess it's time to sleep," he said.

After a moment, during which Mary Rose told herself she was a fool to have let Caleb do this to her again, she resolutely shoved aside the almost crushing disappointment she was feeling, closed her book and stood.

"If the roof's fixed over the spare bedroom, you can sleep in there," she said as calmly as she could manage. "There's an extra blanket and pillow on the shelf in the closet. If the roof's still leaking in the bedroom, use the living room." She started for the door, then paused and without turning added, "You'll put out the lamp?"

Caleb stifled a sigh of regret and emptiness. "Yes, I'll put out the lamp," he answered, adding silently, *in more ways than one...though it isn't going to be easy.*

"Good night," she said as she disappeared through the door.

"Good night, Mary Rose," Caleb replied, liking the sound of her name on his lips. He knew he would like the taste of her on his lips, as well, certainly more than would be wise for him to...certainly more than he could justify, considering the circumstances.

It was a long, long night. And the next morning, when it was still raining hard, Caleb didn't know whether to be glad or sorry he couldn't work on the roof that day.

"Well," Mary Rose said at breakfast, her tone philosophical, "the rain should be good for the garden."

Caleb merely smiled thinly. He hadn't gotten much sleep, and his mood hovered somewhere between a surliness over being forced into such close contact with Mary Rose and a muted anticipation at spending the day writing instead of pounding the wrong nails into the wrong shingles over a spot where they probably didn't belong in the first place.

"Will you write again?" Mary Rose inquired as she looked doubtfully at a biscuit that had gotten a little brown since it had been in a part of the oven that got hottest.

"If you don't mind," Caleb answered, and he was dismayed when the remark came out sounding almost sarcastic.

Mary Rose looked at him, clearly startled.

He grimaced. "I apologize," he said quietly. "I'm not in a very good mood, but I shouldn't take it out on you."

Mary Rose started to ask him why he was in a bad mood, but something stopped her. She wasn't in exactly a sparkling frame of mind herself. She was tired from having spent half the night tossing and turning, unable to forget that Caleb was so close...and so desirable. "I think," she said as she carefully reinspected the overbrown biscuit, "I may go back to bed for a nap after breakfast. Rain always makes me feel sleepy."

Caleb covered his eyes with his hand. He wished to hell he could sleep. It would be a relief to block out the feelings that shot through him every time he looked at Mary Rose. But he knew he couldn't.

There was no relief for Caleb until breakfast was over, Mary Rose had finished the dishes and she took herself off to her bedroom. Then, finally, he was able to write.

But what he was writing didn't prove to be as much of an escape as he'd hoped. Although his story was set in the past, its heroine was recognizably Mary Rose and its hero was recognizably Caleb Anderson. And soon the imaginary Mary Rose and the imaginary Caleb were making imaginary love.

In the middle of the lovemaking, Caleb threw his pencil down in disgust and got up to pace the small kitchen. He felt like a tiger confined in a very small cage.

Before he'd paced for very long, he found his legs carrying him in a direction his brain and conscience both felt it unwise to go.

MARY ROSE was having no better luck sleeping now than she had the previous night. Yet she didn't want to get up and rejoin Caleb in the kitchen. She was weary of having to fight the desire to look at him. She was tired of having to watch the tone in her voice when she spoke to him so she wouldn't reveal what was going on inside her. And she didn't want to have to endure any more of those soulful glances between them that stirred her up, then dropped her thudding to the ground.

Not having ever wondered much about how men thought, she had no idea what was going on inside Caleb. One moment he seemed to want her, but the next he turned away. No wonder she was confused!

A slight sound at the doorway made Mary Rose open her eyes, and when she did, she caught her breath. Caleb was standing there staring at her with the look in his eyes that always made her think he wanted her. But she wasn't going to be fooled again!

"What is it, Caleb?" she asked without sitting up. Though she hadn't slept, her voice was drowsily husky, as if she'd just awoken.

He didn't answer. He felt caught in an emotional slingshot. The lines were taut, but he couldn't yet release them. Then Mary Rose sat up, and though she was frowning, he didn't notice. He was staring at her hair. She'd undone her braid and the silky white-blond mane framing her lovely face was incredibly enticing.

"Caleb?" she said, puzzled. "What do you want?"

He couldn't help his answer. It came of its own accord.

"You."

The one word served to release the taut control he had been holding over himself. He crossed the room before Mary Rose could respond with anything other than a widening of her eyes. She still hadn't said anything by the time he had stretched out on the bed beside her and taken her in his arms. And then she couldn't say anything, because her gaze was locked in his again, and this time he didn't look away.

The first touch of Caleb's mouth on hers affected Mary Rose almost as though his lips were an electric brand rather than human flesh, and she gasped and automatically drew back. The look on Caleb's face echoed what she was feeling, and at seeing it, Mary Rose's eyes widened in surprised delight.

"It isn't possible," Caleb whispered dazedly, but he knew what he'd felt was possible, because his senses didn't lie.

He gathered Mary Rose closer to prevent her from drawing back again, and kissed her hard this time, trying to discharge that electric feeling with sheer pressure. But it didn't work...not for him and not for Mary Rose.

She felt as though she were drowning in a pool of sensation. It was the first time in her life a man's mouth on hers had had the power to make her feel dizzy. But she was perfectly willing to submerge herself in this all-consuming bath.

Caleb was not so inexperienced. He recognized what he was feeling, but had just never before felt these emotions with such intensity, and the experience was subtly frightening. But not so frightening that he could control himself and stop his need from escalating.

Even if Caleb had remembered that he had earlier wondered about the extent of Mary Rose's sexual experience, her reaction to him now wiped out any such consideration. When he touched her breast for the first time, she made a little sound of aching pleasure. When he caressed her body, she moved eagerly beneath his hands. Consequently Caleb behaved as hungrily and abandonedly as he would have with any woman of whose experience he had incontrovertible proof.

To Mary Rose, it was as though what was happening was as natural as breathing...as though she'd been waiting all her life for this moment. She didn't give a thought to protesting. She accepted Caleb's possessive, intimate touches and his deep kisses as though he had a right to take whatever he wanted. She moved to his rhythm quite naturally. It was all as it should be.

Caleb's fingers trembled as he unbuttoned Mary Rose's blouse, and that surprised him vaguely. But when she was completely undressed he forgot to wonder why he should be so shaken. He stared hungrily at what he'd uncovered, and barely noticed that she was intent upon undressing him. "You couldn't be this beautiful," he whispered wonderingly.

Mary Rose had no reply. Her mind was not on her beauty. It was intent on uncovering Caleb's. "Help me," she said when she'd done as much as she could on her own.

Absently Caleb undressed. And when he was naked, he didn't notice the look of wonder in Mary Rose's eyes. He was still too absorbed in her beauty.

"Kiss me," Mary Rose whispered, and he obeyed eagerly.

The contact with Mary Rose's open, seeking mouth and the brush of her warm, naked body against his sparked the desire he'd felt earlier. He couldn't get enough of kissing her. He devoured her mouth and then went on to taste the rest of her, feeling as though he were feasting on love.

Caleb's mouth on her breasts soon made an urgent tension arise in Mary Rose that she was afraid would be released too soon. Her senses were stirred beyond what she could ever have credited was possible, and she was once again drowning in a storm of delicious sensation.

She had a momentary twinge of hesitation when, at last, Caleb turned her on her back and covered her body with his. Wasn't he going to use something? But he made love to her so ardently, she had no time to warn him she was unprotected.

Caleb paused when he realized the extent of her inexperience, and he looked at her with a sort of sensually remote puzzlement. But his excitement and hers was at a peak, and he couldn't stop.

Mary Rose let the pleasure build, then explode within her, then fade gently away on a cloud of innocent, hazy joy.

Chapter Ten

As Caleb cuddled Mary Rose, his mind wasn't nearly as relaxed as his body was. He didn't want to remember that she'd been a virgin. It made him feel responsible for her in some way he hadn't counted on and even more guilty about withholding the truth of his intentions from her. And he didn't want to believe the lovemaking with Mary Rose had been as fantastic as he knew it had been. But there was no way around the truth, even if he wasn't sure what that honesty implied about his deeper feelings. Then he had a thought that brought him up on his elbow. He stared down at the soft, wondrously delighted look on her face, and for a moment almost didn't have the courage to spoil any of this for her. But he had to know.

"What is it?" Mary Rose was puzzled by the expression on Caleb's face. After the wonderful lovemaking between them, why should he look so anxious?

"Mary Rose, I'm sorry..." Caleb said awkwardly. "I didn't know you'd never... I mean, if I'd known, I would have..." Would have what? he asked himself bewilderedly. Stopped? He knew better than that. Nothing short of an earthquake could have made him stop loving her.

Mary Rose smiled understandingly. "It's all right, Caleb," she said, trying to soothe his conscience. "There's nothing for you to be sorry about. I'm old enough to decide when and with whom I want to lose my virginity. And I'm not at all sorry I chose you and now."

The statement pleased Caleb enormously. But there was still another matter to discuss. "Well, but..." He finally blurted out his concern. "Mary Rose, are you protected? I didn't think to ask...and I didn't use anything..."

Mary Rose felt a sudden dart of apprehension. She wasn't sure how she would feel if it turned out she'd gotten pregnant the very first time she'd ever made love. But she couldn't change anything now, and for the moment she couldn't make herself regret what had happened, either.

"No," she admitted, "I'm not."

Caleb groaned and closed his eyes. "Ah, Mary Rose," he said softly. "You should have told me."

"Yes, I should have," she agreed on a sigh. "I just somehow thought you'd... And then it was too late..." But what was the use of quibbling over the matter now? Instead she leaned up and kissed Caleb's cheek. He opened his eyes and looked at her soberly. "Let's not look for problems just yet, Caleb," she said with a soft smile. Then she pushed him gently aside, got up, strode to the door, grabbed the white lab coat off the hook on the back of it and departed the room, heading for the kitchen.

Caleb stayed where he was for a few moments to give Mary Rose some time alone, and as he lay there, he felt bewildered. No woman had ever affected him in the way she had. For the first time in his life he'd completely lost

control of himself. Hell, she could have told him she
was unprotected before it was too late and he still might
not have been able to stop himself from loving her. He
didn't know whether he could have stopped or not. He
didn't *want* to know.

The implications of his loss of control made him feel
off-balance. For they meant that either he was falling
in love with Mary Rose, or was already in love with her.
And that realization took him completely by surprise.

"Well, at first I thought I was in love with Alicia, too,
didn't I?" he muttered to himself. "And it turned out I
was fooling myself."

But that didn't help him feel more centered. What he
had felt with Mary Rose was nothing like what he'd felt
with Alicia. As a matter of fact, it was nothing like what
he'd ever felt with any woman, or had ever expected to
feel with one. So would he be glad or sorry if Mary Rose
turned out to be pregnant?

Caleb groaned. He didn't know the answer to that
question.

WHILE CALEB was dealing with his feelings, Mary Rose
was dealing with hers. She washed, poured herself a cup
of coffee, sat down at the kitchen table and was trying
to think calmly about what had happened. It wasn't
easy to think rationally, however, because she kept remembering what an absolutely fantastic experience
making love with Caleb had been.

But what if she had gotten pregnant? How did she
feel about the fact that she might, even now, be carrying his child, when she didn't know whether he wanted
their relationship to deepen or not? She also didn't
know whether he'd want to have any part in raising their

child if it turned out he didn't want the relationship they'd just begun to deepen.

Abortion was not an option for Mary Rose. So, after thinking about it for a short while, she calmly decided that the idea of being an unwed mother—aside from the obvious disadvantage to the child in not having a father—didn't dismay her as much as she previously would have thought.

Perhaps it was because her own father had died when she was so young. To her, having only one parent had been sufficient because that was all she'd ever known past a certain age. And she'd had a delightful childhood. True, for the child it would probably be better if there were two parents. But almost nothing in life was perfect, was it?

"Mary Rose?"

She was so wrapped up in her thoughts that the sound of Caleb's voice startled her. She turned to look at him. He was standing fully dressed in the doorway, and the expression on his face made her smile. *Oh, Lord,* she thought half humorously, half sadly, *he's feeling so guilty it's pitiful.*

Caleb crossed over to her and gently pulled her to her feet. "I'm sorry," he said in a husky voice. Then he wrapped her in his arms for a long, tight hug.

"It's all right, Caleb," she murmured. "I told you, there's nothing for you to be sorry about. And there's nothing for you to feel guilty about, either."

Caleb drew back and looked at her searchingly.

"However," Mary Rose added, "I have to admit, if you're feeling guilty enough to want to give up ice in your tea for a few days as penance, or else get it yourself from now on, that's fine with me. I'm really getting tired of hiking up and down that hill every day."

Caleb smiled. "I'm not willing to give up my ice," he said, "but I will go for it myself from now on."

"Wonderful!" Mary Rose tried to step back out of his arms to clap her hands together in delight over his offer—and because it was getting disturbing to remain so close to him—but Caleb tightened his arms and wouldn't let her go.

They fell into one of those long looks that had previously been the source of so much disappointment for Mary Rose. After a moment she said in a soft, inviting voice, "If you're going to get me all stirred up looking at me like that, then disappoint me, I won't stand for it. Enough's enough."

Feeling as though he were the victim of some magical spell that reduced his free will to ashes, Caleb drew her closer and placed his mouth over hers. He was startled at first, then accepting, when he felt the same wonderful sensations he'd experienced earlier. Mary Rose's mouth was a soft touchstone that drew from him deeper feelings than he'd ever known he possessed. Wherever her warm, womanly body touched his, he felt an actual tingling sensation.

Because Mary Rose had never felt, when any other man had kissed her, even an approximation of the excitement Caleb inspired in her, she was aware of everything. She liked the way his mouth was softly warm yet firm underneath and the way it dominated her own without being hurtful. She liked the exploring touch of his tongue against hers. She liked the scent of him, the way his body was taut but yielded to hers, the male strength and human warmth of him.

Caleb drew back a little and stared down into her warmly accepting gaze. "Are you a witch like your mother?" he murmured, and his eyes, though lit with a sensual glow, displayed his bafflement over his incredible physical reaction to her.

Mary Rose started to smile, but Caleb's mouth returned to hers and prevented it. When he stopped kissing her, he raised his hands to cup her face and studied it in a serious manner. She was lovely, of course. Fair skin, pinkened over the cheeks right now. Beautiful hair; gorgeous green eyes; pert, straight nose; sweetly, generously curving feminine mouth. But she was no lovelier than hundreds of women he'd met, and shouldn't have been so much more exciting than the other women to whom he'd made love. Why was it, then, that she had this electric, stunning effect on him?

"I don't understand," he said softly.

Mary Rose was puzzled by Caleb's manner. "What don't you understand?" she asked.

But it was too soon to be making declarations. Caleb wanted to do a lot more thinking, and spend a great deal more time with Mary Rose before he made a commitment. She was not a woman he wanted to hurt.

"Nothing," he said, and to cut off any further questions, he kissed her again. And went on kissing her, with the predictable result that they were both soon thinking of returning to the bedroom.

"I guess you don't have any protection here at the cabin, do you?" Caleb whispered as he held her tightly against him, rocking her, aching for her.

Mary Rose shook her head. Her eyes were closed, she clung to him so tightly her arms ached and she wanted him desperately.

Caleb sighed. "I don't have anything, either. And we probably shouldn't take any more risks."

They stood together for a few moments longer, then he finally found the strength to put her away from him.

The expression on her face echoed what he was feeling, and he took a deep breath. "I think I'll walk to town," he said, looking toward the window to judge how heavily the rain was falling. But he didn't really care if there was a typhoon raging. He would have risked anything to get what he needed so he wouldn't have to sleep apart from Mary Rose that night.

She smiled. "To get ice for lunch and supper?" she asked lightly. "We used all we had for dinner last night."

Caleb looked back at her and smiled, too. "Yes," he nodded. "To get ice...and a few other things we need."

Mary Rose didn't look away from the meaningful warmth in Caleb's eyes. "Be careful," she whispered. "The road gets muddy."

"I'll be careful," he promised.

After donning his slicker, all he dared permit himself was a goodbye kiss on Mary Rose's cheek before he left the cabin.

As Mary Rose watched him walk away, her whole body felt warm and tingling and alive, and joyously glad to be so.

If it hadn't been raining so hard, she would have walked to her mother's grave and related this marvelous new development in her life to the one person she was certain would be as delighted for her as she was for herself.

CALEB THOUGHT he'd seen a pharmacy section in the supermarket, and he was relieved that his memory had served him correctly. After picking up a few other things he thought went with the occasion, he went to the front of the store to check out.

As he walked back to the cabin, the rain pouring down over him and wetting the brown paper bag containing his purchases could have been rays of sunshine for all the attention Caleb paid to it. How could I possibly take the cabin from Mary Rose now? he was thinking.

Under these new circumstances, the only way he could see for everything to come out perfectly was if he fell in love with Mary Rose and she with him, he sold his book and others after it, and her practice became a success. Then the question of buying the cabin needn't come up—they could share it.

But life seldom worked out that neatly, and Caleb had the uneasy fear life wouldn't oblige his wishes in this case, either.

At the top of the hill, the cabin, looking darkly veiled by the rain, came into view, and Caleb paused and stared at the small dwelling. Why should anything so outwardly unprepossessing have the power to capture the lives and hearts of two otherwise sane, sensible people? he wondered. Surely no one should put as much emotional energy into a dilapidated heap of wood as he and Mary Rose did.

Shaking his head, feeling more confused than he could ever remember, Caleb trudged the last few yards and mounted the porch steps. He knocked on the screen door, and when Mary Rose came to answer he handed her the sodden sack. "I need to take off my boots," he explained when she looked at him in surprise.

Mary Rose laughed at the sight of globs of mud on his boots.

As he got out of his boots, Mary Rose took the sack to the kitchen table. The brown paper bag was falling apart, so she emptied its contents onto the table. There were two expensive steaks, two baking potatoes, salad makings, a bottle of wine, a plastic bag of ice and, of course, the items Caleb had gone to purchase in the first place.

In short, it looked very much as though they were going to have a celebration, and Mary Rose smiled with delight. How thoughtful he was. How sweetly romantic! And how practical now that it might be too late to matter.

She quickly took one of the purchases to the bedroom and put it in the bedside table drawer, then returned to the kitchen, arriving just as Caleb came in in his damp stocking feet, his dripping slicker in hand.

"Here, give me that," Mary Rose said as she reached for the garment.

Caleb handed it over and she took it and hung it on a hook on the back of the kitchen door.

While she was doing that, Caleb looked over the table and smiled when he saw what was missing. Then he took a step forward, so that when Mary Rose turned from hanging up his slicker, she found herself in his arms.

"I worked up an appetite coming up that hill," he said softly, and though he'd planned to wait until that night to make love to her again, now he knew he couldn't wait. He pulled her even closer, leaned down and kissed her hungrily.

By the time he drew back Mary Rose was breathless. "If you're hungry, you'd better let me fix lunch," she said shakily. "It's already two o'clock, so—"

"Let's skip lunch and make the most of dinner," Caleb whispered, smiling, and he kissed her again.

After that kiss, and several more like it, Mary Rose didn't protest when Caleb drew her to the bedroom.

Nor did she protest when he undressed her, then himself, and snuggled the two of them under the covers.

"Listen to the rain on the roof," he murmured between kisses, but his hands, stroking her, made it impossible for Mary Rose to hear anything other than her own heartbeat. "Feel how warm and comfortable and safe we are," he added huskily. But safety and comfort were the farthest things from her mind. However, she did feel warm. In fact, she felt on fire.

"Your skin feels and tastes delicious," Caleb whispered as he kissed her shoulder, then moved lower, and Mary Rose could relate to that statement wholeheartedly. The touch of his mouth on her body, the feel of his warm skin under her palms, were better than delicious. The sensations tingling through her were maddeningly marvelous.

Because he was Mary Rose's first lover and he wanted her to have joy in the experience, Caleb took his time. He experimented, searching out what she liked best. He dived into new heights of creative loving in an effort to please her. He fought the excitement flashing through his body like lightning so he could prolong her pleasure. And he stopped often to allow them both to recover slightly before he began again.

Mary Rose almost couldn't believe this much pleasure was possible. And she was amazed she'd never suspected it. But during the pauses in the lovemaking she became almost frightened. Despite the tender, wonderfully exciting sensitivity of Caleb's touches, she didn't want to fool herself it meant he might want to go on making love to her on a permanent basis.

Caleb's patience and willpower didn't extend as far as he'd hoped. Try as he might, he couldn't stop himself from taking everything. Then, enclosed and shel-

tered by the warm welcome of Mary Rose's body, he
experienced a new combination of feelings he'd never
known before. Coupled with his all-consuming excitement was a sense of contentment. Before now he would
have said one couldn't experience such feelings in con-
cert. Feeling them, however, there was no contradic-
tion . . . there was only the reality of the experience.

Mary Rose, operating on the principle that if she had
in the near future to do without what Caleb brought her
now, melted totally into her senses. She let go of self, yet
never experienced self more vividly. She let go of Caleb
in one sense, yet melded with him ever more completely in another. Without him, she knew, she could
not have had what she was having . . . would never have
known what she now knew.

Later, enfolded in his arms, smiling and contented,
she felt such warmth for him, she knew she would always love him in some sense, even if they never went
further with their relationship.

Caleb lay silent, once again emotionally stunned.

"Caleb."

He turned to look at her, but his gaze was more distant than focused. "Yes?"

"I have the feeling you think too much," she said
quietly, her tone warm and accepting. "Just enjoy this
gift we've both gotten out of the blue."

Caleb blinked, and now he did focus on Mary Rose's
face. "Gift?" he questioned thoughtfully. "Is that what
you think this thing between us is?"

Mary Rose nodded, smiled and snuggled closer. "My
cabin has always given me everything I've needed and
most of what I've wanted. I'm not in the least surprised that my introduction to womanhood came

here...or that it gave me you. This house has always nurtured the most important gifts.''

Caleb tightened his arms around Mary Rose. *My* cabin, she'd called it. But surely it was his, as well. Hadn't it nurtured his gift? Hadn't it given his writing back to him? Yet wasn't it too much to hope for that it would also give him the one woman in all the world who was exactly right for him?

It seemed perfect. And Caleb distrusted anything that appeared so ideal. Again a foreboding settled in his mind.

''You're thinking again,'' she whispered against his shoulder.

''Yes.''

''Why?''

''Because...I'm worried that this is too good to be true, Mary Rose.''

She thought about that for a moment. Did he mean what she hoped he did? ''Do you mean,'' she finally answered, ''that you're afraid it's too good to last?''

Caleb nodded and felt relieved that she understood. ''That's it,'' he said. ''That's exactly it.''

Mary Rose felt the joyous beginning of hope rising in her heart. But she was afraid to say anything too revealing of her own feelings yet. ''Does it really matter?'' she asked.

Caleb frowned. ''What do you mean, 'does it matter'?''

''I mean, are we supposed to ruin the present by worrying about the future?'' she explained. ''This time tomorrow, you or I or both of us could be dead. I know it's not likely, but what if it were true? Wouldn't you be glad we'd had this before it happened?''

Caleb shrugged, his smile noncommittal. "Well, I guess that's one way of looking at things," he said wryly. "But the odds are that we'll both still be alive this time tomorrow...this time twenty years from now. So do you blame me for thinking about the future?"

Mary Rose shook her head. "No, I don't blame you...I just think it's sort of foolish to worry now," she said lightly. Then she leaned over and kissed Caleb. While she was kissing him, she realized it was the first time in her life she'd ever initiated a kiss with a man.

She was smiling radiantly when the embrace was over, and Caleb looked at her, his gaze curious. When she'd explained, he smiled. "Try it again," he teased. "Good things should come in pairs."

So Mary Rose kissed him again, and went on kissing him, and finally took advantage of her newfound power by seducing him.

Afterward she laughed delightedly. "That was wonderful!" she cried as she held up her arms and stretched luxuriously.

"It was that," Caleb agreed, unable to help laughing with her.

"And now I'm starved," she added, jumping up from the bed. "Let's have our celebration, even if it isn't suppertime yet."

"I thought we just celebrated," Caleb said with a grin as he sat up.

Mary Rose grinned back. "Yes, but let's have the wine and steaks," she suggested. "Then we can come back to bed and celebrate more."

He was all for that idea, and was on his feet in an instant.

Chapter Eleven

"I need to go into town and phone my agent," Caleb informed Mary Rose over breakfast one morning a week later...a week he considered had been one of the most glorious in his life. He had somehow managed to tear himself away from her long enough to finish the roof, but mostly he had concentrated exclusively on her.

"Oh...that's right!" Mary Rose beamed at him. "I'm confident the news will be good, Caleb." Then she had the first serious thought about her own career she'd had in a week. She really did need to get over to the county seat and see about that loan, she told herself. She was amazed she'd allowed such an important matter to slip for so long. But she'd had other things to think about this past week—glorious things she would never forget if she lived to one hundred like Grandma Bolling.

Caleb smiled. "I wish I were," he said, shrugging. "But the publishing business has a way of knocking one's confidence for a loop."

"Everything has a way of doing that some of the time," Mary Rose answered. "I've always wondered how I'm going to take it the first time I make a mistake. I just pray it won't be a serious enough one that a patient of mine is really hurt.''

Caleb stared at her thoughtfully, realizing she was right. A mistake he might make in his writing would only hurt himself. The kind Mary Rose might make as a physician could have much more serious consequences, which, he imagined, would be very hard for her to deal with unless she had someone to help her.

Caleb looked down at his plate, sure he wanted to be that someone. Judging from the past week, he would be a fool to deny that what was between Mary Rose and him was too special to dismiss as just another affair. Over the years, some of the intensity in their sexual relationship might wane. But he loved Mary Rose in other ways than just the physical. So the waning would barely be noticed now that he couldn't imagine living in this cabin, or anywhere else, without her.

"What are you thinking about, Caleb?" she asked curiously. "Are you really worried about the book?"

Caleb raised his head and saw once again what he had been seeing every day for the past week. A woman's face he would never tire of looking at every day for the rest of his life.

"Caleb?" Mary Rose was smiling as she studied his expression. He looked so serious . . . so like a little boy who has just discovered one of the great secrets of life.

He shook his head as though to clear it. "What?"

"I asked what you were thinking about," Mary Rose repeated, her smile broadening. Then it faded a little. "But if you don't want to tell me, that's all right," she added quite seriously. "I don't want to pry."

"You aren't prying, Mary Rose," he said. "But if you don't mind, I'll wait just a little longer to tell you what I was thinking . . . until after I find out about the book."

Suddenly the book was even more important than it had been previously, if that was possible. Once Caleb had wanted enough money to buy this cabin. Now, if things worked out the way he hoped, he wouldn't be buying the cabin, but he had other things he wanted to do. Mary Rose intended to take out a loan to modernize the cabin. Why should she have to get money from a bank to do that when he intended to share in the benefits of their modernized home?

"Fine," Mary Rose said simply. "Would you like some more coffee?"

"No," Caleb said, getting up from the table. "I want to go make that call."

She grinned. "You *are* anxious, aren't you?" she teased.

"More than you know." Caleb smiled back. *But not more than you'll ever know,* he added silently. *If the news is good, you'll be the second person to hear it . . . and what it means for us.*

Mary Rose walked him to the door, and Caleb kissed her goodbye as though he were departing for China rather than Sweet Water, just two miles away.

"Wow," she whispered against his shoulder as he held her close to him afterward. "You sure know how to say goodbye."

"That wasn't goodbye," Caleb said. "That was 'so long for a while.'"

"Oh. Pardon me," Mary Rose apologized. "And what's your goodbye kiss like?"

He laughed and stepped back. "You'll never know," he said lightly, reaching up to tug a strand of her white-blond hair. "At least, I hope you won't."

His words pleased her enormously, but Mary Rose was afraid to respond in kind just yet. She knew how she felt about Caleb, but she didn't want to push him into declaring his feelings until he was ready. "Hurry back," she said, instead. "And don't forget to get some ice."

Caleb gave her a chastising look. "Remember who you're talking to," he said.

"The King of Iceland, I know. I'm biting my tongue, see?" And Mary Rose mimed just that.

"So you should," Caleb said with a grin. Then he pecked her cheek and walked away.

On the way down the hill, he met the woman and her little girl who had come to see Mary Rose several days back.

"Is Dr. Perkins to home?" the woman asked, eyeing him appreciatively.

Caleb paused. "Yes, she is," he replied, his glance straying curiously to the woman's plump daughter.

"Good. Me'n Beth wanta thank her," the woman said. Then she asked, "Ain't you got that roof done yet, young man?"

"Uh, almost," Caleb answered warily. The roof was finished, but he didn't want to answer the next logical question, which was why was he still here?

"Well, yore a good-looker, but yore sure slow." Mrs. Mullins shook her head, her eyes twinkling. "Couldn't be you just like the company of your boss, could it?"

Caleb grinned. "She is a lovely woman," he agreed.

Mrs. Mullins nodded. "Smart, too," she said. "She told just by lookin' at Beth here that my girl had somethin' wrong with her."

He glanced at the little girl, who smiled up at him shyly. Caleb smiled back, which made the little girl's face flame into color before she hastily looked away.

"Beth was dang near havin' to go without a thyroid," Mrs. Mullins said emphatically. "So me and Beth and the rest of our family is gonna take our medical bizness to Doc Perkins from now on."

Caleb smiled, as pleased as though someone he respected had praised one of his books in a knowledgeable fashion. "I don't think you can go wrong with her," he said, adding silently, *I don't think anyone who puts trust in her can*.

"You betcha," Mrs. Mullins said firmly. "Well, we won't keep ya no longer. We're both anxious to git up thar and thank the doc."

"I'm sure Mary Rose will appreciate that," Caleb responded.

He smiled all the rest of the way to the pay phone in town. The news that Mary Rose's first venture into doctoring in Sweet Water had been a success seemed to him to bode well for the future.

MARY ROSE was delighted by the visit of Mrs. Mullins and Beth. And she didn't have to fake an interest when Mrs. Mullins recounted the details of the thyroid test. She was glad to hear that the small hospital in the county seat apparently was up-to-date in its methods and equipment.

Later, as she stood on the porch, watching Mrs. Mullins and Beth walk away, she wondered what had happened to their battered pickup. Since it had looked to be on its last legs the time before, she assumed it had either died for good or was in the shop for repairs. The thought that the Mullinses had walked all the way up the hill to tell her the results of Beth's tests made her feel both slightly guilty for not having visited them herself, and inordinately pleased that they had thought her worth a personal visit to thank her. How nice to have such people for patients!

All such thoughts left her mind an instant later, however, when she saw a familiar car top the hill. Mary Rose's eyes opened wide with delight. It was Aunt Sarah! Coming here must mean that she had forgiven her! With that happy thought, Mary Rose started running down the lane to meet the oncoming car.

SARAH ZIMMERMAN watched her niece racing toward her and felt a sharp twinge of conscience over the happiness she saw on Mary Rose's face. It wasn't going to be easy to see that look wiped away and replaced by one of shocked disbelief. But it was for the best, Sarah firmly reminded herself. If Mary Rose was too idiotic to take care of her own best interests, then it was Sarah's job to do it for her. Mary Rose might hate her for a while, but Sarah was prepared to endure that hatred in the short term, given the long-term advantages to be gained. And of course it helped to know that Mary Rose didn't have it in her to hate anyone for very long, especially a member of her own family.

"CALEB, WHEN YOU MAKE a comeback, you really come back!" Ted shouted over the phone. "This one's better than either of the first two!"

A sense of relief so strong that he had to lean momentarily against the phone booth to support himself brought a weak grin to Caleb's lips.

"You wouldn't kid a kidder, would you, Ted?" he asked.

"Hell, no!" he roared back. "We're talking best-seller here!"

Caleb closed his eyes and tilted his head back, his expression beatific. "Keep talking, Ted," he urged his agent. "Your words are music to my ears."

But as Ted ranted on Caleb barely heard him. He was busy formulating the words of his confession and his proposal to Mary Rose. He only wished he'd taken care of the confession a lot earlier. Yet when he told Mary Rose how much he loved her, maybe she would be willing to forgive him for his slight lapse in timing.

SARAH WAS ANNOYED with herself. It was proving to be a great deal more difficult than she'd envisioned to utter the words that had brought her to Sweet Water. Every time she looked into those large, sparkling green eyes of her niece, so like Mary Violet's, Sarah had the uneasy feeling that her sister, were she still alive, would condemn her for what she was about to do. It wouldn't matter to Mary Violet, of course, that what Sarah was about to do was in Mary Rose's best interests. Sarah and Mary Violet had always disagreed about what was most important in life.

Still, it was a relief to have the coming confrontation delayed by the arrival of a tall, good-looking man Sarah had never seen before—a man who looked as happy as Mary Rose did—even though Sarah did wonder why the man hadn't knocked but had walked into the cabin as though he owned the place.

"Oh, Caleb!" Mary Rose cried when she saw the look on his face. "It's good news then?"

"Very good news," he answered with a grin before turning politely to the stranger sitting at the kitchen table. He wished that this woman, whoever she was, weren't here. He wanted to get on with telling Mary Rose just how good the news was, then proposing to her and confessing to her...in that order. But maybe this was a new patient, so he supposed he shouldn't resent her too much. And maybe she would leave fairly quickly.

"Oh, let me introduce you two," Mary Rose said when she saw Sarah and Caleb looking curiously at each other. "Caleb, this is my Aunt Sarah Zimmerman. And Aunt Sarah, this is Caleb Anderson..." Her voice trailed off as Mary Rose considered how to finish the introduction where Caleb was concerned. Should she describe him as her roofer or her lover?

The thought made Mary Rose want to giggle, but she didn't have time to do anything but look at her aunt in surprise as Sarah quickly got to her feet and went to Caleb, holding out her hand to be shaken.

"Mr. Anderson!" Sarah said enthusiastically. "It's nice to meet you in person! But what are you doing here?" she asked, feigning innocent curiosity. It was obvious there was something going on between Mary Rose and Caleb, a prospect that alarmed her. "Didn't you believe me when I told you Mary Rose wouldn't sell you this place?"

Caleb's grin had faded the moment he heard Mary Rose pronounce Sarah Zimmerman's name. *Oh, God!* he thought, a presentiment of overwhelming disaster coursing through him. *God, no! Please, no. Let me tell Mary Rose in my own way...don't let it come out like this.*

Mary Rose looked at her aunt, then Caleb, in disbelief. "You and Caleb have spoken before?" she asked Sarah, praying it wasn't true. "About...the cabin?"

The last three words came out slowly... with dawning sick recognition. Because it was clear from the expression on Sarah's face that she had spoken to Caleb, and it was even clearer from the expression on Caleb's face what the conversation had been about.

"Oh, yes," Sarah said lightly, her sharp eyes and ears at full alert. She had a pretty good idea what was going on here. Now if she could only make it work to her—and Mary Rose's—advantage. "He called to ask about buying the cabin the day you left home to come back here."

Mary Rose suddenly felt as though everything inside her had frozen over. She looked from Caleb to Sarah and back to Caleb, unable to speak for the moment.

"Mary Rose, let me explain..." he said, and he knew his expression showed the guilt he was feeling. He just hoped it also showed the love he had for her.

"Yes, I think you'd better," she said, her voice faint... distant.

"Sit down, Mr. Anderson," Sarah invited, pretending she didn't notice the tension in the air.

Caleb ignored her. "Mary Rose," he said, holding her frozen gaze, willing her to trust and believe him, "it's true I lied to you. I didn't stay overnight just once. I lived in the cabin for quite a while, writing the book my agent just told me is sure to sell. I... this place did something to me," he added, his voice pleading with her to understand. "Before I stumbled onto this spot I hadn't written anything worth publishing in two years. And I'd been here no more than a night, when the dam burst. I couldn't *stop* writing, and it was good, Mary Rose. It was the best writing I've ever done."

She merely stared at him, still having trouble believing he had been lying to her all this time, though it was obvious he had.

"When I finished the book," Caleb went on, "I didn't want to leave here. I told you before that this place drew me, and that wasn't a lie. I don't understand it, but the cabin has become *home* to me...the first real home I've had since I grew up and moved away from my parents' house. And since it didn't seem as though the place had been occupied for a long while, I thought the owner might be willing to sell it to me."

As Caleb paused for breath, Sarah jumped in. She was alarmed by the potential damage to her plans this new development could have. If Mr. Anderson and her niece were as seriously involved with each other as they seemed to be, and he loved this cabin as much as she did, Sarah had to drive a wedge between them. Otherwise, though she was positive the legal action she'd set in motion the preceding week would have a favorable outcome and the cabin would be unavailable to either Mary Rose or Caleb, it was just possible these two people would build another home around here, and then she'd never get her niece out of this one-horse town!

"Caleb called me, Mary Rose," Sarah quickly spoke up. "And at the time I had to tell him he was probably never going to be able to buy this cabin and the surrounding property because of you. But since then things have changed." Abruptly Sarah turned her attention to Caleb. Although it annoyed her, she found it impossible to look at Mary Rose as she imparted the next bit of information. "Mary Rose no longer owns the cabin. I do."

It was a lie, of course. Sarah had merely started the proceedings that would eventually result in her owning the cabin. But she was counting on Mary Rose not checking at the courthouse. And whatever legal papers the court sent to Mary Rose informing her of the filing and inviting her to respond would be sent to Sarah's home. Therefore her niece would never see them, and would do nothing to interfere.

For a long moment both Mary Rose and Caleb were too stunned to react verbally. Then Mary Rose spoke.

"That's impossible, Sarah," she said, shaking her head over and over again. "That can't be true."

"Yes . . . well, I'm afraid it can be," Sarah said, still not looking directly at her niece. "You see, I'm the one who paid the taxes all those years you were growing up, remember? Besides that, though I never pressed my claim to this place when Mama and Papa died, it *was* half mine. I simply let Mary Violet and Tom live here as though it were theirs, because they didn't have any-place else to go and I didn't want any part of the cabin."

Abruptly Caleb found his voice. "But at the court-house," he said, his voice strained and harsh, "Mary Rose was listed as the sole owner."

Mary Rose barely heard him. She was staring at Sarah as though at a stranger. "You told me it was mine," she whispered. "When you came to get me and I asked you if the cabin was mine, you said it was."

"And so I considered it at the time," Sarah said stiffly. She glanced up at Caleb. "The courthouse rec-ords listed Mary Rose as the owner because her mother—my sister, Mary Violet—couldn't have gotten state assistance after her husband died and she was in-capacitated if the state had known she owned this much property. And without assistance, Mary Rose and Mary Violet would have starved. So she and I agreed to put the place in Mary Rose's name. I handled the legal details."

Mary Rose felt sick. "That's not true," she said, shaking her head. "We lived off the land . . . off Ma's medicines."

Sarah grimaced impatiently. "Don't be naive," she said shortly. "You could never have survived on just that. And at the time I couldn't help enough financially to be of much use to the two of you."

"But no checks came!" Mary Rose cried. "I would have seen them if they had!"

Sarah sighed. This was so much harder than she had expected. "The checks were automatically deposited to a bank in the county seat, Mary Rose. I'm not sure how Mary Violet managed to pay for things out of those funds without your knowledge—possibly you can tell me. But I know why she did everything without telling you. She didn't want you to grow up thinking of yourself as a welfare child. She thought it might humiliate you or affect your character adversely or something. She wanted you to be proud and learn to work hard— oh, you know what her values were as well as I do!"

Mary Rose was stunned. Numbly she whispered, "I knew she had a bank account because she gave me checks to pay for groceries at the general store. And sometimes she had me mail things already sealed in envelopes—and she never allowed me to open any mail she got. She said children shouldn't worry about business. I suppose she burned everything after she'd looked it over because there weren't any papers here after she died."

"She didn't burn them," Sarah said shortly. "She sent them to me. I handled anything she didn't want you to know about. I canceled the whole business when

Mary Violet died. In fact, I had to repay the government for the checks that came during the months you didn't tell anyone about her death.''

Mary Rose had told Caleb what she'd done when her mother had died, and he had admired her courage and resourcefulness enormously. He was beginning to hate Sarah Zimmerman. How could the woman do something like this to her own niece! An instant later he remembered the look on Mary Rose's face when she'd found out he'd been withholding the truth from her all this time and he wondered how he could do something like that to the woman he loved.

"That still doesn't explain how you came to own the cabin," he grated, taking up the cudgel on Mary Rose's behalf, since she was merely staring into space, looking numb.

Sarah shrugged. "I told you, I paid the taxes all those years. That fact, coupled with my original claim to half the property, made it a simple matter to have the deed changed to my name." Under the table Sarah had her fingers crossed, though she was ashamed of such a childish gesture.

Caleb was disgusted, but if what this woman was saying was true, he didn't know what could be done to right matters.

Mary Rose was devastated. She got to her feet, her eyes never leaving Sarah's face.

"I don't have to ask why you've done this," she said so quietly that Caleb and Sarah barely heard her.

Perhaps it was her conscience that made Sarah react so angrily. "No, you don't have to ask!" she responded, furious. "Since you're not willing to act in your own best interests, I have to do it for you, just as I have since you were fourteen years old! And make no mistake, my girl! I'll continue to do anything I have to to pry you out of this God-forsaken backwoods and out into the world, where you belong. You're not going to make the same mistake your mother did! Whether you like me for what I've done or not, my conscience is clear!''

Sarah only wished that were true. She also wished she didn't have to see that horrid stricken expression on Mary Rose's face. But she didn't have to look at it for long, as it turned out, because her niece started to rush out of the cabin.

Caleb couldn't stand seeing that look on Mary Rose's face, either, and as she attempted to brush past him, he grabbed her arm to stop her, intending to fold her into his arms and tell her it didn't matter about the cabin... that as long as they had each other they'd be all right. But the look of betrayal that came over her face when he touched her argued against his being able to comfort her for the present. It argued against his getting the chance to say anything at all that she would be willing to listen to... at least for the time being.

Mary Rose wrenched her arm from Caleb's grip, then slammed out of the cabin, running as hard as she could toward the family cemetery.

Sarah got up from her chair and went to the door. ''She's going to try to get some comfort from Mary Violet,'' she said to Caleb. She was striving for a dry tone, but she was failing. Her voice broke.

Caleb stared at Sarah as though at a creature beyond his understanding. ''How could you do that to her?'' he asked.

Sarah turned her head to glare up at him, and there were tears in her brown eyes. But her gaze was also fiercely determined. ''Do you think it was easy to hurt her like that?'' she demanded. "To take the chance that she'll hate me for the rest of her life? I've raised her from the age of fourteen! I consider her as much my child as Mary Violet's! I love her! And that's why I don't intend to stand by and see her make the biggest mistake of her life.''

Caleb shook his head wearily. He didn't understand that kind of love. "Surely what she does with her life is her decision,'' he said, his voice quiet, tinged with a guilt of his own that ate at him.

"Not when she does something as foolish as burying herself in this backwater!'' Sarah grated. "Do you know how good a doctor she can be?''

"I have a pretty good idea,'' he responded dryly.

"I don't think you do,'' Sarah shot back, her expression grim. "I'm the one who talked to her professors, to the doctors she worked with during her training. They all said the same thing. Mary Rose was born to be a physician . . . she has a gift. They couldn't believe she would bury all that potential in a place like this!'' Sarah looked around the cabin and glared as though it were her enemy.

Caleb looked around him, as well. He well knew the spell this place could cast. He was in the coils of its charm himself. Perhaps Sarah was right about Mary Rose. It would be an unconscionable waste for her to bury herself here. But he couldn't get around the fact that such a decision should be made by Mary Rose herself...not anyone else. He also couldn't get around the fact that he wanted Mary Rose to marry him and for the two of them to continue living here together for the rest of their lives.

Sarah turned abruptly from the screen door and went to the sink to begin making a pot of coffee. As she worked, Caleb watched her, his back to the door. He was thinking hard about how best to handle Sarah Zimmerman in order to get what he and Mary Rose wanted from her. It wasn't going to be easy, but it had to be done.

HER EYES STREAMING TEARS, Mary Rose fell on her knees at her mother's grave. "Why, Ma?" she got out through her sobs. "I know I'm supposed to be here. Why can't Sarah understand?"

But for once, no familiar, comforting voice in her mind answered her tortured questions.

"And how could Caleb...?" Mary Rose couldn't get all the words out. Only silence and emptiness greeted her question, but it didn't matter. She thought she knew the answer anyway. Besotted by the love she felt for him, she'd imbued him with qualities he didn't really have. In truth, he was simply a self-centered hedonist who believed he was entitled to anything he wanted, whether it was the cabin, or sex with a woman he intended to betray.

Trying to dismiss Caleb from her mind, Mary Rose went back to the question about the cabin. Wasn't there anything to be done? she asked her mother in an anguished tone. Anything at all?

But the silence persisted, which was an answer in itself. Finally Mary Rose stumbled to her feet. She had to return to Sarah and Caleb and face the inevitable. She knew that. But in that moment she would have given almost anything to be returning to Caleb for help, instead of to end what was between them.

After retracing her path and climbing the steps to the porch, Mary Rose stared through the screen door at Caleb's broad back, and she hesitated. How was she going to find the courage to say what she had to without bursting into tears and betraying her own pride? Then he spoke to Sarah, and with every word he said, the pain in Mary Rose's heart grew.

"HOW DO YOU FEEL about selling me the cabin now?" Caleb asked.

Surprised, Sarah turned to look at him. She couldn't tell much from his expression, but she felt very wary of his motives. And even if she hadn't been afraid that if she sold him the cabin he would share it with Mary Rose, thereby subverting her plan, she was in no position as yet to do so. Of course she couldn't tell him that. He might tell Mary Rose.

"I didn't go to all this trouble and inflict so much pain on Mary Rose for nothing," she said grimly. "I won't sell you this place. You might turn around and give it back to her."

"What makes you think I would do that?" Caleb asked dryly. He didn't like what he could see he would have to do. But if it meant that Mary Rose would get the cabin back, he was prepared to do almost anything. He would explain to her what his plan was after he got her aunt to agree to sell him the cabin. "I want this place for myself."

Sarah eyed him in a hostile, suspicious manner. "Love can lead people to do some very stupid things," she responded tartly.

At that moment Caleb shifted, and Sarah caught a glimpse of Mary Rose's white face on the other side of the screen door before he moved again and hid her from view. Sarah almost warned Caleb that Mary Rose was listening. Then her instincts told her to keep quiet about her niece's presence.

It took Caleb a moment to carry out the next part of his deception because it went so much against his grain, but finally he said with a shrug, "You're making an assumption, Mrs. Zimmerman. Just because I sleep with a woman doesn't mean I'm in love with her."

Sarah stiffened. She knew how much those words must have hurt Mary Rose, and she regretted causing her niece any further pain. On the other hand, it was better for her to know the truth about Caleb's feelings...if he was telling the truth. Sarah still wasn't prepared to take his words at face value. Apparently Mary Rose had, though, because Sarah saw a flash of movement behind Caleb and knew she'd left the scene.

Sarah sighed. On the one hand she felt fiercely protective of Mary Rose and was indignant with Caleb for sounding so cavalier about what must have meant a great deal to her niece. But however Caleb Anderson really felt about Mary Rose, it wasn't likely to do him any good now, considering what she'd just heard from his lips. Mary Rose might have a forgiving nature, but no woman could forget something like that.

"I don't know how I feel about selling you the cabin at the present," Sarah lied, her voice harsh because he had hurt Mary Rose so badly. "I still don't trust you."

It cost him a lot, but Caleb managed to smile. "Mrs. Zimmerman," he said in a level, reasonable tone, "I don't know how much you know about people who are consumed by their careers, but there is nothing more important to me than being able to write. I wasn't lying to Mary Rose about how this place affects me. I really did have a prolonged dry spell before I stumbled up here one evening, and this cabin really did help me get over that dry spell with a vengeance. I'm superstitious," he added, managing to inject a tone of amused self-tolerance into his voice. "Therefore I don't want to give up a place that has such a beneficial effect on the most important thing in my life. I have this feeling that I can't write anywhere else."

Sarah's absorption in the world of ivory towers and book knowledge played her false at this point. She believed Caleb. "I see," she said thoughtfully.

He was somewhat astonished by her gullibility. Then, remembering that what he had just said had been true before he'd fallen in love with Mary Rose, he didn't find Sarah's reaction so strange, after all. He still wanted the cabin, if it was possible to have it both for himself and for the woman he loved. But he'd just learned that this place was less important to him—everything was less important to him—than Mary Rose's happiness. With her he thought he could write anywhere. Without her he doubted if even the cabin would help him much. Yet Mary Rose's happiness rested within these walls and the surrounding acres. Therefore Caleb was prepared to do anything to get back the property and restore her happiness.

"Let me think about it, Mr. Anderson," Sarah said, interrupting his thoughts. She was staring at him speculatively. "Once I've gotten Mary Rose away from here and started on her career somewhere else, if you still want the cabin, contact me. I might be more willing to believe you if it turns out you can stay away from her."

Caleb immediately felt a great upsurge of anger. Sarah Zimmerman's determination to run Mary Rose's life infuriated him, as did the prospect of having to sneak around to see her until all this about the cabin was settled. But he was careful to let nothing of what he was feeling show. The cost of indulging his temper by telling this woman just what he thought of her would be too high.

"Very well," he somehow managed to say nonchalantly. "I can understand your concern. I need to go to New York for a while, anyway. I've got a new book—the one I wrote here," he added with a smile, "that I need to shepherd along as fast as possible. It's what's going to earn me the money to pay you for this place when you're satisfied that I really do want it for myself."

"Wonderful," Sarah responded dryly. She didn't like Caleb Anderson's attitude toward Mary Rose, but she could see why her niece had fallen for the man. Besides being physically attractive, that selfishness of his would appeal to any woman who didn't have the sense to look out for her own interests. It was always the charming rotters who had the most success with that type of female.

"Would you like some coffee?" Sarah asked with stiff politeness.

"No, thank you," Caleb answered, trying to make his smile natural. "I think I'd better go and say goodbye to Mary Rose. I expect I'm not very popular with her at the moment and had better be on my way voluntarily before she throws me off the place."

"I expect you're right," Sarah agreed rather shortly. "Good luck," she added, an unpleasant smile appearing on her lips. "I hope you get away from your goodbyes unscathed."

Caleb frowned, wondering what Sarah meant by that. He knew he was going to have some tall explaining to do to Mary Rose beyond telling her why he'd lied to her from the beginning. But he was confident she would eventually forgive him for being less than honest with her once she heard that he loved her and wanted to marry her... and once he told her about his plan to get the cabin back for both of them.

He found her at her mother's grave, but this time she wasn't talking to her. She merely sat on her knees, her head down, looking so vulnerable Caleb's heart contracted.

"Mary Rose," he said gently as he sat down beside her. "There's no need to give up hope. I'm going to—"

But he had to stop speaking when Mary Rose lifted her head and gave him a look that nearly destroyed him. After a moment he got control of himself, but his voice was shaking as he said, "Darling, please listen to me. Please let me explain."

Mary Rose turned her face away. "I've heard all I need to already," she said dully. She swallowed, then added, "I realize I don't have the right to throw you off this land anymore, Caleb. But I wish you would find someplace else to be until I've moved out myself."

Caleb sighed. "Mary Rose, you must listen to me," he said, keeping his voice gentle. "I know you'll forgive me once I tell you—"

That statement brought Mary Rose's eyes abruptly to his, and she had such an incredulous, contemptuous look on her face that Caleb paused.

"You think I'll forgive you?" Mary Rose shot back disbelievingly. The next instant she jumped to her feet and stared down at Caleb as though she found him repulsive. "You're something," she said bitterly. "One moment you're telling Sarah that just because you slept with me it doesn't mean you're in love with me, and the next moment you're asking me to forgive you for lying to me all this time. Do all writers live in some sort of fantasy world that makes no sense at all to normal people?''

A shaft of pain pierced him. "You heard that?" he whispered.

"I heard," she said, "and I wasn't all that surprised. I'd already learned how far you were willing to go to get the cabin.''

Caleb winced. "Mary Rose, please...none of this is the way you think.''

She closed her eyes wearily and whispered, "Please be quiet. I can't take any more right now.'' Then she opened her eyes and took a step back from him. "I hope you get the cabin," she added, her eyes and voice unutterably sad. "Despite your lack of character I believe you do love this place. And if I can't have it, I'd like to see it go to someone who will appreciate it.''

Abruptly she pivoted on her heel and began walking away. Caleb scrambled to his feet and started after her.

At hearing him behind her, Mary Rose paused and looked over her shoulder. "Just go, Caleb," she said, her voice breaking. "Please...leave me alone. You can be that honorable at least, can't you?''

Caleb wanted to pursue her as he'd never wanted anything else in his life. His whole body strained toward her. But his instincts told him it would be a waste of time. For the present Mary Rose wouldn't believe him or trust him. And he couldn't blame her.

Yet as he watched her disappear from view, he vowed to himself that a time would come when she would believe him and trust him more than she ever had before. Justice might now be served by his doing without the one woman in the world he should never have deceived at all, but he'd be damned if he'd do without her forever.

Chapter Twelve

Upon arriving home from the university a few months later, Sarah Zimmerman checked her mailbox as usual. The official-looking envelope sitting on the top of the pile of mail brought an anxious frown to her face until she ripped it open. Then the frown turned to a relieved smile. The cabin was officially hers now. Mary Rose was safe.

Later, as Sarah sat in her favorite chair, a drink in hand, her mind turned bleakly to the situation that existed between her and Mary Rose. How much longer, she wondered, was it going to take before her niece forgave her and came to see her?

Regardless of Mary Rose's coldness toward her, Sarah still didn't regret what she'd done. And now that the cabin was safely in her name, she intended to continue to protect Mary Rose.

Just two weeks earlier a female colleague the same age as Sarah had died of a heart attack. It had made her realize that Mary Rose would inherit the cabin if she, Sarah, should die unexpectedly. Therefore she had decided the safest thing to do to protect Mary Rose was get rid of the cabin as quickly as possible.

Sarah narrowed her eyes thoughtfully. Caleb Anderson had written and given her the phone number and address of his agent, who would know where to contact him, since he had no fixed address at the time. What would be the harm in contacting the man to see if he was still interested in the cabin? It might take months to sell the property going the regular route through a realtor—if anyone was even interested in buying such a run-down place. And as far as she'd been able to find out from people in relatively frequent contact with Mary Rose, Caleb and her niece hadn't spoken with each other since that day at the cabin. So apparently it was safe to trust him after all.

CALEB SAT WEARILY back from his typewriter and gradually came out of the world he'd been creating on paper into the real world surrounding him. Getting up from his chair, he went to the kitchen of the small apartment he'd rented once he'd gotten an advance on royalties for the book he'd written at the cabin. Considering the size of the advance, no one could understand why he'd chosen to rent such a small apartment. They didn't realize he was merely biding time…waiting, hoping, praying that one day he'd get a call from Sarah Zimmerman.

As Caleb opened a beer and sipped it while throwing a sandwich together, he was very much aware that even if Sarah eventually sold him the cabin, whereupon he would immediately turn around and deed it to Mary Rose, there was no guarantee Mary Rose would want to have anything to do with him again, despite his gift. After he'd traced her to Rockville, Maryland, he'd called her repeatedly, but she hung up on him every time. And his letters were returned to him unopened.

But giving her the cabin would be a start. If that wasn't enough to make her listen to him, he planned to haunt the place, and her, until she could no longer continue refusing to hear him out. If nothing else, maybe she'd get so used to him hanging around that she would soften.

Meanwhile he was working on the book he'd started at the cabin in which Mary Rose was the heroine and he was the hero. It was a historical, completely outside the realm of anything he'd ever done before or had ever expected to do. And once he finished it, he would probably never do a book like it again. He wasn't even sure if he'd try to sell it. It was so different from what he normally wrote that Ted was puzzled as to why he was writing it at all. Caleb hadn't attempted to explain to his agent that the book made his lonely existence without Mary Rose bearable. If he could have her only in fiction, he would take what he could get.

The phone rang, and Caleb picked up the receiver, hoping it wasn't his friend John, trying to fix him up with yet another woman. None of them were right, or ever would be.

"Hello?" he said.

"Mr. Anderson? This is Sarah Zimmerman."

Caleb leaned against the wall, weak with relief.

MARY ROSE WEARILY unbuttoned her white coat, preparing to leave her office for the day. Not that her day was likely to be over. She fully expected to be called to the hospital sometime during the evening, since she was on call for two other doctors, who were on vacation. An undisturbed night's sleep was a luxury she seldom enjoyed.

But that was the way she liked it. Work was the only thing that dulled the persistent ache plaguing her heart over the loss of her cabin...Caleb...and even her Aunt Sarah, whom Mary Rose had been unable to forgive as yet. She knew she probably would reestablish contact with her someday, but not now. The hurt was still too fresh.

Meanwhile she was gaining quite a reputation for herself as a good doctor. And that was some satisfaction, if not enough to make her anticipate the coming Christmas season. Thanksgiving had taught her how deadly a holiday could be with no one to share it. Yet she hadn't even been able to feel guilty that Sarah might be having the same sort of lonely holiday. Probably her aunt had been invited to spend the day with one of her colleagues, she'd rationalized.

Mary Rose had turned down all the invitations to Thanksgiving dinner she'd received and had spent the day remembering the long-ago celebrations she'd shared with her mother. She had long since gotten over feeling a little hurt that her mother had been less than truthful with her about the welfare money. But she understood her mother's reasoning, and besides, her mother was one person Mary Rose could forgive for anything.

The apartment she'd rented was within walking distance of her office, which was located in a building owned by the physician who had offered to take her in with him, even though she couldn't afford to pay for a partnership as yet. But she was doing her best to justify his faith in her and was putting money aside to buy into the partnership eventually. Mary Rose had chosen to live close to work because she didn't trust the old secondhand car she'd purchased, and was afraid that some morning she'd wake up and wouldn't be able to get the thing started.

Letting herself into her small apartment, she threw her mail onto the kitchen table without looking at it— it was probably mostly bills and Christmas cards from her colleagues, anyway—and popped a frozen dinner into the oven.

After showering, she donned a warm, comfortable sweatsuit and sat down to watch the news as she ate. The food was barely edible, but Mary Rose didn't have the energy to cook these days—she spent too much of herself on work, and ate half her meals at the hospital cafeteria or in restaurants, anyway.

Half an hour later, she remembered her mail and went to fetch it, thinking she shouldn't wait too much longer before she bought and mailed some Christmas cards of her own. It just seemed there was never time to shop. Wryly she thought that since she never got to shop, it was lucky she had no one to buy a Christmas present for. This was one year she planned to skip buying for Sarah.

Halfway through the pile, she came upon a large card with no return address. Her name and address were typed, which was unusual for a Christmas card.

After she opened the envelope, it took Mary Rose several long moments to get over her shock, but she finally had to accept that what she held in her hands was the deed to the cabin and a loving Christmas card, with only the words "Merry Christmas...I love you" and Caleb's signature below the verse.

The deed was wrapped in a red ribbon.

CALEB DROPPED OFF the manuscript of his historical at his agent's office on his way out of town.

Ted looked at it in a disgruntled manner. "You sure you want to do this?" he asked.

"Don't knock it until you've read it," Caleb responded cheerfully.

"You changed your mind about having Christmas with me and Elsa?" he asked. "She cooks a mean turkey. And the kids are crazy about you."

"Thanks, Ted, but I have other plans. I'll be gone over the holidays and probably for quite a while afterward. I'll check in with you from time to time, though."

Ted looked curious. "Where you going?" he asked.

Caleb didn't answer the question. He merely grinned and said, "Merry Christmas." He had no intention of telling his practical friend what he had planned. Ted would think he'd lost his mind. "I left presents for you, Elsa and the kids with your secretary," he added as he headed for the door. "Hope everybody likes what I bought."

"Ah, Caleb, you shouldn't have done that," Ted said, following after him. He grinned as they stepped into the outer office. "But since you did . . ." and he went over to the small tree his secretary had set up and fetched a package from beneath it, which he handed to Caleb. "Merry Christmas yourself."

Laughing, Caleb tucked the box under his arm, and then, since he was in such a good mood, he grabbed Ted around the neck and gave him a hug. "Happy New Year," he said as he left.

"Happy New Year yourself," Ted replied.

Caleb smiled. If things worked out as he hoped, the next year might just turn out to be the happiest one of his life.

IT WAS APRIL before Mary Rose could get away from her commitments in Rockville. She didn't mail the letter she'd written to her aunt until she was on her way out of town. Starting from the time Caleb had sent her the deed to the cabin, she had begun softening toward Sarah. She hadn't seen her yet, but she knew now that she was a lot closer to a reconciliation than she had been. Of course, once Sarah got her letter, she might be the one who needed to soften awhile before a reconciliation could be affected.

Mary Rose drove her clunker at a leisurely pace on her way to Sweet Water. She'd taken it into the garage, and everything the mechanics could find to fix had been repaired. That, Mary Rose had figured, was cheaper than buying a new car. Still she was conditioned to treat the vehicle gently, and besides, she didn't feel the urgency she once had to get to the cabin and tear into her new life. She was looking forward to getting there, of course, and she was looking forward to her new life. But for a while she expected the cabin to deluge her with painful memories of Caleb.

Mary Rose had come to no definite conclusions about why Caleb had bought the cabin from Sarah, then deeded it back to her, Mary Rose. She imagined the "I love you" at the bottom of his card was nothing more than a writer's extravagance with words. Maybe his conscience bothered him...or maybe, once his writing career had taken off again, he'd decided the place was too primitive for him, after all. She hadn't been able to reach him to ask him why he'd done it or to thank him, because he hadn't put a return address on the envelope the Christmas card and deed had come in, and he wasn't listed in the New York City telephone directory. When she'd asked an operator for his number, she had been told it was unlisted.

The gift had done much to ease her heart where Caleb was concerned, but Mary Rose didn't fool herself that he'd ever intended for the two of them to get together again. If he'd had any plans in that direction, he would have contacted her once he was sure she'd had time to get the card and the deed. She was just glad to know he wasn't as insensitive as she'd thought for a while. And she was quietly happy to know that he must have cared for her to some degree to have made her such a precious gift ... even if he'd made it because he no longer wanted the cabin for himself.

It was late when Mary Rose drove into Sweet Water, and Ina's store was closed. So she stopped by the twenty-four-hour supermarket to get a few supplies until she could shop more extensively.

She was tired and slightly sleepy as she drove up the lane to the cabin. So she might have put down what she saw as she topped the hill to an illusion brought on by fatigue. Except that she wasn't *that* tired, or *that* sleepy.

"What in the world...?" she said aloud as she slowed the car almost to a standstill and stared, her green eyes wide.

The cabin was lit up like a Christmas tree...literally. There were Christmas lights outlining the roof. And that wasn't the only thing that convinced her some genie must have wired the place for electricity during her absence. The windows—far more windows than the cabin used to have—radiated light no kerosene lamp could provide.

Mary Rose automatically killed the motor of her car, but she made no move to get out of it. She kept looking around her, wondering bewilderedly for a moment if she could somehow have taken a wrong turn and ended up at some place other than her own cabin. But that was clearly not so. She recognized her home, although it was now much larger than before.

Absently, her eyes still glued disbelievingly to the cabin, Mary Rose opened the car door and stepped out. And then she started walking toward the porch.

THE SOUND of a car door outside made Caleb look up from his book. He was lying on the new couch he'd bought, which rested in the newly decorated living room. The lights on the fake Christmas tree in one corner of the room were blinking merrily and the new television set in another was spilling laughter from a sitcom. But Caleb hadn't been paying any attention to the show. He just had the set on for company.

His heart rate sped up for an instant as he wondered, as he always did when someone came to the cabin, if it could be Mary Rose. Then he grimaced in disappointment. She didn't have a car, so it had to be only Todd or somebody else stopping by for a visit.

Caleb got up and walked to the kitchen. The new refrigerator, gas cooker, stainless steel sink with hot and cold running water, and gleaming cabinets made the room look as though it belonged in the twentieth century now. But the scarred table and ancient chairs made by Mary Rose's grandfather kept the improvements from destroying the old-fashioned homey feeling of the room.

Opening the kitchen door, Caleb came face-to-face with Mary Rose, who was just opening the screen door. For an instant neither of them said a word. They just looked at each other as though for the first time.

Then Mary Rose found her voice. "Caleb?" she said disbelievingly.

Caleb didn't answer for a moment. He was too busy drinking in the sight of Mary Rose and turning a slow smile into a jaw-breaking grin, which gradually faded into an expression of quiet joy.

"At your service," he finally said, speaking softly, a wealth of emotion beneath his quiet tone. "Absolutely at your service." Then he gently took her hand to draw her into the kitchen.

Had her mind been working in top form, Mary Rose would have deduced in an instant the reason for his being there and for the changes she saw in the kitchen. But her mind wasn't working at all, much less in top form. She merely stood in the kitchen, blinking at the changes, feeling stupid.

"How do you like it?" Caleb asked, trying not to sound as anxious as he felt. All through the remodeling he'd had the fear he wasn't doing things the way Mary Rose would want them done. Now he couldn't tell anything from her expression. She just looked blank.

Mary Rose didn't answer. Actually, she hadn't even heard the question. Her ears weren't working any better than her mind.

"I had a new roof put on, too," Caleb said, finally breaking the silence. "By someone who knew what he was doing."

She still didn't answer, and after looking closely at her, Caleb had an idea she was in shock. He wasn't sure what one did for someone in that condition, so he did the only thing he could. He pretended it wasn't so. Taking Mary Rose's hand, he drew her toward the bedrooms, saying, "Come see what else I've done."

The beds still had the original frames made by Mary Rose's grandfather, but they obviously now had new mattresses and covers. And there was a modern bathroom complete with large closets off each bedroom.

Mary Rose looked around dazedly, but she made no comment.

The living room looked much the same to her, except for the pretty new wallpaper, new couch and two matching chairs, television set...and Christmas tree twinkling with lights in the corner.

"That's a Christmas tree," Mary Rose said at last, sounding as though she were a wise child who was sufficiently advanced in her knowledge of the world that she could now recognize one when she saw it.

"Yes. Pretty, isn't it," Caleb commented, acknowledging the obvious. "If you'll notice, it's even got presents under it. Most of them are for you. But they can wait. First I want to show you the pièce de résistance."

A door had been cut into one wall of the living room, and Caleb ushered Mary Rose through it into a completely new wing he'd had constructed. A hallway intersected two areas. On the right was a small bathroom, a small waiting area, an examining room, unfurnished except for an examining table, and a small office lined with empty bookshelves.

Mary Rose didn't say a word. She just walked around with a blank look on her face, touching things.

Her silence was making Caleb more nervous by the moment. But he didn't speak, either, as he led Mary Rose across the hall to his own domain.

His office was as much den as office. It, too, had its own bathroom, as well as a fireplace, a comfortable couch and two chairs. Aside from the windows, the walls were completely covered with filled bookshelves. At one end of the large room was a work area, with a computer, desk, printer, file cabinets and a closet for storing supplies.

When Mary Rose saw this room, she at last turned to look up at Caleb. There was a wealth of anxiety in his light brown eyes... but there was also a wealth of love.

"You plan to live here with me, don't you?" she asked matter-of-factly.

Caleb nodded. Then, as though that weren't enough, he said, "Yes." Then he nodded again, emphatically.

Mary Rose blinked at him. "You signed your Christmas card 'I love you,'" she reminded him.

"And I meant exactly that." Caleb's tone was very firm.

"You're not really a total low-down dirty scumdog then?" Mary Rose asked, and again her tone was calm and matter-of-fact.

Caleb winced. "I hope not," he said quietly. "But I know you thought I was."

She nodded. "For a while."

Caleb took a very deep breath. "Do you still think that?" he asked.

"No. I haven't since I got the deed in the mail with your card."

He hesitated. "What did you think about me when you got the card and the deed?"

"I didn't know what to think."

"Not even when I signed the card 'I love you'?"

Mary Rose sighed. "I thought it might be just..." Her voice trailed away. She felt very tired, yet very peaceful.

"It wasn't 'just' anything," Caleb said softly, taking a step nearer to her. He took one of her hands in his own. "I told you ... it meant exactly what it said."

She looked down at the hand he was holding. "But if you meant for us to live here together, why did you put the deed in my name only?" she asked. "And how did you manage to get all this work done when you don't even own the place?"

"I put the deed solely in your name because I wanted you to know I love you more than I love the cabin," Caleb answered in a gentle voice. "And I hired the contractors when the deed was still in my name."

Mary Rose at last began to smile. It was a tremulous smile, but in his relief at seeing it, Caleb thought it was the most beautiful one he'd ever seen in his life.

"Aren't you going to kiss me hello?" she asked.

Caleb felt as though a two-ton weight had been lifted from his shoulders. But he didn't move to kiss her. "I'm afraid if I do, I won't be able to stop," he informed her with quiet sincerity. "It's been so long ... and I've needed you so badly ..."

Mary Rose shrugged nonchalantly, and a warm look of love began to glow in her green eyes. "Who said you had to stop?" she asked. But the blasé tone she'd intended gave way to a sudden storm of tears that took her as much by surprise as it did Caleb.

He immediately wrapped his arms tightly around her, and he held her closely while she cried. When she was done and had lifted her face to his, he kissed her at last and broke the final barrier between them.

"COME ON, get up," Caleb said. Standing beside the bed in a brown velour robe, he reached down and pulled the covers off Mary Rose. "You haven't opened your Christmas presents yet."

Mary Rose put out a languid hand, searching for the covers to draw back over her. Her eyes were closed. "I'm sleepy," she mumbled. "The presents can wait till morning, can't they? Besides, you already gave me the best gift."

Caleb pretended to misunderstand her. "Why, thank you, darling," he said, beaming at her as he pulled her into a sitting position. "I knew I was a good lover, but it's sweet of you to compliment my expertise like that. A man always likes to know he pleases."

Mary Rose sighed and opened sleepy green eyes. "I meant the cabin," she said as Caleb lifted her to her feet and started stuffing her arms into the new robe that matched his own.

"Ouch!" He feigned hurt. "Then you're just a mercenary woman out for what she can get? You'd sell your body for four walls and a few acres, wouldn't you?"

She smiled and leaned against him, wrapping her arms around his waist. "Yes," she said simply. "But the price wasn't hard to pay."

"I'm glad to hear it," he drawled, unwrapping himself from her and guiding her toward the door of the bedroom. "Because I've got something else to give you, for which I'm going to extract like payment."

Mary Rose sighed again. "You're a hard man," she complained.

"No, I'm a lovestruck callow youth," Caleb said, grinning.

He took her into the living room and made her sit down on the couch. But when she promptly tried to lie down, he hauled her off the couch and deposited her in a chair, instead. Mary Rose gave him a disgruntled look and tried to keep her eyes open.

"What have you been doing to yourself in Maryland to get so worn out?" Caleb asked as he went to the Christmas tree.

"Doctors never get enough sleep," she said on a yawn. "And I've had to work harder than usual lately in order to leave things in good shape when I resigned from my medical practice."

In a moment Caleb was back with a very small present in his hand. He pulled Mary Rose up from her chair, sat down, then put her on his lap.

She leaned her head against his shoulder and looked at the small present he held up in front of her eyes.

"That doesn't look worth what you're going to charge for it," she complained.

"Wait and see," Caleb said with a smile. "Open it."

Mary Rose did, knowing even before she raised the lid on the ring box what she was going to find. She smiled with happiness...and then she gasped. The diamond on the engagement ring Caleb had bought her was enormous. "Caleb!" she exclaimed.

"What? You don't think you're worth it?" he asked teasingly as he took the engagement ring from her, leaving the plain gold band where it was, and promptly slid it halfway onto her ring finger. He paused. "You are going to marry me, aren't you?" he asked sternly. "Because if you're not, I don't think a quick roll in the hay can justify a diamond this size."

Mary Rose raised stunned eyes to his, glanced back at the ring, then returned her gaze to Caleb. "I guess I'd better," she said shakily. "And if I don't get enough patients and you don't sell enough books to make a living, we can always sell this and live off the proceeds for years.''

Caleb smiled and, with his hand on the back of her neck, drew her a breath away from him. ''This,'' he said, looking at the ring, ''and this...'' and his eyes swept over the cabin, ''are two things we never sell. Agreed?''

Mary Rose took in a deep, trembling breath. ''Agreed,'' she said, and Caleb kissed her mouth as he slid the ring the rest of the way onto her finger.

After the kissing had gone on awhile, he got to his feet with her in his arms. The ring box was cradled in her lap, and Mary Rose picked it up so it wouldn't get lost as Caleb carried her to the bedroom.

When he set her on her feet beside the bed, she held up the box. ''Here,'' she said, smiling gently. ''Keep this for me.''

Caleb merely tossed the ring box into the drawer of the bedside table, then began untying the belt of her robe.

''At least the wedding band is relatively modest,'' Mary Rose teased him as he stripped the robe from her shoulders. ''I think I'll just wear it when I'm working. I don't think the folks in Sweet Water are ready for an engagement ring that costs more than a pickup. They'll say I'm putting on airs.''

Caleb had his robe off now and he pulled Mary Rose into his arms. As their bodies touched, they both gasped.

''I'm glad to see this hasn't changed between us,'' she said shakily against his neck. ''I hope it never does.''

''Same here,'' Caleb said huskily before taking Mary Rose's mouth in a deep, probing kiss that lasted even as he was lowering her to the bed.

"Oh, Caleb," she whispered hungrily a few moments later. "If the people of Sweet Water could see me now, my reputation would be ruined for sure. I'd never get any patients."

"What's a little thing like a reputation against what we feel when we're together like this?" Caleb murmured against her breast. "Would you trade?"

A shudder of sheer delight rippled through her body as he touched his tongue to the tip of her nipple.

"Trade?" she gasped. "Are you crazy?"

"No." Caleb smiled his satisfaction over her answer. "I'm just a man in love."

"Ditto," Mary Rose answered inaccurately, and it was the last coherent thing she said for quite a while.

JUST BEFORE falling asleep, Mary Rose had a thought. "Caleb," she mumbled drowsily against his shoulder, "why did you leave the Christmas tree up so long? And why the Christmas lights on the cabin?"

Caleb smiled. "Because I considered last Christmas our first holiday as a married couple. I just didn't plan on it taking you so long to get here so we could celebrate it together. Besides," he added, gathering her closer and kissing her forehead, "I wanted the proper atmosphere for my gift giving."

Mary Rose's eyes blinked open and she stared at him in dismay. "But I didn't give you anything," she said guiltily.

Caleb grinned. "Didn't you," he replied as he ran his hand meaningfully along the length of her body.

"That's not the same," she protested.

Caleb chuckled and kissed her. "Don't worry about it, honey. Your cabin gave me all the gifts I'll ever need."

"What are they?" Mary Rose's eyes were wide and curious.

"It gave me back my writing first, you afterward, and peace and love for all time," he said quietly. "That's more than enough for any man."

Mary Rose stayed silent for a moment, hugging Caleb tightly. And then she murmured, "But you gave the cabin away to me."

Caleb nodded. "That's how you keep any of the really important gifts, Mary Rose. By giving them away."

He kissed her . . . and she understood.

Epilogue

In the family cemetery the wildflowers were blooming. Mary Rose knelt by her mother's grave, wishing with all her heart that Mary Violet could be at the wedding. Looking up at Caleb, she asked, "When do you want us to be married, darling? And where?"

"As soon as possible, and right here where your mother can join us, of course" was his answer.

Mary Rose smiled happily, loving Caleb anew for his generosity and his sensitivity. Then she had a thought. "I wonder if Sarah will come," she said.

Caleb frowned. "Do you want her to?" he asked, puzzled.

She thought a moment, then nodded. "Yes...now that she can't change anything, I do. She's all the family I have left. Though I can't agree with what she did, I know she thought she was doing the best thing for me. So if we can make peace, I'd like to."

Even though he was grudgingly grateful that Sarah had sold him the cabin, Caleb wasn't particularly interested in making peace with her. But if that was what Mary Rose wanted, he wasn't going to protest.

"Call her or write her then and ask," he said. "But I'm not going to delay our wedding to give her time to come to terms with what's happened, if you've got that in mind."

"No, I'm willing to go only so far," Mary Rose said, smiling elfishly.

"Good." Caleb was relieved and gratified by her attitude. Then he changed the subject. "Do you want to buy a headstone for your mother?" he asked.

Mary Rose shook her head. "No, I want to plant a redbud tree at the head of the grave," she answered. "We can nail a plaque to it when the tree gets big enough. And since this is the right season to plant trees, I guess we should go to town and buy one pretty soon."

Caleb nodded, not in the least surprised by her intention. He knew he had captured an original, and he wouldn't have tried to change her into someone more conventional for anything in the world.

THEY STOPPED by the gas station on the way to buy the tree, and Todd was delighted to have Mary Rose back. "Ain't been the same around here without ya," he said shyly.

She smiled fondly at him, then invited him to the wedding.

"Hey, yore plan worked, huh, Caleb? Good goin'." Todd grinned and winked. "Shore, I'll be there."

Laughing at the look on Mary Rose's face, caused by Todd's comment, Caleb started pulling her out of the gas station. "See you later," he said. "We've got to go buy a tree."

"A tree?" Todd responded, frowning in a puzzled fashion. "Looks like that's one thang ya'll got plenty of already."

"You can never have too many trees, Todd," Mary Rose said.

"I reckon not," he answered, but he didn't look as though he believed his own words.

"I thought Caleb was gonna die of the lovesick blues if you didn't show up soon," Ina declared as she hugged Mary Rose hello.

"Pretty mopey, was he?" Mary Rose smiled, pleased.

"Pshaw! 'Mopey' ain't the word fer it. He'd done gone into a full-blown de-pression," Ina declared. She glanced at Caleb then and grinned. "But he's lookin' right perky today, ain't he?"

"And feeling it, as well," Caleb said, grinning complacently.

After Mary Rose had caught the ever nosy Ina up on what she'd been doing for the past few months and invited her to the wedding, she and Caleb left to go to the hardware store, where Ina had told them trees were for sale.

An hour later Caleb had the hole dug and Mary Rose held the tree in place while he shoveled the dirt back around it.

"There!" Mary Rose said, pleased with their work. "Ma would love knowing her future son-in-law had a hand in erecting her monument."

"Then why don't you tell her?" Caleb suggested. When Mary Rose looked at him in surprise, he added, "I know you talk to her. I came upon you doing it one day."

"Did you think I was crazy?" she asked curiously.

"At first," Caleb acknowledged. "And then it just seemed sort of... natural, I guess."

Mary Rose nodded. "I needed her," she said simply. "But I don't seem to need her as much now as I did then," she added, giving him a look that expressed her meaning.

Caleb was humbly, quietly pleased. "I'm glad to hear it. But if you want to talk to your mother, Mary Rose, go ahead. I'm not the jealous type... at least not of another woman."

He kissed her, then walked away. And Mary Rose had a long, satisfying chat with her mother before she went in search of her future husband.

As SARAH READ the letter inviting her to Mary Rose and Caleb's wedding, some of the rage she had felt since receiving her niece's last letter—the one explaining that Caleb had given the cabin back to Mary Rose—finally began to dissipate. She began to accept that she had lost and to turn her mind to gaining something from the ashes of defeat. After reasoning things out to her satisfaction, Sarah went shopping for a dress to wear to the wedding.

AMONG THE ITEMS Mary Rose purchased with the money she'd been saving up to buy into the practice in Maryland—money she was now using to equip her medical office—was a microscope. And on the day after she and Caleb went to the county seat to take out a marriage license as well as present Mary Rose's medical credentials to the hospital there, she was using the microscope to study a glob of mud from a nearby stream.

Caleb wandered into the room and stared in puzzled distaste at what was on the slide. "What *is* that?" he asked.

"Mud," Mary Rose answered absently.

Caleb sighed. "Mud," he repeated. "Of course. Why didn't I think of that?" And then he got an alarmed look on his face. "That isn't a new medical treatment you're trying out, where I'm going to be the guinea pig, is it?" he asked.

Mary Rose glanced up at him, her thoughts elsewhere until she saw the alarmed look on his face. That brought a smile to her lips. "No, my darling," she assured him. "It's just that a fungus in some mud in Norway is now being used to produce a medication that helps prevent organ transplants from being rejected. I was curious to see if the mud around here might have anything similar in it."

Caleb breathed a sigh of relief.

Mary Rose patted his cheek. "Don't worry," she told him fondly. "I would never use you as a guinea pig. You're too precious to lose."

"How about trying something out on Sarah then?" he asked slyly.

"Caleb!" Mary Rose chided.

Grinning, he shrugged unrepentantly and left the room. As he came out into the hallway, the door to the medical office opened and Mrs. Mullins and a woman Caleb didn't know came in. He greeted them, and Mrs. Mullins introduced her companion, a small, nervous-looking woman, as Mrs. Winans.

"I heered Doc Perkins was back," Mrs. Mullins said.

"Yes, she is," Caleb acknowledged. "Did you want to say hello to her?"

"Yep. And I brung my friend here to talk to her about somethin' if she ain't too busy."

"I'll ask her," Caleb said, and he returned to Mary Rose to tell her she had visitors, one of whom was possibly a new patient recommended by Mrs. Mullins.

Mary Rose was delighted. "God bless Mrs. Mullins," she said happily, and went out to say hello and meet the new patient, who, it turned out, had a lump in her breast.

After examining Mrs. Winans, Mary Rose was fairly positive it was nothing more serious than a cyst, but since she couldn't get anything by aspiration, she called up the hospital in the county seat to schedule a mammogram.

"You're to go in tomorrow afternoon," she told her patient, "and I've asked that they send me the results as quickly as possible."

Then she spent a good half hour explaining various possibilities to Mrs. Winans and answering her questions to reassure her. After that Mary Rose invited both women to her wedding. Mrs. Mullins was delighted Mary Rose had managed to capture the handsome roofer with the broad, manly shoulders.

As the women were about to leave the office, Mrs. Mullins said, "I sure am glad you're back."

"I'm glad I'm back, too," Mary Rose responded sincerely.

Mrs. Winans timidly seconded the opinion. "I don't much like to go to men doctors for things like this," she said, blushing. "And I liked the way you took the time to explain things to me. I never would have had the nerve to ask a male doctor all those questions."

Mary Rose was pleased. After the two women left, she went to look for Caleb, and found him in the kitchen, having a cup of coffee. She kissed him, then got a cup for herself and sat down beside him.

"With Mrs. Mullins's recommendations," Caleb said, "You'll probably soon be so busy doctoring everybody in Sweet Water, you won't have much time to sit and drink coffee with me anymore."

Mary Rose wrinkled her nose at him. "I'll always have time for you," she promised. "By the way, have I told you lately how much I love you?"

Caleb looked ostentatiously at his watch. "Not in the past four hours," he responded, giving her an exaggeratedly disgruntled look.

"I love you," Mary Rose said softly.

Caleb then gave her a considering look. "Prove it."

She gazed primly down at her cup of coffee. "My Aunt Sarah always told me if a boy asked me to prove my love in an indelicate fashion, it meant he was just out for what he could get."

Caleb shrugged. "I'm not a boy," he reminded her. "And you're wearing my engagement ring, so I'm obviously not just out for what I can get. Besides, your aunt has been wrong on more than one occasion."

Mary Rose raised her green eyes to Caleb, her expression bland. "On the other hand," she went on as though he hadn't spoken, "my mother always told me to trust people and most likely my trust would not be in vain."

"I'm positive I would have *loved* your mother," Caleb said emphatically.

Mary Rose smiled. "Yes, so am I," and she got to her feet, reached for Caleb's hand, drew him around the table and started pulling him toward their bedroom. "Unfortunately you're going to have to settle for me."

A short while later Caleb said sleepily, "Do you suppose people in town are scandalized because we're so obviously living together before the wedding?"

"I don't know," she answered drowsily. "And I don't care."

Caleb smiled, but before he could say anything more, Mary Rose continued. "Of course, if you're worried about *your* reputation, you could sleep outside in your sleeping bag again," she suggested.

Caleb frowned. "You've got to be kidding," he grumbled. "It's supposed to rain tonight."

"But if you got pneumonia and I treated you successfully..." Mary Rose said, brightening.

"With axle grease and turpentine?" Caleb sighed.

"And an antibiotic slipped in on the side just to make sure," she said complacently.

"No, thanks."

"You don't want an antibiotic?"

"I don't want pneumonia. It might interfere with my honeymoon."

"But we're staying here for our honeymoon," Mary Rose pointed out.

"Exactly. Right here." Caleb pointed at the bed. "And I don't care to gasp and wheeze my way through the sealing of our nuptials."

"I don't think I've ever heard of a disease called 'nuptial,'" she said on a yawn. "What are the symptoms?"

"If you'll be quiet for a moment, I'll demonstrate."

"Are they catching?"

"Very. Now shut up and pay attention."

The phone rang the next morning, and Mary Rose sleepily reached out a hand to answer it. But it wasn't a patient asking for an appointment. It was Caleb's agent.

When Caleb took the phone from her, Ted started out by asking, "Who's the new woman?" He hadn't spoken particularly softly, and Mary Rose heard him. Her eyes widened in a glare.

Caleb pretended not to notice the look. "That was my fiancée," he said, yawning. "You and Elsa want to come to the wedding, Ted?"

"The wedding!"

"Yes, the wedding," Caleb said patiently. "It's going to be held in Sweet Water, West Virginia, next Saturday. You can be my best man."

"Next Saturday!" Ted sputtered. "Sweet Water, West Virginia? Where is that?"

"If you want to come, I'll give you directions. Otherwise it's not worth the trouble." Caleb smiled, then reached down and kissed Mary Rose's flushed cheek. He followed up that kiss with one on each of her eyelids to get rid of the only slightly abated glare still aimed at him.

"Hell, Caleb, first you disappear for months, then you come up with a fiancée in some backwater!" Ted grumbled. "Are you going through a midlife crisis or something?"

"Nope...I'm going through the happiest time of my life...so far," he amended, thinking the years ahead might turn out to be even better.

Mary Rose misunderstood and glared at him again. Caleb grinned.

Ted sighed. "Well, Elsa and I will be there if she hasn't already made other plans," he said resignedly. "It's kind of short notice, you know."

"For me, too." Caleb's grin broadened. "Why'd you call, Ted?" he asked, changing the subject.

"Oh. I finally found a publisher for that historical you wrote."

"No kidding." Caleb smiled with satisfaction.

"The book didn't thrill me, but you never know what these editors are going to like. I'll bring the contract if we come to the wedding. If we can't come, I'll mail it to you."

"Fine," Caleb said, then added. "say, Ted, I want to insert a dedication in the book. You got a pencil?"

"Yes."

"Then write, 'To Mary Rose and Mary Violet... heroines both.'"

"Who are they?" Ted asked.

"My fiancée and her mother," Caleb answered.

"You're dedicating a book to your future mother-in-law?"

"Yes, and it's not as strange as it sounds. She passed away a few years ago."

"Then how'd you get to know her? You were living in New York then."

"I never knew her, Ted," Caleb said. "I didn't have to. I know her daughter."

He was gratified to see that the glare was completely gone now from Mary Rose's eyes. So this time he kissed her mouth.

Caleb felt he knew what Ted was probably thinking about the two names—too sweet, too old-fashioned, to be believed. But he was confident that once his agent got a good look at Mary Rose, his opinion would undergo a drastic change. He gave Ted directions to the cabin and the two men signed off.

"That's a sweet thing to do, Caleb," Mary Rose said softly after he'd hung up the phone. "Ma would be pleased."

"And is her daughter pleased?"

"Very. But what's the book about?"

Caleb smiled. "Wait and see. If you're good to me, I might even give you an autographed copy."

"Ha! Promises, promises."

"Which I always fulfill. I want you to read my other books, too." He grinned. "But save them and this latest one for after the honeymoon is over and you begin to get bored with me. Maybe they'll put some excitement back into your life."

"Just how soon are you expecting the honeymoon to be over?" Mary Rose inquired indignantly.

Caleb managed a thoughtful look. "Well, one can never be sure about these things," he said, "but I'm fairly positive that in about fifty years..."

Mary Rose gave him a smart rap on the shoulder. "I'm going to read them before that!" she vowed. "And don't count on getting bored with me in fifty years, either. If I sense it happening, I'll just dig into my bag of folklore tricks and come up with a love potion to get you back on track."

"Oh, God." Caleb sighed. "I suppose it will be something that looks and tastes perfectly disgusting."

Mary Rose smiled evilly. "The more disgusting the better," she said. "It will be both revenge and cure."

"Then I guess, as a matter of self-protection, I'd better learn to pretend interest whether I feel it or not,"

Caleb said, beginning to kiss Mary Rose where he knew it would have the most effect.

She retaliated in kind until she was positive he wasn't pretending anything. "I don't think you're bored yet," she murmured delightedly. "It's kind of hard to pretend when you're a man, isn't it?"

"Impossible," Caleb agreed, his tone ragged. "And I suggest you use this method to check on my boredom quotient as often as possible."

"Oh, I will." Mary Rose smiled languidly as she kissed the corner of his mouth. "I certainly will."

SARAH SHOWED UP at the cabin two days before the wedding, and when Mary Rose opened the door, she blinked in surprise.

"I wasn't sure you'd come," she said.

Sarah's expression wasn't particularly encouraging, especially when she looked at Caleb, who had come up behind Mary Rose. But his expression wasn't exactly welcoming, so Mary Rose wasn't sure she could blame her aunt for looking less than pleased.

Without greeting Caleb formally, Sarah held out her car keys to him. "My bag is in the trunk," she said.

Mary Rose heard his sigh and knew how he must feel. But she was terribly grateful to him when he didn't say anything. He just took Sarah's keys and walked outside.

Sarah was gazing around her, frowning. "What in the world has happened to this place?" she asked wonderingly. "It looks almost habitable."

Mary Rose smiled. "Caleb modernized the cabin for me," she said lightly. "Doesn't everything look nice?"

Sarah studied her, still frowning. "But when? I thought he gave you the deed immediately after he'd tricked me into selling the place to him."

"He got the construction work started before he transferred the deed to my name," Mary Rose explained.

Sarah was flabbergasted. "He did all this without even knowing whether you'd marry him?"

Mary Rose nodded happily. "He's fantastic, isn't he?" she said, and it wasn't a question at all.

Sarah didn't respond. Without asking for permission, she began a tour of the cabin, instead, frowning all the while.

It was clear to Mary Rose that her aunt was torn in her reaction to the changes. While she obviously approved on one level, on another she hated the fact that the place would now probably appeal to her niece more than ever. The negative reaction was clearest when she inspected Mary Rose's medical office. Her brown eyes were sad and resentful and resigned, all at the same time.

"I've almost got all the equipment I need now," Mary Rose said, refusing to give in to Sarah's mood. "But there are a few things still on order."

Sarah looked at Mary Rose, her expression clearly conveying that what she thought her niece needed wasn't to be found here.

At that Mary Rose looked at Sarah in a calm, but firm way and stated her terms for their reconciliation.

"Until I have children," she said quietly, "you're the only blood relation I have. And I love you and am very grateful to you for all you've done for me. But unless you accept what I've chosen to do with my life—unless you accept Caleb as my husband—I'd just as soon you left here now. I don't intend to have the happiest time of my life tainted in any manner whatsoever because I refuse to do things your way. And if you really love me, as you say you do, you'll focus on how happy I am doing things my way, rather than on how happy you are when I'm doing things your way."

Sarah stared at Mary Rose for a long moment and weighed her options. No matter how much she would like things to be otherwise, it was clear that her niece was prepared to sever their relationship rather than put up with Sarah's tendency to try to run her life.

"All right," Sarah finally said, her voice husky. "I won't pretend I like how you've chosen to live your life...or that I approve of what Caleb did. But I will hide my feelings if that's the only way we can be at peace again."

Mary Rose studied her aunt's face for a long moment, and gradually began to smile. "Good," she said quietly. "Then why don't you come with me and greet Caleb in a civil manner. I'm not the only one who has to be convinced you've decided to accept the inevitable."

Caleb was relieved by the change he saw in Sarah when she and Mary Rose came into the spare bedroom, where he'd just deposited the luggage. But he was surprised when she came toward him and extended her hand. He took it hesitantly and shook it, as she seemed to want him to do.

"Hello, Caleb," Sarah said, her tone neutral, neither overly warm, nor noticeably reluctant. "Welcome to the family."

Caleb looked at her closely, and had a pretty good idea of what their future relations would be like. There was not likely ever to be any real affection between them. They would conduct themselves in a polite, civilized manner, weapons sheathed. But that was far better than he'd expected, so he was gracious when he answered.

"Thank you, Sarah," he said. "I'm very pleased and proud to be included in this family."

Mary Rose was very proud of him. And she was very relieved that Sarah had elected to behave as she had. But she was also aware that it might be politic to keep them at arm's length, except when impossible to do otherwise.

Caleb excused himself from the room, and Mary Rose and Sarah began to further heal the rift that had grown between them by talking about practicalities for the wedding.

EXCEPT FOR Sarah and Mary Rose, the wedding party was gathered at the family cemetery.

As Caleb looked around at the guests, he smiled, positive that almost everyone was having trouble understanding why he and Mary Rose had chosen to exchange their vows in a graveyard. Ted still looked stunned, in fact. But his wife, Elsa, had recovered from her shock and was admiring the flowers and trees.

Ina shrugged and said to Mrs. Mullins, "It don't surprise me none. Any little gal that can handle a buryin' at the age of fourteen all by herself is likely to do anythang."

Beth Mullins, considerably slimmer and more animated than the last time Caleb had seen her, was all dressed up and looking self-important over her role as flower girl, and her parents appeared just as pleased as their daughter.

Todd, however, seemed uncomfortable. He kept running a finger around the tight collar of his white shirt and stretching his neck. The pretty young lady who'd come to the wedding as his date was too shy to look anyone in the eye. Todd's father and Mr. Phipps from the hardware store wore identical expressions of resignation over having to dress up and were idly discussing local politics.

The pastor worried Caleb. The man had to be in his nineties if he was a day. White-haired, he stood with a Bible in his hands and an absent, otherworldly look on his sweetly aged face. But the man had baptized Mary Rose, so it had seemed only fitting that he should perform the ceremony. Caleb only hoped the old fellow would be able to remember all the words, since so far he hadn't gotten Caleb's name right once.

Catching sight of Mary Rose and Sarah approaching, the young choir director began to strum his guitar, playing the "Wedding March," and at that Caleb forgot everything but his beloved. As he gazed lovingly at her, he thought she looked as though she had stepped out of the last century, rather than being a modern woman who was a physician.

Dressed in a quaintly old-fashioned pink-and-ivory dress, Mary Rose wore a hat instead of a veil, and she carried a matching parasol in one hand, a bouquet of pink and white roses in the other. On her face was a radiantly alive, glowingly joyous expression.

She took Caleb's hand as she joined him beside her mother's grave. The pastor stood on the other side.

After exchanging a long, mutually loving look, they held tightly to each other as they turned to face the elderly man.

" 'Dearly beloved,' " the pastor began, intoning the ceremony in a strong, deep voice at odds with his shrunken frame. " 'We are gathered here today...' "

Caleb's fears that the pastor would forget what to say evaporated as the ceremony proceeded without a hitch, and he relaxed. Mary Rose had a nervous moment when the pastor asked if anyone objected to the union, but Sarah remained silent. Then suddenly it was over, and time for the kiss.

Mary Rose swept her hat off as she faced Caleb. "I don't want anything to get in our way," she whispered exultantly.

"Nothing will, my love," Caleb whispered back, his voice unsteady. "Nothing can...not ever." He kissed her, and the kiss was long and thorough enough to make the guests look at one another and smile in amusement.

The reception afterward was held in the yard around the cabin. It was a beautiful May day, not hot and not chilly, and no one minded in the least being outside. Even Sarah, who had thought it tacky not to erect a canopy, eventually took off her fancy hat and let the gentle breeze caress her hair.

Around five in the afternoon, people started to leave, and Mary Rose was content to see them go. She'd loved having them at her wedding, but she wanted Caleb to herself now. Then she remembered that Sarah would still be their guest, and though she tried not to mind, she was greatly relieved when it turned out that her aunt had the sensitivity to leave with everyone else.

"Are you sure you want to drive back all that way tonight?" Mary Rose asked politely. "It's getting late."

"If I get tired, I'll stop somewhere and take a room," Sarah said as she opened the door to her car—she'd put her bag in the trunk earlier. She hesitated a moment and met her niece's eyes. "I hope you'll be very happy," she said quietly.

Mary Rose smiled and stepped forward out of the encircling warmth of Caleb's arms to hug her aunt. "Thank you," she murmured softly. "Thank you for everything. I mean that."

Sarah's brown eyes teared, and after hugging Mary Rose once more and kissing her on the cheek, she quickly got behind the wheel of her car.

When Sarah's car had disappeared down the hill, Caleb headed for the cabin, his arm around his new wife, but Mary Rose steered him away. "It's too nice a day to go in just yet," she said, hugging him close, her arm encircling his waist. "Let's walk for a while. I'll make up to you for the delay in our honeymoon later."

"I know you will," Caleb said, squeezing her back. "You make up to me for everything, Mary Rose...always."

Pleased by his comment, she paused and lifted her face for a kiss. Then they walked on to the place she had in mind...the view of the mountains to the east.

They stood quietly together, enjoying the sight, and then Mary Rose suddenly caught her breath and pointed. "Look, Caleb!" she exclaimed softly. "Oh, just look."

A doe and her fawn were outlined against the ridge for a long moment before they disappeared from sight.

"Lovely," he said softly. "Absolutely lovely."

Mary Rose was too choked up for a moment to respond. Then she shook her head. "They're more than lovely, Caleb. They're a gift...a promise that all will be well with us."

Caleb didn't ask for any further explanation. He was merely thankful from the bottom of his soul for one more gift among the many his new home and his new wife had given him.

Harlequin American Romance

COMING NEXT MONTH

#301 CHARMED CIRCLE by Robin Francis

One relaxing month by the sea was all Zoe Piper ever expected from her four-week stay at Gull Cottage, the luxurious East Hampton mansion, but it turned out to be a month that would change her life forever. And then there was Ethan Quinn, the skeptical Scorpio with the dreamer's eyes.... The first book of the GULL COTTAGE trilogy.

#302 THE MORNING AFTER by Dallas Schulze

The morning after Lacey's thirtieth-birthday bash, her head pounded, her eyes ached—and she awoke in a Vegas hotel room. When a man groaned beside her in the bed, she thought she knew the worst. But it was yet to come. She was married—to a man she had met at her party. Last night's revelry must have affected her groom's brain—because Cameron wouldn't admit they'd made a mistake.

#303 THE FOREVER CHOICE by Patricia Cox

Christine Donovan had run away from Detective Paul Cameron, the only man who had captured her heart. Now she was face-to-face with him again as they tried to find out who was embezzling money from her aunt's perfume company. They were both determined to play it cool, but what they hadn't counted on was a love destined to be, and a criminal in the family....

#304 TURNING TABLES by Judith Arnold

Amelia's outrageous sister had done it again. But to get herself out of jail this time she hired a lawyer determined to take her case to the Supreme Court. Before the incident became fodder for the tabloids, Amelia had to stop Patrick Levine. But Patrick had his own plan—and a passionate desire to see how straitlaced Amelia would react when pushed too far.

Your favorite stories with a brand-new look!!

H A R L E Q U I N
American Romance®

Beginning next month, the four American Romance titles will feature a new, contemporary and sophisticated cover design. As always, each story will be a terrific romance with mature characters and a realistic plot that is uniquely North American in flavor and appeal.

Watch your bookshelves for a **bold** look!